About the author

Katy A. Mitchell grew up in a small seaside town in Lancashire, England. Katy has always had an interest in travel and she has lived and worked in various countries around the world. She is a teacher and has been working in education for the past eleven years.

Katy got the idea for *Blackout* and the character of Cecily Stalks while at university. It took her eight years to complete the first book of *The Light and Dark Narratives* and different parts of the story have been imagined and written in several countries across the world.

THE LIGHT AND DARK NARRATIVES: BLACKOUT

Katy A. Mitchell

THE LIGHT AND DARK NARRATIVES: BLACKOUT

Vanguard Press

A CIP catalogue record for this title is
available from the British Library.

ISBN 978 1 784652 89 0

*Vanguard Press is an imprint of
Pegasus Elliot MacKenzie Publishers Ltd.*
www.pegasuspublishers.com

First Published in 2018

**Vanguard Press
Sheraton House Castle Park
Cambridge England**

Printed & Bound in Great Britain

Acknowledgements

I owe a great deal to my family and friends, who were there for me throughout the duration of this project. It has been a long road thus far and, at times, I have needed a lot of support and encouragement to make it happen. Without you, I'm sure I would have given up on Cecily Stalks long ago.

Many thanks to my friend, Joe Falconer, an amazing artist who illustrated the map of Bramblegate. Also to my publisher, Pegasus Elliot Mackenzie, for their belief in my writing.

A final mention for those who have already read Cecily's story; your support and feedback means the world.

Thank you all from the bottom of my heart.

For those who believed

Prologue

The battle cries of war rang in her ears. She took a moment out of the fight to take a look around and gauge their situation. Her army had taken a massive hit. All around her lay decapitated, broken bodies. The metallic smell of fresh blood filled her nostrils as she looked down in order to carefully place her feet, not wanting to tread on one of her recently deceased comrades. As she turned around, full circle, she saw them gathering in the shadows of the tree line, a threatening black mass. This meant that he would not be far behind. She could not... no, she would not let him win this war. She could not even contemplate the disastrous consequence of such a victory on his part. Thrusting this terrifying thought to one side, she urgently scoured the combat field for her friends, inwardly praying that they were safe. She could not do this without them. She instinctively felt danger. She spun around just in time to see her cowardly attacker run at her from behind. She reached out her hand which held her long, sharp sword and hit her adversary on the head with the hilt of the powerful weapon. She skilfully twisted the sword around in both hands and directed the blood-spattered blade into the abdomen of the enemy soldier. He never stood a chance. He was no match for her.

Chapter One

Cecily Stalks stared at herself in the bathroom mirror. Another Monday morning had arrived, an indication that life does, indeed, go on. She decided that she looked a bit peaky today. As she stuck her tongue out and examined its health in the reflection, she wondered if she was well enough to make the twenty-minute walk to work. She then considered whether she could persevere through the eight-hour shift that lay ahead. However, her conscience had already made the decision for her.

"Come on, Cecily," it chided. "There is nothing wrong with you. Now brush your teeth and wash your face… and for heaven's sake, put a brush through that mop you call a hairstyle!"

Cecily went over this same routine every morning, bound to it. She despised her job at the local tourist spot. She even more loathed the drove of tourists that poured through the doors every day of the week, rain or shine. Weekday visitors comprised of noisy, reckless groups of school children who crashed about as if in their local playground. Also, there were the well-off, middle-aged housewives who had no need of work and who had plenty of time to spare. They discussed the latest fashions and charitable causes of the moment. Cecily would often eavesdrop on their meaningless babble and in a way, she envied their seemingly trouble-free lives. Then there were the dear old folk, who would come in early and make a pot of tea for two last well into the afternoon. Cecily always wondered how they managed this feat. It was as if they possessed magical powers which they could channel into the ability of refilling a teapot at will. Cecily knew there was little hope of any tips when this happened, but somehow, she did not mind. They were kind and knowledgeable and instead of cash, they gifted her with stories about the past. If the weather was nice, they would attract students skiving from the local college. They would while the afternoon away, sunbathing and chatting in their small social pods. This, at the very least, gave the middle-aged housewives and the old folk additional conversation pieces to discuss about 'the youth of today'. Cecily snapped out of her premonition about what this Monday held in store for her. Predictable, as always. Predictable, just like every other day. The fact of the matter was that they needed money and she would have to go out and earn it.

Where had the weekend gone? she mused to herself. It was far too short. Cecily now stood in the bomb site that resembled her bedroom. Everything in here was familiar to her: the beaten up old rocking chair, once her grandmother's, that now sat by the window, the three-quarter size bed which was full of lumps that she had slept in for as long as she could remember, the mismatched wooden furniture that inhabited every nook and cranny of her room. Here, she was safe. But as Cecily gazed around the room, surveying the numerous piles of clothes and subconsciously deciding what to wear, a niggling feeling probed from the back of her brain. It was like this feeling was attempting to escape that closed off place and make a run for the forefront of her mind and freedom. It was that same feeling that told her all was not well. But, of course, she was being ridiculous. That is what her mother told her anyway.

Eighteen-year-old Cecily had been having the same dreams since her father died three years ago. Vivid dreams of battlefields and a struggle between good and evil forces. A tremendous weight lay heavily on her shoulders and that burden was the victory of this most significant war. And then there were the shadows; the shadows were most disturbing. Her mother had sent her to a psychiatrist when these dreams began at the age of fifteen. The doctor, unsurprisingly, interpreted these dreams as a manifestation of guilt, that Cecily blamed herself and ultimately felt responsible for the death of her father. The reoccurring dream was her anxiety playing itself out, over and over whilst she slept. But Cecily felt no guilt or blame about her father's death. She only discovered his body; she did not kill him.

Cecily pushed all thoughts of her father and her dreams out of her head. Aware that she was running late, she threw on a pair of old, worn jeans and a t-shirt. As Cecily grabbed her bag, her eye caught the reflection in the full-length mirror by her desk. Cecily was so pale she was almost translucent. She had the loveliest colour of auburn hair which fell in a straight bob midway between her chin and shoulder. As was the latest fashion, she had a thick fringe cut in. When her hair caught the light, it was like a disco ball, reflecting the different natural highlights in Cecily's hair of golden and brown. She had a small nose, dotted with a few red freckles, high cheekbones and a pale pink mouth. However, it was Cecily's eyes that were her most stunning feature; big, wide, lustrous eyes, the colour of ripe limes, framed by long, dark lashes. Her eyes set off her heart shaped face perfectly. Cecily was very pretty and one day, she would be a beautiful woman; however, at the moment, Cecily was much the tomboy and at five feet six inches, she had a lean, almost gangly frame. She adjusted her thrown together outfit in the mirror, slung her bag over her shoulder and ran down the stairs. If she was quick, she might be able to avoid her mother. No such luck.

"Cecily, I'm not going to be home until late tonight. You will have to get your own tea," she called from the kitchen.

"Right, OK, Mother!" she huffed under her breath as she pulled her trainers on by the front door.

"But there is no food in. I haven't had time to go shopping." Cecily could hear from her mother's voice that she was getting closer.

"No change there then," she muttered as she was tying her laces.

"What was that?" said her mum, who was now stood behind her.

"Nothing!" snapped Cecily. "Don't worry about me!"

"Cecily," began her mother in lecturing mode, "if you have something to say to me, then spit it out!"

"I haven't got time for this!" retorted Cecily. "It's ten to nine. I have to go. Don't want to lose my job now, do I?"

And with that, Cecily belted down the garden path, through the gate and onto the gravel track that led through the wood, her mother left standing in her wake.

Chapter Two

Cecily was resigned to the fact that she was going to be late for work again. This meant she could expect the usual lecture on tardiness from her boss. Time management skills were not Cecily's strong point. In fact, she was surprised she still had a job to go to at all.

It was a splendid spring morning. April was one of Cecily's favourite months by far. Everything smelt so fresh and new. The woods were revitalised, free once more to share their beauty after being held prisoner by the long, cold winter. Bluebells began to raise their heads, shades of blue as magnificent as a clear summer sky. Crocus, pure and white, reflected the morning sunshine through the dazzling dew that lay delicately upon them. The grass was green once more and the trees were showing signs of life, budding after their long slumber. Cecily had always been in tune with nature. It was as if she could hear every sound in the woods as a separate entity: the blackbirds singing their spring melody, the spiders spinning glossy webs, waiting patiently to snare their prey, the squirrels digging furiously in search of sustenance, the breeze gently rustling through the uppermost treetops, the unfurling of the spring buds of wildflowers and trees alike, the babbling of the brook on its way downstream. All of these sounds came together in a wondrous harmony that thrilled Cecily to the very bone and made her calm, almost serene. Cecily had an affinity with nature. She felt as if she belonged.

Cecily thought about her home and how lucky she was to be surrounded by such breath-taking nature. The scenery seemed to melt her troubles away. She lived in the heart of the Lancashire countryside, in a tiny village called Bramblegate. Bramblegate was old. In fact, it was very old. But, old as it was, so was it unremarkable. Cecily should know, she had lived there all her life. Her parents, both writers, had relocated from the nearby city to Bramblegate shortly before Cecily was born. They felt that the tranquil atmosphere of the country would be an inspiration for their writing and they also felt that in these 'modern times', it would be safer for their child.

Bramblegate: population, 386. And this number was at an all-time high due to baby booms in the seventies and eighties. Still, it was a small village with a small population and as you may well guess, everybody knew everybody else. At times, the advantage of living in a small village was evident, like the episode outside the village hall a few years ago, when Maxine Matthews was about to wallop Cecily. Maxine Matthews was, without a doubt, the most feared school bully in years and you did not have to do much to upset her. Cecily had simply been in the wrong place at the wrong time. And as Maxine was two years older than Cecily and distinctly taller, it was rather unfortunate that Cecily had stumbled upon an irate Maxine whilst taking a shortcut home. Luckily, Mr Jefferies was walking his beautiful Border Collie, Alfred (who did not like bullies), at the time and he had managed to call off Maxine before the blow landed. At times like these, Cecily was grateful for the interfering inhabitants of Bramblegate.

However, she was not so grateful when Mrs Gibson-Brown caught her kissing Joel Worthington in the church graveyard. She promptly dragged them both to confront Joel's parents about 'inappropriate, blasphemous behaviour'. Mrs Gibson-Brown was quite certain that the once respectable, now dead villagers of Bramblegate would be turning in their graves. Incidentally, the Worthingtons were quick to contact Cecily's parents; it would not do for Joel's name alone to be dragged through the mud. Cecily found that she was the subject of whispers and disapproving glances for a good month after the event, that is, until the next scandal gripped the village. At times like these, it was a definite disadvantage to live in such a small village. Everyone knew everyone else's business.

The local amenities in Bramblegate consisted of: St Peter's Church and its attached graveyard, the primary school, the village hall, the Bramblegate Village Store, which also housed the post office, the local pub called The Bramble Arms, which had rooms above and so also served as a bed and breakfast, Maddy's Coffee Shop, which was actually a small café and the fish and chip shop, aptly named 'Good Cod', its location being opposite the church. Nothing ever seemed to change aesthetically in Bramblegate and if someone decided they wanted to change something, then there would usually be a squabble with the locals. The largest upheaval in recent years was the addition of a petrol station, just half a mile out of the village on the approach. Some of the villagers actually staged protests against the building work. However, after all the fuss, the villagers now seemed content not to have to drive five miles to the nearest pump in order to fill their vehicles.

Cecily complained about a lot of things and as she thought about the village of Bramblegate, with its inquisitorial inhabitants and almost stagnant nature, she also thought about her affection for the place, how she cherished it and how she would not want to be anywhere else on Earth. However, on this Monday morning, there was no time to appreciate Bramblegate or to enjoy the divine spring weather. She was late and so she half-ran, half-walked the rest of the way to work.

Chapter Three

Cecily arrived at work at 9.04 a.m., precisely four minutes late. Little beads of perspiration were beginning to gather on her top lip. Perhaps if this were the first time Cecily had ever been late for work, then four minutes would not have been that much of a big deal. But as Cecily was late on a daily basis and sometimes more than four minutes late, it was a travesty, or so her manager, Acantha Sims, thought. With the efficiency of a hawk swooping down on its prey or the prowess of a tigress leaping in for the kill, Acantha Sims cornered Cecily in the back corridor by the staff room.

"Cecily, really!" puffed Acantha. "How many times do I have to tell you to BE ON TIME? It will not do! We have an obligation to our reverent employers, the Bramble family. They are good to us, Cecily. You shouldn't take advantage."

Cecily looked blankly at Acantha. *This is the part where you are supposed to reply,* Cecily thought to herself as her brain clicked into gear. She had witnessed this speech of Acantha's a million times. She could repeat it backwards, verbatim, in her sleep. Cecily especially liked the part where Acantha placed her right hand over her left breast as she talked about the Bramble family, with a far off look in her eye.

"I'm so sorry, Ms Sims. I don't know why I'm late. I've really no excuse. I promise I will be on time for the rest of the week," implored Cecily.

"Oh, Cecily!" sighed Acantha. "You say that every time you are late. As your manager, it is my job to ensure that you abide by the rules. There aren't that many rules, Cecily. All I ask is that you arrive to work on time. Do you know how many people would kill for your position here?"

That last assertion of Acantha's was not strictly true. No one wanted this job. Most of the villagers commuted the twenty-five minutes, either by car or bus, to the nearest city for work. Obviously, there was a larger variety of better paid jobs than the ones available in a tiny village. Cecily's 'reverent' employers, the Bramble family, only paid minimum wage for her job and as she was under twenty-one years old, it did not amount to much for a full-time position. However, the work was easy and she was close to home. At the end of the day, it was money.

"I'm truly sorry, Ms Sims," said Cecily. "It won't happen again."

"It had better not, Cecily or I really will have to take action. Now put on your pinny and get to the floor. We already have customers in."

Cecily watched Acantha waddle off. She was a portly lady of middle-age with short, curly, blond hair and round blue eyes. She reminded Cecily of a cherub angel. She always dressed in smart suits and she spoke with a bogus upper class accent. Most of the time, she behaved as if she were a member of the aristocracy, which was quite comical to watch, especially when she was in the presence of the Brambles, who actually were the aristocracy. But for all her affectations, she was benevolent and she had been good to Cecily. After all, she should have been fired many times over. Cecily took a deep breath and went into the staff room to stash her bag.

"Here we go again," she murmured, as she lowered her pinny over her head.

Once out on the floor, Cecily executed a quick survey of how many customers were seated. She was quite surprised to see that it was fairly busy, with half of the tables already full. It then dawned on her that this was the first week of the Easter holidays. How could she have forgotten? Cecily groaned. She knew from

23

experience that it would be heaving all day, not only with the regulars, but also with families taking their bored children out for the day.

"Cecily!" She turned around at the sound of her name and came face to face with a very red-faced Joan, who was her supervisor. "You're late! Take section A today."

"But I was on section A all last week, Joan!" Cecily pointed out irritably.

"Well if you were on time once in a while, you would have a say in the matter!" retorted Joan. "Now get to work! There are three new tables in!"

Quite frankly, Cecily felt like crying. She did not want section A, this week especially, because it was the biggest. It was only ten past nine and this Monday was already shaping up to be a terrible day.

It took Cecily a few minutes to get her bearings and think about what had to be done. As she looked around, she realised that the college students who usually worked at the weekends were in, all dashing about, balancing plates of food with cups of beverages. Through the kitchen hatch, she noticed that John, the chef, was not alone today, as he usually was during the week, but that he was accompanied by Millicent Poole. Millie was in charge of the kitchen on the busy weekends and she filled in for John when he took his holidays. As Cecily did not work weekends, she rarely had the pleasure of the weekend staff. It was the Easter holidays and personalities would clash; the weekday staff versus the weekend staff. *Great!* And with that less than harmonious thought in her head, she grabbed an armful of menus and went to serve her customers, smile intact in the hope of large tips.

Cecily worked at the legendary Lancashire manor house, Bramble Hall. Bramble Hall was a magnificent Tudor house, still independently owned by the Bramble family, which is more than could be said for other manor houses throughout the county. The Bramble family used to own much of the land surrounding the manor, including the village of Bramblegate (hence its name); however, over the years, the Brambles sold off their land in order to pay for the upkeep of their ancestral home. Nowadays, the house was open daily to the general public for tours. The Brambles had always been survivors.

The house sat in twenty-six acres of gardens and ancient woodland. It took a team of six gardeners to tend the grounds of Bramble Hall, which included ponds and rockeries, lawns, gardens and the capacious Bramble Lake. The gardens were stunning and they encompassed the most beautiful flowers and plants all year round. The gatehouse to Bramble Hall stood at the far end of Bramblegate High Street. From there, the approach to the house was a gravel driveway that wound on for three quarters of a mile, up a slight incline and through the dense woodland. The woodland then opened up to reveal the magnificent manor house, accessible through the avenue of aged and sturdy oak trees, which towered over the remaining driveway like protective giants.

Both the family and the house certainly had a chequered history. In their time, the aristocratic Brambles had been landowning gentry, collectors of taxes, advisors at court, artists, poets and writers. They had been involved in the slave trade, they had been members of Parliament and also patrons of leisure pursuits. The Brambles were infamous throughout the ages. This only added to the mystery and intrigue surrounding Bramble Hall, making it popular with the tourists and a very successful business indeed.

Cecily worked in the Dairy, one of the outbuildings at Bramble Hall. This had been transformed into a tea room when the house first began to admit visitors nineteen years ago. During the last five years, the Dairy had been renovated to give it a more pleasant, sophisticated atmosphere as opposed to one that smelt like it still housed the cows. Cecily had been working at the Bramble Hall Tea Room for three years, since her last year at high school. It was just after her father had died and her mother had desperately needed some extra money. After she left school, her mother had still needed the extra money as 'writing is an unstable business' and so Cecily began to work at the tea room full-time and here she was still.

***

Cecily had not stopped since she had arrived at the Dairy (as it was still often referred) that morning. She glanced at the clock. It was nearly eleven o'clock. She had not had a chance to speak to her regulars who usually tipped well as she had been so busy and now she had a headache from all the caterwauling children. She also felt faint and dizzy, owing to the fact that she had not had time for breakfast. Therefore, she was not in the mood when someone quite pointedly tapped her on the shoulder. Cecily inhaled deeply in order to keep her short fuse intact, when a voice said, "All right love, come here often?" Cecily spat out the breath she had just respired in a hysterical giggle, for she knew before she even turned around, that the voice which uttered this line delivered for her amusement, meant that the rest of this Monday at work would be bearable. For that voice belonged to her best friend in the whole world, Kaden.

Chapter Four

Cecily and Kaden had grown up together. Their mothers had become acquainted after the Stalk family moved into one of the three cottages in the dell, just below the village. The ladies were pregnant at the same time and so had a lot in common. You could not exactly call them friends though as Cecily's mother was a difficult person to get along with at the best of times. Kaden and Cecily became firm friends over the years, always looking out for each other. Kaden arrived in this world precisely two days before Cecily and as the oldest of the duo, he always had the final say. Cecily was by no means a pushover and she could certainly take care of herself, it just seemed that Kaden had all the answers and he was usually right. Cecily felt blessed to have such a good friend. She would not have made it through the rough times without him.

However, Kaden had experienced his own fair share of hardship. Kaden's mother had died eight years ago. She had been battling breast cancer on and off for a couple of years when it finally took her. Kaden was devastated by the loss of his mother, but he remained stoic. He was ever the perfect son, even in the face of such adversity. Cecily truly did not feel worthy in his presence. She admired him for the way he composed himself, but at the same time, she could not wholly understand his calm and almost controlled behaviour.

Kaden's mother also left behind a husband, Kaden's stepfather. They did not get on or see eye to eye on any subject. The truth was that Kaden's stepfather drank a lot. He was retired early from his job as a factory worker after sustaining a back injury and he could no longer work for a living. Coupled with his wife's death, the man was a shadow of his former self and he did not really seem to care if he lived or died. This attitude annoyed Kaden, but out of respect for his mother's wishes, his stepfather remained at their home, although Kaden and he barely spoke.

Even through all his struggles, Kaden was still there for Cecily. He was angelic. She often felt like she did not match up in the friend stakes. After her father's death and the discovery of his body, she went to pieces. But that was all in the past now. Even if Cecily felt like she could never live up to Kaden, their bond was stronger than ever. They had both lost parents they adored; a tragic fact, but something they had in common nonetheless.

"You didn't tell me you were working today," said Cecily in an accusatory tone.

"I didn't know I was," drawled Kaden, looking over Cecily's shoulder at the ever-increasing crowd of tourists seeking a table. "Acantha called me forty-five minutes ago and told me you were short-handed in here. And there was me thinking I'd get the first day of the holidays in bed! Not to worry, I could do with the cash anyway!" he added cheerily.

Kaden had been studying for his A levels at the local college for the past two years while Cecily had been working at the Dairy. He worked part-time at the Dairy for a few hours on a Saturday and Sunday and he sometimes filled in at the gift shop. Cecily and Kaden rarely had the opportunity of working together, only during the holidays. However, this did not stop them spending the rest of their time together.

"Has it been busy then?" enquired Kaden.

"Horrendous!" replied Cecily. "And I was late again. Joan put me on section A. I haven't stopped yet. Has she given you a section? You can cover for me if you like. I'm so tired. And hungry. I didn't have time for breakfast this morning…"

Cecily was so desperate for a break and something to eat that the words powered out of her mouth like a high-speed train. Kaden and Cecily looked at each other for a moment and then burst into laughter. In turn, this eruption earned Cecily the dirtiest of looks from both Dawn and Cherry, two girls who were at college with Kaden and who were also weekend staff at the Dairy. However, Cecily was used to receiving less than complimentary comments from jealous girls when she was in Kaden's company. To say he was handsome was an understatement.

Standing at six feet and one inch, Kaden resembled a Greek god. He was of medium build, he was toned and muscular and he had a slight tan no matter the time of year. Kaden had bright blue eyes and a strong jaw which was set with two dimples, one either side of a mouth full of white teeth. A mop of floppy, blond hair only added to his appeal. But Kaden's most attractive features were his charisma and presence. He radiated warmth. He was also a genuinely nice guy. Cecily often felt like she had been robbed when she was with him. How could so many good qualities belong to one person? It did not seem fair.

"You go and ask old Joan if you can have a break then. I'll cover your section," said Kaden.

He must have noticed Cecily looking over at Dawn and Cherry.

"What's wrong?" he asked.

"Oh nothing!" sighed Cecily. "Just the usual."

"Ignore them," smiled Kaden, taking her by the shoulders and rocking her gently back and forth.

"Oh, don't worry, I will!" replied Cecily. "Right, I'll go and find Joan. What kind of name is Cherry anyway?" Cecily commented as she loped away. "It's a fruit, not a name."

She heard Kaden laughing at her perception of the matter.

***

Five minutes later, Cecily was sitting at the back of the tea room in the quietest corner, away from her customers. She was perusing the menu, trying to decide what she wanted for her lunch. However, no matter how hungry she felt, she just could not focus on the menu. Now she had time to think, her feelings from earlier that morning were beginning to manifest themselves again. Deep down, Cecily knew these dreams were a problem. As she played the images out in her head, she realised how vivid they were becoming. She wondered how long it would be before she could piece the images together in order to form a story. This thought worried her. Surely her imagination was not that good. What concerned her the most though was the idea that she was, in fact, crazy. Just like everyone thought. Just like her mother thought.

Cecily was so deeply lost in the corners of her mind, she did not realise that Kaden was stood in front of her.

"Woo hoo, Cecily… Earth to Cecily… are you receiving me?" Kaden was waving his hand up and down furiously in front of her face.

"Oh sorry," said Cecily in a monotone voice. "I didn't see you there. I was daydreaming."

"Or worrying about something," muttered Kaden under his breath. "Why were you late again this morning, Cec? It's not like we had a late one last night."

"I didn't sleep very well so I just couldn't get up with my alarm clock when it went off."

She felt Kaden eyeing her suspiciously, probably searching for any hint that would give her away.

"It's the dreams, isn't it? Cecily, if they are bothering you, go and see that doctor again. You can't carry on like this. You're practically a zombie!"

"I'm not going back to that doctor, Kaden!" snapped Cecily. "I'm not crazy!"

"I didn't say you were! He could help you! Christ, I could help but you won't talk to me! I don't know what to do!"

"I'm fine."

"Well, what happened last night to keep you awake? The dreams, are they getting worse?" The cautious manner of Kaden's question was evident in his tone of voice. In turn, Cecily averted her eyes from Kaden's prying ones.

Every time she drifted off to sleep, she could hear the cries of war. She could smell the sweat and blood and she could feel the harsh resistance of the sword as she plunged it into the broken body beneath her. But it was the shadows. She just could not fathom the shadows. When she first started to have the dreams, the shadows were present, but they seemed to be in some far off place, like she could only see them out of the corner of her eye. Now when she awoke, it was as if the shadows crossed the boundaries of dreamland into her reality and into her room. She felt them everywhere. Cecily was frightened. Yet should she be scared of the shadows because they were real, or should she be scared because they were not? The latter meant she was clinically insane.

The mental showdown played itself out in her head.

"In the red corner, we have rational thinking and in the blue corner, we have preposterous thought!"

It felt like a psychological boxing match and she could even imagine the commentator, complete with tuxedo and microphone. Once the bell rang, Cecily's two lines of thought would meet in the middle and thrash it out to see who would be the winner in all of this madness. And that is what it was, utter madness. Cecily's rationality told her that shadows only existed when an object or person blocked the light. They did not have a life of their own and they were certainly nothing to be afraid of. But then her fantastical thoughts and feelings, the ones that kept her company in the dark, dead of night, urged her to fear them. She could feel it in her gut. There was no such thing as reason in the dark, dead of night. And so, the battle between rationality and the nonsensical, reality and the fantastical, raged on in her head on a daily basis. One thing was for sure, if she did not find a resolution soon, she would be donning a straitjacket and travelling on a one-way ticket to crazytown..

This thought made her head hurt.

"I'm fine, Kaden, really." Cecily's retort made it clear to Kaden that she did not want to discuss the matter any further. But this fact did not discourage Kaden from his course. Although Cecily's eyes were fixed on the menu, she could detect that he was hovering. After a couple of minutes' silence, he tried tentatively to strike up their conversation again, only she was ready for him.

"Cecily…"

"I don't want to talk about!" she snapped.

"Listen, I was just going to ask you if you wanted to get some fish and chips tonight. Then maybe meet up with the others for a couple of hours? It would take your mind off things."

"I don't know, Kaden. I really should try and get some sleep."

"Please, Cec! I'm worried about you." Kaden's pleading made it very difficult for Cecily to say no. That and the fact that the last thing she wanted to do was sleep. Plus, there was no food in the house anyway.

"OK,' she agreed. "Call round for me at six."

Cecily stalked over to the counter to order her lunch. It seemed today that even Kaden could not improve her mood.

***

Cecily barely saw Kaden for the rest of the afternoon, the lunchtime rush saw to that. But every time they passed each other, in the kitchen or on the floor, she was aware of the worry lines furrowing Kaden's brow. Should she talk to him and reveal her craziness? He was her best friend, maybe he could help. But to say it out loud would be to make it real.

Around quarter past four, the crowds had depleted and this gave the staff in the Dairy an opportunity to clean up and get ready for the next day. As the tea room closed at five, the part-time workers had been sent home an hour before. Cecily was performing the tedious task of refilling the salt and pepper pots when she heard Acantha's navy-blue court shoes trotting towards her.

"Cecily!" shrilled Acantha. "Joan said we are out of serviettes. Be a dear, run along to the store and fetch a box, would you?"

"No problem," she sighed.

Cecily put down her funnel and walked over to the door of the Dairy. She bounded out into the fresh spring air for the first time since arriving at work that morning. The store was in the main kitchen of Bramble Hall. Cecily ambled round to the back of the house, enjoying the warm sunshine on her face as she went and made her way down the stone steps of the basement entrance of the kitchen. She looked around the deserted kitchen for signs of life, although she knew that no one would be there. All of the preparation for the evening meal was done and the day shift had gone home. In an hour or so, the night shift would arrive to cook the Brambles their evening meal. The usually bustling kitchen was as silent as a graveyard at midnight.

Cecily passed the large butcher's block in the middle of the main area as she headed towards the door of the store at the back of the kitchen. As she rounded the corner, she suddenly yelped out in pain. "Ouch!" Someone had left a mop bucket in the middle of the floor and she had kicked it. Hopping on one leg whilst nursing the other injured one, she noticed that she had spilt dirty mop water all over the floor. *Fantastic,* she thought to herself. As Cecily bent down to pick up the mop, which was now strewn across the floor, she had a feeling that she was not alone. It was a fleeting moment. The hairs on the back of her neck stood on end as she shuddered. Cecily got up quickly and looked around. She was always freaked out by Bramble Hall, especially when she was in some part of it by herself. It was all the legends and ghost stories she had been told a million times over playing tricks with her mind. She reprimanded herself for being so silly, after all, she had never seen one ghost in the three years she had worked at the house. She resumed her task of mopping up the smelly water, when without warning, there it was again. She felt invisible eyes boring into the back of her head. She hastily finished cleaning up and removed the mop and bucket so no one else would fall over it.

Hurriedly, she continued along to the store. Cecily opened the door and flicked on the light. She scanned the room in order to locate the serviettes and she noticed that the boxes were in the far corner of the store on the uppermost shelving. The kitchen staff were always moving things around, so she knew she would have to check each box until she found what she was looking for. Leaving the door ajar, she grabbed the step ladders and carried them over to the shelves. She climbed steadily up the ladder, trying not to put too much pressure on her now sore shin. By this point, Cecily had scared herself half to death with her spectral fancies. She wildly searched through the boxes, looking for one containing the much sought after serviettes. As she went, she muttered the contents of each box out loud to herself. "Disposable gloves, candles, paper plates, plastic forks… ahh, here we are!" She had finally located the serviettes.

Cecily secured the box under her arm and carefully began to make her way down the ladder. She had only taken one step when the light began to flicker on and off. Afraid of having to grope her way through the dusty, cobwebbed room in the dark, Cecily was determined to get out of the store as fast as she could. It was only when she looked down to gauge her footing that she saw them, closing in out of the corner of her eye. She did not register them at first; the flickering light acted as a strobe, making their approach seem as if it were in slow motion. Cecily blinked uncontrollably as she refused to believe what she was seeing. The floor beneath her was rippling in a motion similar to a sea on a calm day, only there was nothing calming about this movement. It was the shadows and they were coming together to form one dark black mass. Cecily's heart was beating violently and as a result, she felt the blood being pumped furiously around her body. As the black mass reached the bottom of the ladder, she heard a bloodcurdling snarl like that of a rabid dog, accompanied by ear piercing shrieks that got louder and louder the closer they came. Somewhere in the distance, she heard the door of the store slam shut. Beneath her she saw the flash of a jaw snap at her heels, a gaping orifice loaded with sharp yellowing teeth, dripping hungrily in saliva. Then the dark stench of evil reached her nostrils, overpowering Cecily.

That was the last thing she remembered.

Chapter Five

When Cecily came to, the first thing she noticed through the fog was the small crowd of staff that had gathered about her. This gathering included Justin Short, one of the kitchen porters, Joan and a frantic Acantha, who was fanning Cecily's face with yesterday's newspaper.

"Oh, she's awake! Thank the Lord, she's awake!" cried an emotional Acantha.

"Yes, we can see that," commented Joan somewhat dryly. "How are you, Cecily? Do you feel OK?"

It took Cecily a few moments to gather her thoughts. She was confused. She had been in the store, up the ladder, yet now she was lying on the kitchen floor… the memory of the incident came flooding back and she almost fainted again.

"Cecily, you are awfully pale," said Joan, cradling Cecily's forehead with the palm of her hand. "What happened in there?"

Cecily did not quite know what to tell them. She was not sure what had happened herself and she certainly was not about to blurt out that she had been terrorised by her imaginary shadow monsters.

"I'm not sure. How did I get out here?" she enquired, deftly changing the subject.

"I carried you out!" said Justin proudly, puffing out his chest. "I offered to come in early today as the head chef needed some of the stock in the store rotating. A blooming good job I did, if you ask me!"

"Yes, well we didn't ask you," said Joan rather curtly, butting in on his tale of heroics. "Now what happened?"

Justin continued with his story, obviously disgruntled at Joan's impatience.

"Well," he sniffed, "I had just arrived when I heard the door of the store slam shut. I was a bit puzzled as to what could have made it slam with such a force. None of the doors and windows in the kitchen were open and even if they were, there is not even a breeze out today. Fine weather we are having…"

"Get on with it," said Joan through gritted teeth.

"OK!" continued a now afraid Justin. "I was just getting there! As I reached the door to the store, I thought I heard growling. It was like the growl of one of those big, vicious dogs, you know, like the ones they use as guard dogs."

As Justin spoke, Cecily's heart began to pound once more. *Surely not*! Her mind was racing.

Justin continued. "Anyway, I thought to myself *that can't be right, there is no such animal at Bramble Hall,* so I tried the door to get in and investigate, only it was stuck."

"So what did you do?" probed Joan, in an attempt to be more patient.

"Well, as you can see, I broke it down."

The small crowd automatically turned their heads to the door of the store and sure enough, the damage caused by Justin was evident. The wood on the frame of the door was split and hanging off where the lock had bust open. At six feet and three inches, Justin was as wide as he was tall. The damage could have been a lot worse.

"But that would have meant the door was locked," pointed out Joan. "Cecily, why did you lock the door behind you?"

"I didn't!" cried Cecily. "I left the door ajar. I mean … I'm not sure… no… I definitely left the door open!"

"The restless spirits of Bramble Hall have been up to their old tricks again," declared an ever dramatic Acantha.

"Don't be so ridiculous, Acantha!" snapped Joan. "Carry on, Justin, if you would."

"Once I got through the door, I saw Cecily wavering at the top of the ladder. She gave me quite a fright, as I wasn't expecting to see her. I was expecting the big dogs. I shouted out, but she didn't seem to hear me. She was white as a sheet, a look of sheer terror on her face and she was staring at the floor. Then she passed out. I ran over to her as fast as I could and caught her just before she hit the floor. She was out cold. I carried her out here to the kitchen and lay her on the floor. I then called the Dairy for you."

"Can you remember what happened, Cecily?" asked Joan, gently. "What scared you?"

"I... I don't remember," said Cecily, quietly. Cecily was aware that she was stammering, but she was still trying to understand what had happened herself, without having to explain it to others.

"It was probably the spirits!" sang Acantha rather loudly. "Was it the spirits, Cecily dear?"

"Erm... I don't think so." *Why can't they just leave me alone,* she thought to herself. *I need to get out of here, now. I need time to think.*

As if reading her mind, Joan said, "Well, I think that's enough questions for today. You obviously have no external injuries, Cecily. Why don't you go home and make an appointment to see the doctor in the morning? Maybe he can get to the bottom of what caused the fainting."

"That still doesn't explain the growling dogs or the locked door," puzzled a dissatisfied Justin. He thought he deserved more praise for his brave deed.

"There are the lost souls of many animals roaming Bramble Hall, Justin," said Acantha in an authoritative tone. "However, I feel that their energy has now passed. We must not be afraid." Acantha then turned to Cecily. "Cecily dear, you gave us quite a fright there. I'm so glad that you are OK. When you are ready, I am here to share your 'experience'." Acantha thought it proper to make quotation marks in the air with her fingers upon speaking the word 'experience'. "Anyway, I must go," she continued importantly. "I have a meeting with Lord Bramble. I shall inform him of your accident, Cecily. Joan, please could you call maintenance and have them fix the door? Very well done, Justin! I'll be sure to mention your service to the head chef. Good day to you all!" With her salutation hanging in the air, Acantha turned on her navy-blue court shoes and trotted off.

"Yes, well done," said Joan to Justin. "I wonder if she would also like me to call a priest and have him perform an animal exorcism?" Cecily noticed that Joan looked at Justin sceptically out of the corner of her eye.

***

A short sit down and two glasses of water later, Cecily was feeling decidedly better, at least physically. Millicent Poole had offered her a lift home, but Cecily was quite resigned to the fact that she would like to walk.

Out once again in the beautiful spring weather, Cecily's problems seemed to temporarily melt away. She closed her eyes, just for a moment and allowed her very being to be revitalised by the warm sunshine. But that was all she allowed herself, one moment. Then the disturbing events of the afternoon crept back into her mind's eye. As she walked through the wood on her way home, she replayed the incident in the store over and over in her head. What on earth had happened? In the light of day, surrounded by the beauty and tranquillity of the wood so familiar to her, she felt ridiculous. What she thought she had experienced, the impending shadows that she felt wanted to in some way harm her, seemed so unreal. Things like that just did not exist, despite what Acantha thought. But then she heard their vicious snarling, saw their hungry rotten jaws and smelt their rancid breath. And so she was back at the scene of the mental showdown. Her only comfort was that Justin had heard the growling too. If these things, these shadows, were real, what did they want with Cecily? How were they connected to her dreams?

The more she thought about it, the less mad she felt, although she was not certain that other people would feel the same way. Cecily immediately thought of Kaden. Should she tell him? Cecily had some decisions to make. She did not feel that the doctor was an option. The dreams were becoming more and more vivid by the day and now the stuff of those nightmares, the monsters that terrified her, were at her place of work. No doctor could help her with that. They would simply commit her. She had to work out what she was going to do next, not only for her sanity, but so she could sleep peacefully once more. How could she sleep? What if they came for her again while she slept? She needed to find out what they were and more importantly, what they wanted.

Cecily was so engrossed in her thoughts that she was not aware she was home until she was walking up the garden path. Glancing at her watch, she realised that Kaden would be calling for her very soon. Cecily groaned. The last thing she felt like doing was socialising. She did not mind Kaden, but she was not sure she was up to facing the others. She silently placed her key in the lock of the front door to the cottage, praying that her mother was still out as she had promised earlier. Indeed, she was another person Cecily did not feel like facing in her current state of turmoil. Cecily did a quick scan of the front room and dining room. No mother. She kicked off her trainers and padded down the passageway, checking the kitchen, the bathroom, her mother's bedroom and finally the back garden. She was alone. Cecily breathed a sharp sigh of relief. It was not that she did not love her mother, she did. It was just that growing up, her father was the one who had always been there for her.

Cecily's mother was an author of romantic novels and she'd had success with them when Cecily was a child. But Cecily always found that her mother was consumed by her writing. She thought her mother self-obsessed. Her father, too, had been a writer, but he was a scholar, an academic. He worked alongside universities and pioneered research in mythology and folklore, his specialty being comparative mythology, in which he would compare myths from different cultures. He was an authority in his field and he used to give lectures on the subject all over the world. It did not seem to matter how much research he had to do or when the next deadline was, he always had time for Cecily. When she felt she needed to be close to him, she would take his books up to her room and read about the gods and superheroes of old. His words reached out to Cecily and as she read them to herself, it was almost as if her father was reading to her, like he did when she was a child.

Since his death, her mother had become more and more distant. She had enrolled herself in ridiculous night classes at the local college and joined clubs such as the Women's Institute. She was barely home and Cecily assumed this was her way of coping. Her mother, Purdey, was in a constant state of writer's block. As a result, she had lost her publisher and although they had some of her father's life insurance money, it was still not enough to make ends meet; hence, why Cecily worked at the Dairy, to bridge the gap. By the time she had contributed to the household, she hardly had anything left for herself. Every now and then, her mother had what can only be described as surges of guilt, because at these times, she tried to over-compensate for the times she was distant by smothering Cecily. It never lasted long though.

Since she had turned eighteen, Cecily had begun to question her life and the point that there must be more to it than working in a tea room every day, handing her earnings over to a mother who did nothing. What would she do if her friends decided to go to university and move away? She would be stuck in Bramblegate with Purdey forever, working at the Dairy. What was that saying? *Carpe Diem;* 'Seize the day'. Cecily had so many decisions to make, only at the moment, the ones concerning her mother and her career were not at the top of her list.

Cecily had time to wash her face and get changed before Kaden was due, so she belted up the stairs to her bedroom and started the proceedings in her en suite. After she had made herself presentable once more, she settled into her grandmother's old chair and rocked herself gently, while looking out of the window for Kaden. Cecily could not see the horizon from her window for the trees.

She lived down in the dell, which was the woodland area below Bramblegate village. If she walked for a mile in one direction, she reached Bramblegate. A mile in the other direction took her to Bramble Hall. The dell was very peaceful, too peaceful sometimes. Growing up here, she would have been bored had it not been for Kaden. Being an only child, Kaden was like her brother. Cecily and Kaden had loved being children in the dell. They'd had many adventures exploring their surrounding wilderness.

There were three cottages in the dell: one belonging to the Stalks, one belonging to Kaden's family, the Quinns and one belonging to the Fanes, a sweet elderly couple who never seemed to change. They had been old for as long as Cecily could remember. Even though the cottages were in close proximity to each other, they were also secluded, due to the dense woodland surrounding them. The cottages were serviced by a gravel track that wound down the one mile from the main road that ran through Bramblegate. The cottages were old and Cecily's, in particular, had needed some modernisation over the years, which had included the addition of the dormer space in the roof of the cottage, now Cecily's bedroom. The cottages used to be owned by Bramble Hall and once upon a time, they were given to workers of the house, that is, before they were privatised and sold off. So it seemed quite apt that Cecily and Kaden should live in the cottages, both being members of staff at Bramble Hall. Even old Mr Fane had been a gardener there before he retired. Cecily loved the cottage. It was the only home she had known and she had many good memories of it, although the past three years, starting with the death of her father, had tainted those memories somewhat and now they were bittersweet.

Cecily got bored of looking out for Kaden and so she let her eyes drift from the treetops and the woodland below to the furthermost corner of her room and the shadows which lay there, caused by the setting sun. She stared at the shadows for a while, wondering what truly lay there, waiting for their animation in the form of a movement or snarl, to creep towards her and engulf her, taking her to God knows where. Staring at the shadows, she realised that things would never be the same again. Even in her own house, her own bedroom, she did not feel safe. The boundaries between the light and dark, between her dreams and her consciousness were blurred. She did not understand anymore. Things had changed. The dark was coming for her.

Cecily was awoken from her trance by a loud rap at the door. Kaden was late.

Chapter Six

Cecily greeted Kaden at the door with a look of disapproval on her face at his lateness. However, Kaden did not appear to notice. He seemed a little on edge and as he waited for Cecily to gather her effects, he shifted his weight from one foot to the other, eager to be on their way. As they strolled up the gravel track to Bramblegate village, Kaden chatted non-stop about a number of inane topics. About how busy it had been at the Dairy that day, about the revision plan for his exams, even about Lady Bramble's new hairdo. Cecily knew instinctively that he was worried about something. She knew him well and he was definitely over-compensating. She would just have to wait until he spat it out, although she could guess the content of the eventual conversation. However, she nodded her head and made appropriate noises where necessary, but her mind was a million miles away. As the trees started to thin a little on the way up hill, Cecily noticed that the sun was already setting on this day. Through the haze of the twilight sunshine, she saw that the sky had a red and orange hue. *Red sky at night, shepherd's delight,* she thought to herself. Tomorrow was going to be another lovely day. As they neared the top of the track, Cecily wondered if Kaden was ever going to ask her about the afternoon's events. He definitely knew something, she could tell by his behaviour. And this was Bramblegate; news, or rather gossip, travelled fast. But he did not mention it. He simply continued to chatter all the way to the High Street.

Once outside the chip shop, Kaden declared, "I'm starving! What are you having?"

Cecily peered through the window and saw that their friends were already there and in the process of ordering their meals. Fen redirected her gaze from the menu on the wall to the window. Seeing Cecily, she waved enthusiastically. As Cecily and Kaden sauntered through the door of the shop, Cecily wondered why Fen even bothered looking at the menu at all. She would order the same dish as she ordered every time they went there. They all would.

Fen was a vegetarian. She would have chips and mushy peas in a tray, only she would be in a quandary over whether to have gravy or not. If she decided on the gravy, she would punish herself over it for the next week for cheating her vegetarian diet, the gravy being made from beef dripping and all. Her boyfriend, Sol, was not a vegetarian. He would have steak and kidney pudding with lashings of gravy. Jedd was a fish man and he would order an extra-large cod with a large portion of chips and plenty of salt and vinegar. Kaden, too, would have the extra-large cod and chips, only he would top his dish with baked beans.

As Cecily queued behind Kaden, she realised that she thought it strange that they never deferred from their food choices in the chip shop. Why did they never order anything different? It was as if they were afraid of change. Or did they just know what they liked? Cecily made a spontaneous decision. She was going to do it. Today, she was going to order something different. As she pondered over this revelation, Fen nudged her and Cecily saw that Graham, the rather unenthused owner of Good Cod, was waiting patiently to take her order.

"The usual?" he asked Cecily in his colourless tone.

Cecily lost her nerve and replied, "Yes please, Graham," slightly annoyed with herself. Jumbo sausage and chips it was then. As Graham wrapped her fare in newspaper, she wondered if she knew her friends well or if they were simply predictable, like everything in Bramblegate. Then her mind drifted to the store at Bramble Hall and she realised that after today, nothing would be predictable again. And then the thought of change terrified her.

The small group of friends decided to take their food to the vantage point, overlooking the valley. Although the day had now lost the warmth of the April sunshine, it was still a pleasant evening and they wanted to grasp the final views of the glorious scenery down in the valley before the night crept in. As they meandered down the High Street, cradling their warm newspaper packages, Cecily examined her friends carefully.

She and Kaden first met Fen Aspey, Sol Forshaw and Jedd Benedict at the tender age of four years old, when they all started at the village primary together. The school was so small that there were only six students enrolled that year. The other student, Elisabeth, had moved away with her family some six months after starting. Cecily could barely remember her, only her tumbling raven curls. That left the five of them and it was only natural that they should stick together. By the time they went to secondary school, strong bonds of friendship had formed between them and so their gang continued to thrive.

Cecily gazed fondly at Fen and Sol. They were two peas in a pod, as her grandmother would say. They had been boyfriend and girlfriend since the moment had they met. A classic case of love at first sight and the truth was, they were made for each other. They even looked alike, in perfect symmetry and harmony, at one. Fen was pretty, without a doubt. She had beautiful, silky, light brown hair which fell naturally about her face in a long bob. She was small in stature and had a slim, petite frame which complimented her delicate features, except for her eyes, which were big, brown and doe like. Sol had similar features and he also had big, brown eyes. Pale golden freckles dominated his face. He was of average height and build, but because Fen was small, he seemed to tower over her. Sol's distinguishing feature was his thick tangle of curly brown hair, which was always wild and unruly. No amount of hair products could ever tame it. They both had sweet and patient characters and they were very wise for their years, Fen not yet eighteen. They had plans for the future. Both clever, they would finish their A levels, go to university and make something of their lives. Cecily envied their steadfastness, knowing exactly what they wanted out of life and aiming for it. Even Kaden had plans to go to university, although he was not as sure about his path. Cecily was not stupid. She knew she had the ability in her deep down, but then she thought about Purdey and the realisation struck that she was being left behind by her friends.

Jedd, on the other hand, was completely different to the rest of them. Cecily doubted that he would have been friends with them at all if they had gone to a bigger school with more children. That said, he did have a close relationship with Kaden. Cecily knew that Jedd told Kaden things he did not disclose to the rest of the group, but Kaden was too kind to repeat them, even to Cecily. Therefore, she did not pry. Although what secrets Jedd could possibly have to confess, she did not know. He came from a good family with money. His parents were both doctors and well-respected. If he just went with the flow, he would have a trouble-free existence, but that was not Jedd's nature. He was rebellious and did the exact opposite of what his parents wished for him. Instead of choosing college and university, he opted to work for a local construction company as a manual labourer. Kaden, Fen and Sol were intelligent, yes. But Jedd was more; he was brilliant. To Cecily, he was truly an enigma, a puzzle waiting to be figured out.

He stood slightly taller than Kaden and his large, muscular build was aided by his labouring job. He had grey eyes the colour of stone which were always angry and his shaved head only made him appear more menacing. Growing up, Jedd could, on occasion, be a bit of a bully. Luckily for him, he had the calming influences of Kaden, Fen and Sol around him. Although he and Cecily were friends, she had always felt that he did not really like her, that he resented her in some way. When she became consciously aware of this feeling, she thought it was because of her close relationship with Kaden. So she duly backed off and gave them some space. However, as they grew, she could not shake the feeling that he disliked her. She frequently caught him looking at her out of the corner of his eye and if Cecily was perfectly honest with herself, she would admit that he frightened her a little. Not just because of his maverick actions, but because of something behind those steely eyes.

It did not take them long to reach the vantage point. Once they were past the High Street, they entered into the small residential domain of Bramblegate, which consisted of five cul-de-sacs, full of stone cottages dating back to the sixteenth century. Monuments to the test of time, these weathered homes afforded views of the valley below, whilst the opposite side of the main road was covered by the dense, ancient woodland which surrounded the dell and Bramble Hall. They continued along the main road, out of the village, until they reached their destination. The vantage point was simply a lay by, where cars could stop and tourists could admire the majestic scenery.

The friends remained silent while they carefully unwrapped their dinner, digesting the breathtaking sight across the valley. For miles, all Cecily could see were rolling fields and hills. During the hours of sunlight, the fields were like a patchwork quilt, coloured with magnificent tones of greens, browns and the odd splash of yellow owing to the corn fields. The hills, green and rocky, were dotted with grazing sheep and solitary trees. However, under the cover of dusk, the earthy tones of the valley were morphing, becoming shades of dark blues and purples under the growing shadow of night.

Once their hungry mouths had sufficiently devoured enough of their food to satisfy their taste buds, Fen was the first to break the silence, with the usual enquiry about her friends' day.

"So, what did everyone get up to today?" she asked, cheerily.

Cecily knew she would be pleased with herself for not succumbing to the temptation of the gravy.

"Same old," replied Jedd. "Some of us are not blessed with the luxury of Easter holidays." Sarcasm laced his words.

"Now, now, Jedd," interjected Kaden. "You're not the only one who has been working today. I got called into the Dairy this morning because it was absolutely hammered. Isn't that right, Cec?"

"Erm, yes. We were really busy today. Tourists," said Cecily, with a mouth full of chips.

"What did you two do today?" Kaden said, directing his question at Fen and Sol.

"Well," said Fen, "something quite exciting happened!"

All eyes were now on Fen and Sol. Something 'quite exciting' had obviously occurred because Fen was effervescent, bubbling over with excitement, like a champagne bottle that had just popped its cork.

"You tell them, Sol," she squeaked.

Sol smiled lovingly at Fen and then turned to the others.

"We had some great news today. We have both been offered provisional places at Cambridge, providing we get the grades, of course."

There was a moment of stunned silence while everyone processed the information, then it was gone, broken by the congratulatory hugs and handshakes offered by Kaden and Jedd. Cecily, however, just sat there. *It is happening,* she thought to herself. *They are going away and leaving me.* Cecily, who had been sat on a rock, rose to her feet. Before she could control herself, the words came tumbling out of her mouth, "You're moving away?" It was both a question and a statement, her voice a whisper, barely audible over the buzzing excitement.

"Hopefully!" said Fen, "Providing we get the grades in our final exams. Isn't it great? We are going to have to study exceptionally hard…"

Fen kept on talking at Cecily, but Sol, who was more sensitive, noticed the look of dismay on Cecily's face. He moved over and stood beside her, gently taking her arm in his.

"You knew this day would come, Cec. You are happy for us, aren't you?"

Cecily made a split-second decision to drag herself out of her own self-pity and she managed a weak smile.

"Of course I am happy for you both. You deserve this." And she too, hugged her old friends, possibly tighter than she would have done ordinarily.

"And it might be Kaden next!" added Jedd, unsympathetically, widening the pit inside Cecily's stomach.

Kaden, who was not unsympathetic to Cecily's feelings, replied awkwardly, "Well, I'm not sure yet. I haven't made any decisions about the future. Hell, I'm just trying to get through the day!" He chuckled out loud at his own joke.

But Cecily had to accept the inevitable. Kaden was going to go to university. What was there for him in Bramblegate? She certainly could not see him working at the Dairy full-time, like her. If she was lucky, he might opt to travel to the local university, but she knew she should not get her hopes up. Jedd was now standing next to Cecily. He woke her from her thoughts with a resounding slap on the back.

"Never mind, Cec, you've got me. It will just be you and me here alone in good, old Bramblegate."

Something about the tone of his voice and the look in his eye unnerved Cecily, but before she had time to think about it, the feeling was washed over by Fen's zealous conversation.

"And there are always the holidays. We will be home then and just think all we will have to catch up on. Oh, and you can come and visit us in Cambridge! That would be wonderful! Please say you'll come and visit, Cec?"

But Cecily did not have the opportunity to answer as it seemed that Jedd had other ideas as to what the topic of conversation should now be.

"Anything interesting happen to you today, Cecily?" he inquired loudly, fixing her with his steely, knowing stare.

Cecily shifted her gaze from his to the valley below, which was now shrouded in darkness, but not before registering the anxious, wide-eyed looks of Kaden, Fen and Sol.

"Nothing special," mumbled Cecily, hoping they could not detect her indiscretion.

"Well," said Kaden slowly, swooping in to save the day, "she did get a good telling off from old Acantha for being late." He let out a forced chuckle.

"Late for work again, Cec?" questioned Sol.

"Erm, yes. I'm just having a bit of trouble sleeping."

"Is it the dreams again?" asked Fen, carefully.

Cecily's dreams were no secret to her friends, only she had not confided their growing severity to any of them.

"Yes, but you know, they are not that bad," replied Cecily, trying to appear chirpy and carefree.

As Cecily turned her back on the valley to face her friends, she was sure she saw a look pass between them, but before she could ponder this thought any longer, Sol said, "Well, our places at Cambridge won't earn themselves! Fen and I are going home now to do some studying."

"But the exams are ages off yet," said Jedd.

"Not really, only a few months," pointed out Fen. "We'll see you guys later."

After they had said their goodbyes and Fen and Sol had taken their leave, Cecily, Kaden and Jedd decided to head to the Bramble Inn for a drink.

"I suppose there is one advantage of Fen and Sol going home early," Jedd joked, as he punched Kaden on the arm. As Fen was not eighteen until next month, she could not yet go to the pub, whereas the others could. Therefore, when she was not around, they took advantage of the situation.

On the short walk back to the High Street, Kaden and Jedd messed around the whole way, shadow boxing and play fighting with each other. Cecily's brain felt numb. She did not know which problem to mull over first. So much had happened that day. As the trio entered through the heavy wooden doors of the Bramble Inn, they were greeted by the smiling face of Joel Worthington, Cecily's short-lived flame of three years ago. He attended the local university and worked nights and weekends behind the bar for extra cash.

"Gosh, am I glad to see you three! It's been slow so far tonight. I'm bored out of my mind!"

As the friends each pulled up a bar stool, Cecily scanned the room for familiar faces. Joel was right, it was quiet tonight. However, it was a Monday and not yet eight o'clock. She noticed old Mr Jeffries sat at one end of the bar, carefully holding his pint of bitter in place as if it might run off at a moment's notice. His dog, Alfred, lay loyally at the foot of the bar stool, snoozing loudly. She could also see into the old saloon from where she sat and she saw that there were a few locals playing pool. It sounded as if they were playing for money as every time a ball was potted, they erupted into cheers.

The Bramble Inn was a traditional English pub. It had a long bar with brass mouldings, traditional ales on tap and endless bottles of spirits on optics along the mirrored wall at the back. Over the far side of the bar, there was a hatch which serviced the old saloon area, a separate room in which the regulars would gather to chat, watch sports and play pool. The main lounge area was a nice size, with plenty of tables and chairs made from the same dark coloured wood as the exposed floorboards. The décor was a bit drab, deep greens and burgundies, which made the inn seem dark no matter the time of day. However, there was a well-stocked jukebox, good home cooked food and a friendly landlord, all of which more than compensated for the less than pleasing aesthetics.

After Joel had settled Kaden and Jedd with a pint of lager each and Cecily with a lemonade, he said with a wide grin on his face, "So what happened to you today, Cecily?"

The words were barely out of his mouth when Jedd jumped in and said, "My thoughts exactly."

Cecily's cheeks coloured red. She had not been expecting to have this conversation here, now.

"What do you mean?" she retorted, defensively.

"Well, I heard you took a swan dive off a ladder at Bramble Hall this afternoon," replied Joel, unaware of Cecily's awkward disposition.

"It was nothing," said Cecily, in an attempt to play down the situation.

"That's not what I heard," goaded Joel. "I heard about the unexplained slamming of a door and the spirits of vicious hellhounds... wooooooo!" He laughed heartily as he did his best ghost impression, looking at Kaden and Jedd to back him in winding Cecily up.

"Yeah, that's funny, because I heard the same thing," said Jedd maliciously, his eyes of stone set upon Cecily.

"Look, it was nothing. I don't really remember what happened. How do you know about it anyway?"

"Oh, Millie Poole was in here earlier, regaling us with the heroic tales of Justin Short, how he broke down the door and gallantly rescued you from the pack of wolves!" Joel clearly found the whole situation highly amusing.

"You know, I was in here earlier too, listening to Millie Poole's gossip," said Jedd, his intonation rising with anger. "Only I'm still waiting for my 'friend' to tell me about it." He stressed the word 'friend' as if it had a sour taste.

"Come on, Jedd, leave it," said Kaden, calmly. "She'll tell us when she's ready."

Jedd's eyes had not left Cecily for a moment and she was feeling increasingly uncomfortable.

"Come to think of it, Cecily," continued Jedd, completely ignoring Kaden, "there is always a drama with you, isn't there? I daren't even guess what caused you to faint. What was it this time? You had to make up a story that a pack of vicious ghost dogs were trying to eat you so you could get some attention? Did you hear Justin coming and pretend to faint?"

Tears began to well up in Cecily's eyes and she was trying desperately to hold them back. She did not understand why Jedd was behaving like this. What had she done to him?

"Are you making up new stories now because the ones about your dreams are getting old?"

"Jedd," Kaden warned, slowly.

"Well, I'm sorry, Kaden!" said Jedd, turning to face him. "I'm sick of it. She's so self-obsessed and she doesn't give a damn about anyone else. You saw her earlier, she couldn't even be happy for Fen and Sol. She always has to have all the attention. She's just like Purdey."

Jedd's final words were a blow to Cecily. Jedd was being unfair. OK, Cecily had not mentioned the incident, but if anything, it was to avoid the attention. Also, she had not said anything to anyone about vicious ghost dogs; that was Justin's interpretation, fuelled by Acantha. Jedd did not seem prepared to hear what Cecily had to say and he was intent on attacking her. She needed to get out of there.

"Look guys, calm down," interjected Joel. "I didn't want to cause any trouble. I was just teasing her."

Old Mr Jeffries had heard the kafuffle from the other end of the bar and he had now joined them, Alfred at his side.

"Come on now, you young'uns. Stop all the noise and leave that poor lass alone," once again coming to Cecily's aid, just like he had when Maxine Matthews tried to bully her.

"It's OK, Mr Jeffries," she choked. "I was just leaving."

As soon as Cecily's face hit the cool night air, her tears started streaming. Behind her, she heard the heavy doors swing open and close. She turned to see Kaden, who had followed her outside. Before he had a chance to speak, she screamed at him, "You knew about this and yet you didn't tell me?"

Kaden could not seem to find any words. He stared at the floor, trying to remove a piece of old chewing gum from the pavement with his trainer.

"Do Fen and Sol know too? Do you all think I'm some kind of freak? Have you all been discussing me behind my back? Is Jedd the spokesperson, or something?" Cecily was now furious.

"Look, I don't know what just happened in there," said Kaden. "Jedd was out of order." He moved forward to console a now sobbing Cecily, but she deftly side-stepped him.

"But that's what you all think, right? That I'm a selfish, self-obsessed, attention seeker?"

"Cecily, you know that's not what we think at all! We understand! You've had a rough time over the past few years."

"Well, Jedd obviously thinks it! You know, Kaden, you're supposed to be my best friend!" yelled Cecily, losing all self-control. "For the others to think or say those things or discuss me behind my back, well the thought devastates me. But you? For you to stab me in the back? I just can't forgive you."

Cecily turned and ran down the High Street as fast as she could, tears blinding her path. She could hear Kaden calling her name, but she did not look back. She could not. She knew she was being unscrupulous, taking her wrath out on Kaden instead of confronting Jedd. Kaden would never intentionally hurt her, no matter what. When she reached the gravel track which led to the dell, she hesitated momentarily. She did not like going down it on her own at the best of times, never mind after what had happened to her that afternoon. But in the wake of her recent argument, she lost all fear and ran down the track in a blind fury. Cecily was deeply engrossed in her thoughts, jolted from them every so often by imaginary shapes coming at her from the dense, dark woodland.

She got home to discover that Purdey still was not back and so she went straight upstairs to her room. Every time she thought about Jedd and his harsh words, they cut. At least his feelings towards her had now been confirmed. But the thought of sweet Fen and Sol and Kaden, her best friend in the world, thinking those things about her, it made her sick to the stomach. She was now sobbing loudly. With no one to hear her cries, she let out her anger, her fear and her sadness in large gulps.

Cecily knew that she had not been easy to be around since her father's death. She knew she had been negative, miserable and depressed about her life in general. She had a job she hated, a mother who was growing more and more distant and if that was not enough, there were her worsening nightmares. She was also well aware that the most important people in her life, her friends, were passing her by and moving on to better things. And after her liaison with the shadows that afternoon, she felt like she was living under a permanent dirty, big, black cloud that would not go away. She had become self-obsessed. Self-obsessed with trying to work out if she was crazy or not. She felt isolated and so alone. To be compared to everything she hated about Purdey was a wake-up call. She had to take control of her life. Things were changing whether she liked it or not. She could either wallow or take action.

First of all, she decided that she needed some time out, some time away from her friends. She did not realise the effect her negativity had had on them. She had to sort through her issues and then she could sort things out with them in a couple of months when she was cheerful, carefree Cec again. Kaden, Fen and Sol would be busy with their studies anyway. At this moment in time, she was not sure if she ever wanted to talk to Jedd again. Next, she would tackle her most pressing problem. She would get to the bottom of her dreams and the meaning of the shadows, but where to start? She was obviously crazy, losing the plot. That evening had shown her that she was a laughing stock in the village. Once she put an end to her nightmares, she could take steps to change the other things in her life she hated.

As she pondered this, Cecily felt a little better for making her mental plan. To think, only that morning, she had cursed the predictability of her life. When she awoke, clever Cecily thought she knew exactly what this Monday held for her. A never-ending cycle of work and bad dreams. After today, that predictability seemed comforting to her. She wanted to give today back and pretend it had never happened, because in the space of this one short day, everything had changed. Things would never be the same again, they could not be. She, Cecily Stalks, had been the one who had longed for change, a break from the monotony of her life. Only she did not realise that change could be bad. Her dreams had come to a climax with the stuff of those dreams attacking her in real life, her friends were moving on and going away, she had been verbally attacked by one of her so-called friends and blamed her best friend in his stead. She was not even sure if her friends would ever want to talk to her again. She could not lose them. They were her life and she needed them now more than ever. Her mind drifted back to the chip shop earlier that evening. She could not believe she thought her friends predictable because they ordered the same meal over and over. She had thought them scared of change. Well, they had certainly shown her. Cecily was suddenly aware that it was she who was afraid of change, despite her thoughts that she wanted things otherwise. At least she could still rely on some things for their predictability. She thought about Bramblegate for the second time that day, only this time around, her feelings were not of love for her home. She wanted to send Millie Poole and the rest of the gossips to damnation, or in the very least, tell them what she thought.

After she had washed her tear-stained face and soaked her puffy eyes in cold water, she pulled on her pyjamas and contemplated sleep. She was exhausted and did not have the energy to dream of wars. Maybe the shadows would just come for her and put an end to her sorrow. She immediately regretted that last thought and looked warily into the corners of her bedroom. She opted to sleep with the light on for comfort and to ward off any dark shadows they may come in the night. But before she could give the matter anymore thought, Cecily had drifted off into a deep sleep.

Chapter Seven

Kaden watched Cecily run down the High Street until he could see her no more. The road was quiet and even when she was out of sight, he could still hear her sobs, Cecily no long holding her emotions in check to save face. After she had disappeared, he stood for a minute or two, digesting the scenario that had just unfolded.

It was true, he had heard the gossip. Jedd had called him at home, just before he left to go to Cecily's. Although Kaden had not had chance to talk to Fen and Sol about it, he knew that Jedd had told them too. It was evident by the look on their faces earlier at the vantage point. Kaden had wanted to ask Cecily what had happened. She would have known that something was up with him by his constant fidgeting and his endless talking, not allowing a quiet interlude for even a moment. In hindsight, he should have just come out with it, but Cecily was not the easiest person to talk to lately. In a way, Jedd was right. She had become a little self-obsessed, depressed even. But Kaden knew that the reason for this was because she was hiding something and it was probably to do with her dreams. He understood Cecily better than anyone.

However, Kaden did not understand Jedd's attack. If he was upset with Cecily for not confiding in her friends, there were better ways of putting it. Comparing Cecily to her mother was possibly the worst thing he could have done. Kaden knew that Cecily was neither a liar, nor an attention seeker. What she was going through was affecting her badly and he was worried about her. Cecily was pale and drawn through lack of sleep and most of the time, her mood was waspish. On top of this, she was dangerously close to losing her job and he knew how much she needed it. But she would not talk to him about it. He had tried. And now, he could not shake Cecily's final words to him. *I just can't forgive you.* She had never said anything like that to him before, upset or otherwise. Her vow was ringing in his ears. Kaden inhaled the night air, a long-drawn breath and then he went back inside the Bramble Inn to talk to Jedd.

As Kaden pulled up his bar stool, he noticed that Jedd was staring stonily at his pint of lager, slowly running his finger up and down the length of the glass, making lines in the condensation.

"So, what was all that about?" enquired Kaden, without looking directly at Jedd.

"I'm tired of her. I'm tired of her constant moods and the whole 'woe is me' act. You know, she never takes an interest in anyone else. She brings the rest of us down with her negativity." Jedd was obviously still angry. As he spoke, he began to raise his voice again. "If she talked to us about it, maybe we could help."

"She's going through a rough time, Jedd," Kaden reasoned. "I think these nightmares are really bothering her again."

"Exactly my point, you 'think'. You don't know for sure, because she hasn't told you. In my opinion, she's changed, end of story."

"Her dad committed suicide just three years ago, Jedd. Cut her some slack. She was so close to her father. We all know that Purdey is a worse than useless parent. To compare Cecily to her was the worst thing you could have done."

"Your mum died too, Kaden, yet you don't act the way she does."

"My mum had been sick with cancer for nearly two years," said Kaden, sadly. "We were expecting her death. I was relieved she wasn't in pain anymore. Cecily came home from school to discover her dad swinging from a tree by his neck in the back garden. It's hardly the same. Christ, that would mess anyone up for life."

"Yeah, but she doesn't do anything to help herself. She even stopped seeing that doctor," said Jedd, defensively.

"Well, we'll be lucky if she speaks to any of us again after your righteous outburst. You were awful to her. And you know, you shouldn't have spoken on behalf of Fen, Sol and me."

"I only said what everyone else thinks," retorted Jedd, wickedly. "If you ask me, we're all better off without her dragging us down."

"Yeah, well I don't agree, Jedd. She's our best friend and if we don't help her, who will? We should be sticking together, not fighting."

Jedd did not have a chance to reply as Joel joined them once more.

"Listen, I'm sorry guys, I didn't mean to cause a row. I was only pulling her leg. I thought Cec could take a joke. She used to be so much fun."

Jedd turned to Kaden, raised his eyebrows and gave him an "I told you so" look.

The boys finished their pints in silence and then headed off home. They parted ways at the gravel track. After an awkward farewell, Kaden took the track and Jedd carried on along the main road. He lived about a fifteen-minute walk out of the village with his parents in a big house on the main road.

Kaden trundled slowly down the path, back to the dell. He was in no rush to get home and he had a lot to think about. The quiet helped. Other than the occasional sound of crickets calling to one another across the dark, the wood was silent. Despite what Jedd's views were, Cecily was his best friend and he wanted to help her. He needed to help her. But unless she talked to him and told him the severity of her dreams, he would not know what to do. You see, there was more to Kaden than met the eye. He knew things. And right now, he needed to know what to expect. What was coming? Were they all in danger? After all, he had not heard anything. And yet he realised that Cecily's increasing nightmares were not a good omen. He had witnessed the dreams becoming progressively worse over the last three years and the effect that they were having on Cecily. He did not know how much longer he could just stand by and do nothing, but he knew he could not risk alerting Cecily, or the others for that matter. He needed to acquire all the facts first, otherwise he would be in serious trouble. He would keep his eye on her for now and try and get her to talk. Only then, could he seek counsel. This was the best he could hope for.

Kaden took a small detour past Cecily's cottage. Her bedroom light was still on, but no others in the house. He stood there for a moment, looking up at her window, resisting the urge to rap on the door. It was not late, but if she had managed to fall asleep, he did not want to wake her. He was also worried about her rejecting him, after what she had said to him earlier that evening. He resolved that he would see her tomorrow and clear the air.

"Night, Cec," he whispered under his breath, up at her window. *She must talk to me.*

Kaden did not see the tall, dark figure watching him from under the wooded canopy. Nor had he noticed that the same tall, dark figure had followed him from the top of the gravel track down into the dell, gliding along silently and unseen at a parallel to Kaden, hidden by the mantle of trees. He now watched as Kaden withdrew from the front of Cecily's cottage, a wry smile spreading across his face. He retreated once more to the cover of the woodland, the shadows recoiling at his command.

***

After Jedd had left Kaden, he did not go home. In fact, he waited for ten minutes, lurking by the side of the road. Then, he doubled back and took the gravel track heading down towards the dell.

Only he did not go the whole way. About a third of the way down, Jedd veered off the track and traversed into the black wood. It was so dark, he could not see to gauge his footing and he kept tripping over the exposed roots of the ancient trees. When he was a safe distance from the track, he pulled out a torch and slid the switch on. He kept his path, walking in a straight line. Even in the dark, he could find his way to the place. He had been there many times before.

It was not long until he reached the clearing. It was only small, but highly distinctive due to the circle of six tree stumps that lay there in a protective ring. These stumps, untamed grass growing wild about them, were once mighty oaks. They had been cut and felled many years since, yet their stumps remained and their roots were twisted, running deep underground. Jedd sat down on one of the stumps, his behind feeling instantly chilled and he waited. He soon distinguished light footsteps coming through the wood towards the clearing from his right-hand side. He knew instinctively who the footsteps belonged to; the man he was meeting. A cold shiver ran down Jedd's spine as he thought about his association, the air suddenly containing an unexplained nip. The tall, dark figure emerged from the right as Jedd had predicted.

"Turn the light off." It was not a request. Jedd quickly did as he was told. "Is it done?" he asked, abruptly.

"Yes, sir," replied Jedd, looking into a face he could not see.

"So, the girl is isolated?" the dark figure enquired further.

"Yes, sir," repeated Jedd. "In fact, my plan went rather well. I'm not sure that Kaden will leave it alone though. The other two, I can handle, but you are aware of Kaden's bond with Cecily."

"All too well," snapped the figure. "Leave the boy to me. You lie low for the time being, as discussed. Do not see or talk to the boy or the girl. Handle the other two. Do I make myself clear?"

"Yes, s-s-sir, p-perfectly," stammered Jedd, exposing his anxiety.

"I'll be in touch."

The dark figure quickly turned and headed back into the trees from the direction he had come. Jedd watched him leave. He could see by the light of the quarter moon that the ground seemed to ripple beneath him, a black mass stirring in a motion similar to the sea on a calm day. A cold shiver, once again, ran the length of Jedd's spine. He stood up and drew his jacket tightly about him. When he was sure the dark figure had gone, he swiftly headed back into the wood in the direction of the gravel track, making sure he was far from the clearing before turning his torch back on.

Chapter Eight

It had been nearly four weeks since the big argument with Jedd and Kaden and Cecily had not spoken to any of her friends since. However, were you to ask Cecily how she was, she would tell you that she was great. In fact, Cecily Stalks was more than great, she was fantastic.

When she awoke the morning after the row at the Bramble Inn, her heart was heavy as she remembered the events of the previous day: the horror of the shadows in the store, her fainting and the gossip surrounding the incident, the news that Fen and Sol were moving away, Jedd's hurtful outburst towards her and worst of all, her falling out with Kaden. These memories stung, but then she recalled the promises she had made herself to sort her life out and to resolve the mysteries that were driving her insane. Only then could she change her life for the better and follow in the footsteps of her friends, whom she held so dear.

As she looked at herself in the mirror through swollen eyes, a realisation dawned on her. She had not dreamed in the night. For the first time since she did not know when, there were no night terrors about battle, no cries of war tearing at her soul, no smell of blood and sweat and no feelings of imminent danger, as the shadows, there but unseen, hunted her down. She had slept straight through the night and despite her troubles, she felt good, almost positive. She was up in plenty of time for work and more importantly, she was alive. Nothing had come for her in the dead of night while she slept, as was her last waking thought of the previous evening.

When she arrived at work that morning, fifteen minutes early,

Acantha and poor old Joan nearly passed out from shock. At first, she attributed the absence of her nightmares to the fact that she was exhausted, therefore she slept deeply, unable to dream. Or maybe, it was because she had slept with the light on. But as the nights turned into days and the days turned into weeks, her nightmares failed to reappear and she actually looked forward to sleep. Cecily felt simply marvellous! On top of the world and full of life, exactly how a normal eighteen-year-old should feel. It seemed that a bit of positive thought, coupled with the determination to turn her life around had worked. And the absence of her dreams, the bane of her life, was a great start. However, there was another reason for Cecily's renewed vigour. She had met someone. A boy.

A couple of days after that dreadful Monday, Joan had to leave the Dairy early, shortly before close, to attend a dental appointment. She entrusted Cecily with the day's takings and asked her to deliver them to Acantha, once she had locked up the Dairy. Acantha was in a meeting with Lord Bramble in his study, so after Cecily had triple-checked that she had locked the door of the Dairy, she went over to Bramble Hall.

She made her way through the Great Hall and up the grand staircase to the first floor. Cecily rarely had reason to go over to the main house, unless of course it was to go to the basement via the back entrance. This was certainly the first time that Cecily had been to the upper floors of Bramble Hall, as they were mostly off limits to the staff and general public. As she turned left at the top of the beautifully polished wooden staircase, she marvelled at the centuries old portraits of various members of the Bramble aristocracy that lined the walls. Curious eyes bored down upon her as she walked across the large, rectangular landing, past the bed chambers and along to the study, which was located in the east wing of the house.

Cecily tentatively knocked on the door. She'd had little dealings with Lord Bramble and although he was quite short in stature, his presence was most certainly intimidating. However, Cecily was quite sure that Acantha would open the door. After what felt like an eternity, the leather-padded door swung open, only it was not Acantha that stood there, with her chubby, round face and nor was it the fearsome demeanour of Lord Bramble. Stood in the doorway of the study was the most handsome boy that Cecily had ever seen in her short life. Cecily thought how very tall he was as she stared up into his ice blue eyes. They were as clear as crystal, except for a thin circle of dark blue that lined the outer edge of the iris. Long, black lashes fringed his eyes and he had thick, shaggy, black hair, which was probably longer than it ought to be, with a smattering of designer stubble to match. When he smiled at Cecily, his eyes smiled too, leaving little creases at the corners.

"Hi there," he said to Cecily, obviously amused at the fact she had coloured up like a beetroot and her cheeks were now clashing with her auburn hair.

"Erm, hi," replied Cecily. "I just brought the, erm, money from the Dairy. For Acantha, I mean, the money is for Miss Sims." Cecily was now unable to meet his crystal gaze and she felt stupid for muddling her words.

"Cecily, dear, is that you?" she heard Acantha screech from the room beyond.

"Yes, Miss Sims," Cecily shouted back, colouring up again.

"Do let her in, Cian, there's a good boy," crooned Acantha, as if addressing her favourite pet.

Cecily tried her hardest to act as cool as possible as she strutted across the cherry parquet flooring. Nothing could ruffle her feathers. But suddenly, all she could think about was exiting the room as quickly as possible. She approached the desk where Lord Bramble and Acantha were sat opposite one another and in her haste, she happened to trip on the corner of the large, heavy rug that lay beneath the desk and chairs. She managed to keep her footing and narrowly avoided ending up in Acantha's lap.

Cecily, who could not be more embarrassed, handed over the takings to her manager, not daring to contemplate Lord Bramble who looked completely baffled.

"Good job, Cecily!" said Acantha, heartily. "We'll make management material of you yet!" Cecily, knowing when she had been utterly patronised, smiled feebly at Acantha and turned to leave the study. However, blocking the exit, with a broad smile across his face, was the handsome boy, who seemed to be enjoying every moment of Cecily's mortification.

As she edged passed him, she glanced upwards in the direction of his face and mumbled, "Thanks", eager to leave the study and the house behind her, as fast as humanly possible.

As she hurried along the landing, she heard footsteps behind her and she knew she was being followed. Turning to descend the staircase, she saw that the handsome boy had followed her.

"By the way, I'm Cian. Cian Bramble," he said in a strange accent, which Cecily thought sounded Irish.

"Cecily Stalks," she replied in a mutter, accepting his hand which was now extended in front of her face. *This guy must think I'm socially inept,* she thought to herself as she blushed deeply, yet again. *What is wrong with me?*

"What are you up to now?" he asked her.

"Nothing," said Cecily, attempting to appear airy and nonchalant. "I'm just about to walk home."

"Well, if you don't mind, I'll join you. I could do with some fresh air."

And that is how Cecily Stalks met Cian Bramble.

***

On the short walk home, Cecily had discovered much about Cian. She found him to be very open and forthcoming about himself. He was twenty years old and from Dublin in Ireland. Cian was Lord Bramble's nephew, being the son of Lord Bramble's younger brother. He was studying at Trinity College in Dublin, but he was currently taking a gap year to do some travelling. Cian was studying 'Ancient and Medieval History and Culture' and had just got back from a trip to Europe after visiting some of the places he had been studying and was yet to study over the final two years of his degree. He'd recently completed his travels with a month in London, so now he was spending some time in Lancashire, at his ancestral home, before going back over to Dublin and university.

Cecily had barely taken note of her beloved wood on that particular walk home. The natural surroundings that usually soothed her: the trees, the wildflowers, the stream, the birds and animals, all paled into insignificance as her sole focus was Cian. And over the past few weeks, since meeting him, so had all other aspects of her life taken a backseat, including her family, her friends and her job. Cecily, who had hardly ever been out of Bramblegate, was mesmerised by Cian and the wondrous tales of his adventures across Europe and back in Dublin. He was like no one she had met before and she was completely in awe of him. When he spoke in his deep, melodious Irish accent, Cecily could not concentrate on anything else. His warm tones compelled her to a place where nothing else seemed to matter. As he told his stories, his eyes danced with enthusiasm, making his whole face smile and Cecily was perfectly entranced by his ice blue, crystal gaze. There was something so familiar about him, as if she had known him forever. But of course, she knew that was not possible, so she took their meeting as a good sign.

Cian had completely swept Cecily off her feet, giving her a taste of a life she had dared not dream of. They often left the claustrophobic atmosphere of Bramblegate and made for the city, Cecily chauffeured by Cian in various classic cars, borrowed from his uncle. Cian was a true gentleman and his advantageous upbringing had afforded him gracious manners. He always opened the car door for Cecily, pulled a chair out for her in restaurants and assisted her with her coat. *Who said chivalry is dead?* she thought to herself on more than one occasion. She often felt clumsy and uncouth around Cian, having grown up in a small village and being very unworldly, but Cian was kind and never made her feel bad. And of course, Cecily was only too willing to educate herself in the etiquette of high society. Sometimes, she felt like she was living in a Jane Austen novel. Cecily was having the time of her life. She had been transported to another world completely and this was certainly more like the change she was craving.

But this was more than about where Cian could take her, what car he drove or who he could introduce her to. Cian seemed genuinely interested in Cecily as a person. He wanted to know everything about her: about her friends, her family, her dreams and aspirations, about her past, present and future. Sometimes, she felt like she had been talking at him for what seemed like hours. He was such a good listener. And this in itself was the perfect therapy for Cecily. She trusted Cian and so told him about her darkest fears, about the death of her father and how the dreams that occurred as a result were affecting her relationships. She shared and let him enter the turmoil of her mind. Even when Cecily talked about the shadows, feeling crazier by the second as she spoke about them out loud, never did Cian judge her. He always had a sympathetic smile and reassuringly squeezed her hand. Cecily felt like she had finally found someone who understood her and she did not want to relinquish this feeling.

That is the reason why Cian had taken priority and all other factors in her life seemed barely important. Cecily did feel a surge of guilt when she thought about her friends. She knew she could not avoid them forever and she also knew that they deserved more than the way she was treating them at the moment. Fen and Sol had made several attempts to contact Cecily, but she had become quite skilled at the art of avoidance. Fen had left her many messages at home, enquiring as to how she was and attempting to make plans to meet up. They had even called into the Dairy on a couple of occasions after college, hoping to see her. But Cecily either found a reason to go over to the main house or managed to swing a break. As the Easter holidays were now a distant memory, Kaden was back at college and working at Bramble Hall on weekends when Cecily was not, so she had not had to worry about bumping into him at work. Also, he had been taken out of the Dairy to work in the gift shop, as Mabel, the old lady who had been running it for years, had retired. Various members of staff were filling in while they were looking for someone to replace her. However, this had not stopped Kaden from calling her incessantly and going to Cecily's cottage at every opportunity. Cecily was rarely home these days, so it had been easy to avoid Kaden. If he called later in the evening, she pretended to be sleeping. Cecily still did this, knowing that Kaden would be lost without her. They had been inseparable since they were children. The only person Cecily had not heard from was Jedd, but she was not surprised about this.

She knew that she would have to face her friends sooner or later, but she was not ready to just yet. She was having the time of her life with Cian and she assured herself that the space would do them all good. There would be time for a reunion later, when Cian had gone back to Ireland, but this was another thought that Cecily was shoving to the back of her mind. She was content living her fairy tale for the time being. Reality could wait.

Chapter Nine

It was a glorious afternoon in the middle of May. The sun was out, baking the world beneath as it shone down. Cian had dropped by the Dairy and invited Cecily to an impromptu picnic by the lake. She was, of course, thrilled and as she was just finishing up at work, she offered to go across to the Hall with Cian and help prepare the picnic basket.

"I've already done it!" Cian informed her. "You go down to the lake and find a spot. I'll join you shortly. I've got to have a word with my uncle about something."

"Are you sure?" replied Cecily. "I don't mind."

"No, it's OK. I'll meet you in fifteen minutes."

Cecily grabbed her bag and trundled slowly down the gravel driveway, glad of the protection of the giant oaks from the blazing sunshine. Although she was excited about the picnic, she was feeling a bit miffed. Cecily had a strong feeling that Lord Bramble did not approve of his nephew's choice. Whenever he saw them together, Cecily felt that he eyed her suspiciously. *I'll show him,* she thought to herself and as she headed for the lake, she daydreamed of some massive accomplishment that would raise her up in Lord Bramble's estimation and make her good enough for his nephew.

Cecily was so caught up in her daydream, that at first she did not notice the girl walking towards her in the direction of Bramble Hall. Just as they were about to walk by each other, Cecily noticed that the girl was looking at her intensely. Cecily could not help but stare back, thinking that the girl looked vaguely familiar.

"Cecily?" asked the girl rather cautiously. "Cecily Stalks?"

"Erm, yes," replied Cecily, feeling rather awkward.

"Oh, thank God! A familiar face! You don't remember me, do you?" she questioned, noticing Cecily's look of dismay.

"Of course, I do!" exclaimed Cecily, stalling for time. "It's…"

"Elisabeth," the girl interjected. "Elisabeth Stone. We used to go the village primary together."

Now Cecily remembered. How could she have forgotten those beautiful ravel curls and the rich, dark brown eyes that were almost black.

"Elisabeth! It's so nice to see you! What are you doing in Bramblegate?"

"I just moved back a couple of days ago with my family. My father's job brought us back here."

"I bet you don't remember much about the place. You were only four when you left, weren't you?"

"Yes, that's right. But I'm so happy to be back. This place feels like home, you know. We've moved around a lot because of my father's work, but it looks like we're here to stay this time! I was hoping to bump into you or some of the others. It's funny, but I remember you really well. Do you all keep in touch?"

"Yes," replied Cecily, feeling rather guilty at her answer. "The others are fine. Kaden, Jedd, Fen and Sol are good friends."

"Excellent!" enthused Elisabeth. "Maybe you could all show me around and fill me in on what's changed?"

Just at that moment, Cecily heard the crunching of footsteps on the gravel driveway, heading towards them at a running pace. She turned and saw Cian coming to join them.

"Who's this then?" enquired Cian.

"Hi, I'm Elisabeth Stone. Nice to meet you," said Elisabeth, offering her hand.

Cecily, who was observing Cian like she always did, thought she saw a flicker of annoyance pass over his handsome face, but Cian, who was always gracious, accepted Elisabeth's hand and said, "Cian Bramble. It's a pleasure."

"Oooo, a Bramble!" cried Elisabeth. "I'm just on my way to Bramble Hall to interview for a part-time job in the gift shop. They need someone for the weekends and it would fit in perfectly with college. Maybe you could put a good word in for me?" she joked.

"Of course," laughed Cian, "but I'm sure you'll have no problem."

"I'd better go," sighed Elisabeth. "I don't want to be late. Can I call you, Cecily?"

"Sure, no problem," she said. "Nice to see you again."

After they had parted company, Cecily and Cian wandered down to the lake. Cian had prepared a sumptuous feast which they devoured whilst chatting and lounging in the glow of the early evening sun. Cecily was curious as to what Cian had been talking to Lord Bramble about, so after they had finished their picnic, she broached the subject.

"Did you talk to your uncle earlier?"

"I most certainly did!" he replied, exuberantly. "In fact, I was just about to mention it. I've asked my uncle if I can arrange Bramble Hall's summer event this year. I have a lot of free time on my hands, especially when you're at work (he winked at Cecily, making her blush) and it's something I can really get my teeth into. I just wanted to run my idea past him and he agreed." Cian was obviously very proud of his uncle's approval.

"So, what will the theme be this year?" asked Cecily, excitedly.

"We are having a Golden Hollywood costume party. I thought that everyone could come dressed as old film stars from the 1930s and 1940s. We'll have a big band, real dancing, a cocktail bar and maybe even finish with a bit of karaoke."

"What a marvellous idea!" said Cecily, clasping her hands together. "I'd better get thinking of a costume!"

"And Cecily, there's one more thing," said Cian, with a

sparkle in his eye. "Miss Stalks, I would like to formally invite you to be my date at the Bramble Hall Golden Hollywood Summer Party." He stood and made a low bow.

"Why, I'd be delighted, Mr Bramble!" replied Cecily, her heart skipping a beat.

As she gazed into his crystal blue eyes, her head still reeling from his proposal, he murmured softly, "You really do have the most beautiful eyes, Cec."

And in the moment that followed, her breath was stolen, as he took her hands in his and kissed her tenderly. As they shared their first kiss, there by the lake, she knew she was in trouble, as she had never felt such elation. There was no doubt that Cian Bramble had her eating out of the palm of his hand.

Chapter Ten

It was a delightful summer afternoon and Cecily was walking home from the Dairy, completely lost in thought, enjoying the serenity of the woodland around her. As Cecily gazed upwards through the trees, trying to spot the birds who were singing such melodious tunes, she thought about the coming weekend. This weekend was the first weekend of June and with it, it would bring the Bramble Hall Golden Hollywood Summer Party. There was a palpable buzz in the air as the villagers of Bramblegate prepared for the event. Lots of tickets had already been sold and Cian and the team at Bramble Hall were working hard to ensure the party was a success. As the theme was old film stars, Cecily and Cian had decided to dress up as Katharine Hepburn and Spencer Tracy. Cecily had opted for Katharine Hepburn as she'd had red hair, like Cecily. Cecily had gone all out for this event and she'd had a beautiful black evening dress made in the style of the 1930s. Cian would be slicking back his thick, black hair and he would be wearing a tuxedo.

All Cecily had thought about was the party, where she would officially be on Cian's arm for the whole village to see. She played the event out over and over in her head, from the moment she and Cian walked in, all eyes on them, staring in wonder and awe at Cecily's magnificent costume and equally magnificent boyfriend, until the end of the evening, when she and Cian would be slow dancing, again being admired by all present. She would be the envy of everyone there and she could not wait.

Every year, Bramble Hall hosted a party for the villagers to mark the beginning of summer. It was a tradition that everyone in Bramblegate looked forward to and most of the villagers would attend. The party used to be held on the summer solstice, but legends tell of mysterious events taking place on one such Midsummer's Eve, so the Brambles, with full agreement from the villagers, moved the event to the beginning of June.

Cecily could not remember being more excited about something for a long time. This was going to be one hell of a party! And deep down, she knew the reason for this was Cian. It was him that had brought excitement into Cecily's life and now the villagers of Bramblegate would experience his influence too. The summer events of Bramblegate in previous years had been dull affairs and Cecily had always dreaded attending them. Kaden, Jedd, Fen, Sol and herself would usually skulk around in the background at some drab garden party with a terrible theme. But this year would be different. This year, she would be with Cian.

As Cecily was thinking about the finishing touches that needed to be made to her costume, she saw that Kaden was coming towards her down the track. Her first instinct was to duck and hide behind a tree, after all, it had been two months since she had seen him, let alone spoken to him, but then she told herself she was being ridiculous. She would have to face him sooner or later; he was her best friend. In any case, he'd already seen her.

"Cec!" he yelled, his face lighting up at the sight of her. "Where have you been? Actually, I was just coming up to the Dairy to find you."

"I've just finished," said Cecily.

"I'll walk home with you!" He then added warily, "If that's OK?"

"Of course it is," said Cecily cheerily, linking his arm. She did not realise how much she had missed him.

"I've been trying to get in touch," said Kaden, "but you've become so good at avoiding me. And the others, come to mention it."

Cecily could detect the note of sadness in his voice.

"I know," she replied. "It's just that I've had a lot of stuff to deal with and I thought that after the big argument at the Bramble Inn, it would be best to spend some time away from you all. I know I've not been the easiest person to be around over the past couple of years. I didn't want to keep dragging you all down."

"Cecily, you're our best friend. We've all been so worried about you."

"Even Jedd?" Kaden's silence confirmed to Cecily that Jedd had not been worried about her at all. "That's what I thought," she said, bitterly.

"Look, I don't know what the deal is with Jedd. He's very angry with you for some reason. But I'm not and neither are Fen and Sol." Kaden averted his eyes as he said this and Cecily knew he was not being entirely truthful. She would not blame them for being mad at her. "We know you are going through a rough time and we want to help you all we can. Please don't shut us out."

"Well, I'm actually doing OK," said Cecily. "The dreams have stopped."

"Stopped?" questioned Kaden.

"Yes, I've not had one since the night of the argument."

"Oh right, that's great news." Although Kaden said it was great news, the tone of his voice did not quite match his words. Cecily was puzzled.

"What's wrong? It doesn't sound like you think it's great news."

"No, it is fantastic news," he said with more enthusiasm, probably not wanting to upset her. "I'm just shocked, that's all. Don't you think it's a bit strange that you've been having these dreams for three years and then they suddenly stop? I mean, the dreams were constant, every night and they were getting worse. I know you didn't like to tell me, but I could see the way they were affecting you."

Cecily laughed. "Kaden, I appreciate your concern, but I'm

certainly not going to question why the dreams have stopped. I thought I was going mad! It's like a weight has been lifted off my shoulders and I actually feel normal again for the first time since I don't know when."

"Well, as long as you're happy," replied Kaden slowly, staring searchingly at her face in case she was about to give something away.

"There's something else I have to tell you," Cecily said to Kaden, finding it hard to keep the excitement from her voice.

"Go on then," said Kaden.

"I've got a boyfriend!"

"What? Who?" asked Kaden, sounding very surprised indeed.

"All right, don't sound too shocked! It's not that unbelievable, is it?" replied Cecily, indignantly.

"I'm sorry, Cec. I didn't mean it like that. I just didn't know that you liked anyone. Who is it?"

"Cian Bramble. He's Lord Bramble's nephew and over here for the summer."

"Ooo Cecily Stalks, going out with a member of the aristocracy. Do tell me more!" teased Kaden.

And so, Cecily told Kaden all about Cian, about how they had met, what they had been up to over the past couple of months and everything she knew about Cian. By this time, the pair had long arrived at Cecily's cottage and they were sat on the wall at the front of her house.

"The thing is Kaden, I like him so much. I can talk to him about anything. He listens and understands me. I think he has really helped with my, erm, problems."

"I'm happy for you, Cec. You seem like you have really got it together. If you like this guy, then I am sure we all will. Although I'm surprised that I haven't seen him around."

"He pretty much keeps himself to himself. Besides, it's not that surprising. You haven't seen me either."

"Yeah, that's true I suppose. So when are we going to meet

him?"

"Are you going to the party at Bramble Hall this Saturday?" Cecily asked Kaden.

"The party! Of course! I almost forgot! That was the reason I was coming to find you in the first place. You've not forgotten that it's Fen's birthday this weekend?"

"Oh, my gosh, I had! How thoughtless of me! It's just that with everything that's been happening. Please don't tell her," implored Cecily.

"Don't worry, I won't!" said Kaden in mock exaggeration. "Well, we are going to the party for her birthday. She's very excited!"

"That's settled then!" Cecily enthused, more excited than ever. "We'll have a reunion at the party on Saturday night to celebrate Fen's birthday. It will be good to see everyone. I've missed you all, you know. Although I must admit, I'm a bit nervous. I hope they don't hate me for avoiding them."

"Who could ever hate you, Cecily Stalks? I'm just glad you are OK." Then he added, "Does this mean you've forgiven me? Last time we spoke, you said you never would!"

Cecily looked sheepish. "I know, I'm sorry about that. I shouldn't have taken it out on you. This party is going to brilliant though!" continued Cecily animatedly. "Cian has been working so hard."

"Well let's hope it's better than previous years for Fen's sake!"

Laughing, Cecily got up from the wall and walked through her garden gate. She was halfway down the path when she remembered something. She called out to Kaden, who was just walking away.

"I forgot to tell you something. Elisabeth Stone is back in the village. Apparently, for good this time."

"Elisabeth?" inquired Kaden. "That girl who used to go to school with us?"

"Yes, I was talking to her the other week. She was going for an interview at Bramble Hall to work in the gift shop."

Cecily waited patiently for Kaden's response, only it never came. He simply stared blankly into space.

"Kaden!" shouted Cecily.

Kaden awoke from his trance. "When did she get back?" he asked Cecily.

"Oh, I don't know..." Cecily mused, trying to remember exactly when she had seen Elisabeth.

Kaden forcefully interrupted, raising his voice. "When did she get back, Cecily?"

"Maybe two or three weeks ago. What's wrong with you? That's the third time today you've acted like the world is going to end."

"Oh nothing. How have I not seen her around?"

"Maybe you haven't been looking in the right places," said Cecily, sarcastically. "You should invite her to the party. She said she remembers us all really well and that she'd like to hang out. As I remember, she had a little crush on you!" teased Cecily.

"For heaven's sake, Cec! We were four!"

"All right, calm down! I was only joking! I guess I'll see you on Saturday." She then added slyly under her breath, "Hopefully you'll be in a better mood."

***

After he left Cecily, Kaden quickly returned home. He walked through the front door and without saying anything to his stepfather, went to his room and closed the door behind him. He began to pace up and down, hoping that this would help him process the information he had just received from Cecily. A couple of hours earlier, he was dying to see Cecily. He had not seen her for two months and in a way, he felt responsible for the argument with Jedd. He should have warned her. He should have defended her. A couple of hours earlier, he would have done anything to talk to Cecily. Now he wished he had not.

Cecily had a mysterious boyfriend that none of them had seen or heard of. Not that this was completely strange, it's just that Bramblegate is a small village and people talk. How come no one had mentioned it to him? Someone must have seen them together. They work at the same place. It was like she had managed to isolate herself completely whilst still going to work every day and having a romance with a prominent member of the aristocracy. Kaden found this strange and something in his head was nagging at him. In all honesty, he was a little bit angry that Cecily seemed so happy and carefree, especially after the worry she had put them all through. Well, Fen, Sol and him anyway. Jedd was quite clearly not bothered in the slightest.

Cecily was not the only one Jedd had shunned since the night of the big argument at the Bramble Inn. Kaden had barely heard from him at all. He had not seen him face to face despite all of Kaden's attempts. Any phone calls or text messages had been met with stunted replies or pathetic excuses as to why he could not meet up. Kaden had not wanted to tell Cecily as this information would have upset her. She would have felt that she had come between them. The only people Kaden had seen were the good, old, reliable Fen and Sol. However, even their behaviour was somewhat changed. After numerous failed attempts to see Cecily, their attitude towards her and the situation was becoming really negative. This was so unlike them. Although Kaden had not seen Jedd, he knew that Fen and Sol were still seeing him regularly. He wondered if this negative opinion had anything to do with Jedd poisoning their minds against Cecily and maybe even him. They certainly seemed changed and less bothered, although he had not wanted to tell Cecily about their newly found attitude towards her.

And if this was not enough, Cecily dropped the bombshell that Elisabeth had returned to Bramblegate. Why was she back? She was, after all, sent away for a reason. Elisabeth coming back to

Bramblegate was another sign all was not well. The pieces were shifting into place and yet the group were becoming fragmented. And from what he had experienced, he had a feeling that Jedd was the problem at the centre of it. Kaden did not understand what was happening.

He was usually so in control. Not this time. Not now. It was his job to keep everything together and he was failing miserably. Something in their sleepy village was about to go seriously wrong. Something was about to happen. But what? The only warning that he might have had had unexpectedly stopped. Cecily said that she'd had no dreams since the night of the Bramble Inn. Not that she trusted him with the content of her dreams anyway. And he knew that whatever had happened at Bramble Hall that day was to do with it. Kaden would have to take action and hope he was not wrong. He would call on Elisabeth and invite her to the party. He would see if she could remember anything as she had done once, so many years ago, before she was sent away. He would be an observer on Saturday night. All of his friends would be in the same room and he would keep a particularly close eye on Jedd. He would be vigilant and look for signs. He would find out if they knew anything; he was determined. And if not, he would seek counsel, although he would be in serious trouble if he was wrong.

Chapter Eleven

Lord Bramble sat behind his large, polished, mahogany desk. He was a slight man, dwarfed by the high back of the green, leather, padded swivel chair that he sat upon. The room was in darkness, except for a small table lamp whose green shade cast a sickly glow over the aristocrat's face, giving him an impish look. Lord Bramble was pensive, his eyes staring at, but not seeing, the far wall of his office. His fingers were pushed up together in front of his face, forming a church steeple and he was using this structure to rest his lips on. When Lord Bramble finally awoke from his daze, he noticed that his leg was moving nervously up and down, the way it usually did when he was worried. Lady Bramble hated this nervous leg and always tutted loudly when it took on a life of its own. However, this evening, he was aware of his drumming leg as the butterflies inside his stomach flapped their wings to the same beat.

The cause of Lord Bramble's anxiety would be arriving at any moment. He had been turning over and over in his mind the deal that he had made with the stranger who had crashed into his life but a few months since. When the man first presented himself, Lord Bramble had thought him a crazed lunatic, appearing from nowhere with a ludicrous proposition. He claimed that in the past, his family had screwed over the mysterious man and that it was now Lord Bramble's responsibility to put things right and pay his family's debt. Lord Bramble had immediately wanted to have this stranger removed from the premises, but his gut instinct told him not to, even though he felt more than uncomfortable in the man's presence. Part of Lord Bramble was curious about the tall, dark figure. He wore a long, black, hooded cloak and Lord Bramble found himself searching the black hood that surrounded the stranger's head in search of a face. However, as the stranger did not like the light, Lord Bramble only caught an occasional glimmer of bright, unnatural eyes that appeared to see nothing and yet at the same time, saw everything. Now to say the stranger did not like the light only applied when he was swathed in his long, black, hooded cloak. This is when he would appear from seemingly nowhere to discuss the particulars of their agreement.

The mysterious man had attached himself very closely to Lord Bramble under the guise of a nephew visiting for the summer from Dublin. As he did indeed have a nephew of the same age, no one questioned Lord Bramble on the matter, including his wife. The truth of the matter was that Lord Bramble had not spoken to, let alone seen, his younger brother for many years. Therefore, no one would recognise his estranged nephew if they fell over him. The stranger had obviously done his homework as he knew all about the aristocrat's family, both past and present and over the last couple of months, he had inserted himself into the Bramble family with uncanny ease, keeping very close tabs on Lord Bramble. When he was parading as the handsome, amiable nephew, charming folk with his witty banter, only Lord Bramble knew the true malice that lay behind those crystal blue smiling eyes. He also noticed that the stranger's smile did not quite extend over his whole face and that it was tight and false.

However, Lord Bramble could not complain about the stranger's presence as he had taken him up on his offer and agreed to the deal. Lord Bramble had promised to pay his family's debts in order to protect future generations. That was not his only reason though; in fact, it was quite far down his list of priorities. The aristocrat, like his father and grandfather before him and their fathers and grandfathers before them, were shrewd businessmen. How else would they have preserved the family estate over the years, especially in this day and age? The truth was that Lord Bramble was a greedy man and his new mysterious acquaintance had made him such an attractive offer. If he went through with it, he would never want for anything again, in this life or the next. And then after his own needs were sorted, there was the guarantee that the Bramble family name would ensue.

But as Lord Bramble was greedy, so was he cautious. When he had asked his new business partner for his name, the stranger had simply told him, 'Dasrus'. There was no surname. And if this man was who he claimed to be (for Lord Bramble had spent numerous days and nights since pouring over his extensive library), then the aristocrat had certainly done something terrible by entering into the agreement with him. The burden lay heavily on the Lord's narrow shoulders and made him sick to the stomach. He was torn by what he would gain from the deal and the fear that he might have put innocent people in danger. Before Lord Bramble could ponder his situation any further, the lights began to flicker and the tall, black cloaked figure named Dasrus appeared, the floor obscured by black shadows moving at his feet.

Small green dots of light from the table lamp glittered playfully in the unnatural eyes of Dasrus and Lord Bramble suddenly felt the temperature in the room drop significantly, sending a cold shiver down his spine.

"Well, Bramble," said Dasrus silkily, "the time is almost upon us. Tomorrow evening, we will both get exactly what we desire."

The aristocrat was silent. He dared not speak. His presence was terrifying and although when wearing his cloak, his face could not be seen, his stare bore right through the lord, setting his soul on fire. After a few moments, the black hooded figure spoke again.

"I get the feeling that all is not well, Bramble. What is the matter? Maybe my form disturbs you?"

Before Lord Bramble could reply, the black hood which accommodated those unnatural eyes disappeared, morphing very cleverly into the figure of the imposter parading as his long-lost nephew. However, the black shadows did not disappear. They firmly remained, rippling around his feet, giving the impression that he was walking on water, although the Lord could quite clearly hear footsteps on his cherry parquet flooring.

"The preparations for the party are in place. All you need to do is stick to your end of the bargain."

As Lord Bramble spoke for the first time that evening, his mouth felt dry and his voice cracked. Despite these facts, he attempted to command authority as he spoke, even though he was, at heart, shaking, for that was the effect that this individual had on him.

"Your offer is most attractive, Dasrus, and I am grateful for it. My conscience is hounding me though. I must ask, is there any way to complete our plan without innocent people getting hurt?"

He could tell that he had angered his acquaintance as he visibly bristled as Lord Bramble spoke. He turned his back on the lord and slowly walked over to the window.

"Listen to me, Bramble, and listen well for the sake of your family and yourself. We have a deal, an agreement that you will not back out of. I explained the terms very carefully and you agreed to them wholly. The six offerings are necessary at this stage. Any other casualties will be... unfortunate."

Dasrus spoke in a quiet and menacing manner; however, as he was facing the window, looking out over the grounds and not directly at him, Lord Bramble felt a moment of courage.

"I just don't like the idea of innocent people getting caught up in our arrangement. And for that matter, you still haven't told me the significance of Cecily Stalks in all of this. I have many questions left unanswered, yet now we find ourselves on the eve of the event. I cannot move forward without answers." He spoke with the conviction of a lawyer arguing his case in court.

"Answers? You want answers?"

Dasrus was apparently irritated, yet still he spoke in a flat, monotonous tone. He turned from the window and began to sail across the room towards Lord Bramble's desk, the shadows carrying him on his way. The lord was suddenly very aware of his body and he realised he was standing up, leaning forward over his desk supported by his arms.

"After all I have offered you. A lifestyle and riches beyond your wildest imagination. Refuge in a place where all your dreams will become reality. And you want answers?"

Lord Bramble slowly lowered himself back into his chair. A low growl resounded off the study walls.

"I will give you what you want. I just need a guarantee that no one will be hurt."

Like a firework exploding, Dasrus raised himself up and morphed back into his true form. As he did so, the black mass at his feet lurched forward with blood curdling snarls and ear piercing shrieks. Lord Bramble found himself surrounded by gaping jaws on all sides, yellow teeth dripping with saliva, ready to snap him up at Dasrus's word.

"You are in no position to make demands!" he roared, all calm and self-control lost in anger. "There will be blood on your hands, but you made that choice when you agreed to what I asked. Your avarice has far surpassed your morality, Bramble. You are nothing. I need your blood, your consent and nothing more. My end of the bargain will be kept and you will be rewarded handsomely for your trouble."

As he changed back to the personable shell that was assuming his nephew's form, a sinister calm fell over the room. Dasrus turned and moved slowly, resuming his place by the window.

"There is no backing out, Bramble. You have signed the contract. If you question me further or try to sabotage my plans in any way, you will suffer incomprehensible misery for all eternity. Do not test my patience. The sacrifice that you make tomorrow will not be forgotten. It will forge the future of this world and you will go down in history as the person who made it all possible." A repugnant laugh erupted from trickster's face. Lord Bramble could take no more. He cradled his weary head in his hands and as he did so, he reluctantly accepted the situation.

"All right, I will do what you want," he whimpered.

As he looked up, Dasrus had gone, disappearing as suddenly as he had appeared, the study returning to room temperature.

If Lord Bramble were a more scrupulous man, he would have cried in exasperation at his pending crime against humanity. However, he selfishly felt sorry for himself. Why had this curse been placed on his family and more importantly, why did this debt have to come to fruition in his time, while he was head of the family? When the lord had referred to the situation as a curse to Dasrus, he had said it was not a curse, but an honour. Human protectors of the gateway; what did that even mean? All Lord Bramble could think was that he had better be recompensed when all of this stress was done with. He returned his face to his hands, inwardly willing tomorrow to hurry up and arrive and be over with equally as fast. At that moment, he did not feel safe anywhere, not even in the sanctity of his own home. He had been invaded.

Chapter Twelve

Jedd had not slept well and then from the moment he had opened his eyes, he had been engulfed by a feeling of impending doom. Tonight was the party and to say he was nervous about what the evening would bring was an understatement. As he lay in bed, his head propped up by his powerful arms, he thought about how he had betrayed his lifelong friends, wondering if he had done the right thing or not. Although he was plagued by guilt, he could not help feeling relieved, happy even, that he would finally get an answer to his question. There would be no more pain, no more torment and no more having to bottle it all up inside, putting on a brave face for the world to see. They would all be back, reactivated, and he would not have to feel such incredible bitterness that he was the only one who remembered.

Of course, he could have confided in Kaden, but Kaden would have come up with a solution to his problem, a solution that he probably would not have wanted and so he had decided to keep his secret to himself. He would get the answer his way, although his own solution was far from straightforward. His betrayal had come at a price. If he received the answer to his question he desired, then he would have a lot to make up for and a lot of trust to regain, as he was about to do a lot of damage. He would also have a deal to break, which was going to be a very difficult arrangement to get out of and he would need the help of his friends. And with that thought, Jedd's guilt quickly subsided and turned to anger, accompanied by a gut-wrenching pain.

No longer able to contain his feelings, he shot out of bed and stalked to his bathroom. Why doesn't she just remember? He loved her – loves her still. He should not have to go to such extremes. It was her fault he had become so selfish. In a fierce rage, he cleared the items that constituted his bathroom shelf with one swoop of his large hand. As the bottles, jars and tins crashed to the floor, he thought about the ultimate prize offered to him by Dasrus should he not get what he wants. No more memory equalled no more pain. Tonight it would all be over, no more secrets. They would know he is a traitor and the sacrifice would be complete, for now. This evening was about self-preservation and there was no room for feelings of guilt. Which side he gave his loyalty to would depend on her.

With that thought, he picked up the goods he had knocked to his bathroom floor and carefully placed them back on the shelf. While doing so, he caught a glimpse of himself in the mirror and realised that he did not recognise the person staring back. He then wondered if he truly ever had.

***

Jedd was not the only one who awoke with a heavy heart that morning. Instead of looking forward to that evening's party, Kaden was feeling quite the opposite. He was filled with a sense of dread and yet he did not know why. As he had promised Cecily, he went to visit Elisabeth to invite her to the ball. They had chatted and he had quizzed her the best he could without being too obvious. Kaden was convinced that she did not remember anything, although his gut told him all was not well with her. There was something in her behaviour and the way she kept avoiding his eye. Whether Elisabeth was telling the truth or not, or for that matter, whether he liked it or not, all of the pieces were in place. He had no evidence to back up his suspicions and this only brought him full circle again, back to the fact that he was dreading this evening and he did not know why. It was only a feeling and yet he knew something was about to happen. He just could not see it yet. His logic was clouded. He would have to wait and see what tonight would bring. As Kaden churned the information over and over in his head, he absent-mindedly showered and dressed as he still needed to get a costume. However, this seemed the least of his problems.

***

It was lunchtime on her first day at her new job and Elisabeth Stone's tummy was rumbling. She was sat in the gift shop at Bramble Hall, waiting for someone to come and cover her for her thirty-minute lunch break. Elisabeth, probably like most of the other inhabitants of Bramblegate, was thinking about the ball that night. Her costume was ready. As soon as she finished work at four, she would race home and begin her preparations for getting ready. She had been pleased when the rather handsome Kaden Quinn had turned up on her doorstep to invite her to the party. She was a little bit embarrassed at how attractive she found him, so much so, she could not look him in the eye. She had really wanted to go to the party, although she had not wanted to go alone. This evening would give her the opportunity to become reacquainted with her old friends.

As she sat there daydreaming about the forthcoming evening, she experienced the familiar feeling of *déjà vu*. These experiences seemed to be getting worse since she had returned to Bramblegate. There was something niggling at the back of her mind. That niggling feeling was telling her that something had been forgotten, that something needed to be remembered. As she tried to access those elusive memories, she saw something move out of the corner of her eye. This startled her as the gift shop had been dead that morning. She had barely seen a soul. This was not the first time that she had been sure she was not alone since returning to Bramblegate and starting work at Bramble Hall. In those moments when she was by herself, she felt uncomfortable, like she was being watched from the shadows. Not just at work, but at home too. She needed to get out more. Maybe some fun with friends would do her good and make her less paranoid. She had too much time on her hands to think. A cold shiver passed down Elisabeth's spine and as it did so, she heard the trotting of court shoes coming towards her.

"Elisabeth, dear!" Acantha's shrill voice rang out, reverberating off the ancient walls. "I will cover you for your break today! Everyone else is busy with preparations for this evening. Now run along and get something to eat. It will be quite busy in here this afternoon as they will be setting up for tonight. How exciting! There certainly hasn't been a shindig of this proportion in many years! I can't wait for everyone to see my costume…"

As Acantha waffled on to herself, seemingly talking to no one, Elisabeth slipped out of the door and into the grounds of Bramble Hall.

***

Cecily Stalks was beside herself with excitement. She had spent the whole day relaxing and pampering herself in preparation for the ball. Cian had treated her to a manicure and she had saved some of her tips to get her hair put up by the hairdresser. As Cian was busy with the ball, Cecily got the bus into the city on her own. She had returned a couple of hours later, feeling like a million dollars with her newly-styled hair and bright pink nails. She could not believe how happy and lucky she felt. Her life was unrecognisable compared to a couple of months ago. She was now adding the final touches to her outfit. As she applied her pink lip gloss, she tried to put out of her mind the creeping thought that Cian would eventually be leaving Bramblegate. She wanted this happiness to last forever. She took a step back from the mirror and admired herself. This Cecily was a far cry from

everyday Cecily. The hairdresser had managed to pin back her short red bob and the style complimented her lovely heart-shaped face and emphasised the long line of her neck. The black dress she'd had made fitted her perfectly. It slightly skimmed her hips, giving her curves she never knew she had. Combined with subtle make-up that made her skin glow, she looked positively elegant. The tomboy would be staying at home tonight whilst sophisticated Cec would take the stage. She liked the idea of this. As she smoothed her dress down, there was a knock at the door. Cian! Tonight, everything
would be perfect.

***

Lord Bramble stood on the balcony of the grand staircase looking down on the Great Hall. He looked every bit the aristocrat in his smart, black tuxedo. He was carefully observing the arrival of his guests. His emotions were mixed, although none of them were good. What was going to happen this evening? The past couple of months had brought him up to this point. It had all been about this night and now he had never been so terrified in his whole life. From what he could see, the six who were about to lose their lives had not arrived yet. Six deaths were bad enough, but what if there were more? What if he had placed his family in danger? And for what? For the promise of more riches? Now, in the reality of what was about to happen, it hardly seemed worth it. Lady Bramble joined him on the balcony.

"Darling! What a tremendous party!" she cooed. "That nephew of yours has certainly done you proud! I don't ever remember a summer party as wonderful as this! And it's barely begun yet!"

He turned to look at her, beautiful and elegant in blue chiffon, and he felt a powerful surge of love for his wife. Lord Bramble may have been a bit unethical in his business affairs, such was the legacy of the Bramble family; however, he was a loyal family man. No one could deny that. He would do anything for the love of his life and his children. He kissed his wife on the cheek and turned his attention back to the guests. Amongst the gathering crowd, he saw his two young children, Oscar and Delilah, tearing about. He was only half-listening to Lady Bramble, who was gushing about how wonderful the children looked and about how excited they were, for through the door walked three of his young victims, shortly followed by another two. He gazed upon them, marvelling at how they were not that many years older than his own children. Finally, the last of the sacrifices arrived with him. She was positively glowing. Could she really not recognise the evil that lay beneath the handsome exterior of the man she was clutching tightly hold of? Surely, she should be able to smell it at such close quarters? The lord reflected that his business partner looked, well, normal.

The final feeling among the mix of emotions the aristocrat was experiencing was anger. In fact, anger would be to put it too lightly. He was feeling rage. He had a responsibility to his family, guests and employees. He would not allow this ruthless mad man, or whatever he was, to puppeteer him any longer. Greed had got the better of him, but he was quickly starting to realise that some things were simply more important. He had to do something before it was too late, for deep down, he knew he would not be able to live with the aftermath of his decision.

Chapter Thirteen

Cian and Cecily arrived at the party in style. As they pulled up outside the main entrance of Bramble Hall, a smartly dressed valet opened the door for Cecily and helped her out of the car. Cian walked around to meet her and as he did, he dropped the keys of the classic Rolls Royce he had borrowed from his uncle, into the hands of the eagerly awaiting valet.

"Be careful with her!" he joked as he took Cecily's arm in his. This was the moment that Cecily had been waiting for. She was about to enter the most important party on Bramblegate's sparse calendar. As there were not that many social events in Bramblegate to look forward to each year, she knew that a lot of the villagers would be here and she was about to enter with the man of the moment, who had made all of this excitement possible. Not only that, he was, without a doubt, the most handsome man in the village by far. And he was with her. She would never forget the look on his face as she had opened the door to the cottage just a short time ago. He had told her how beautiful she looked, which had made her blush to her very core. At the entrance to the Great Hall, a photographer was on hand to take pictures of arriving guests, with a reporter from the local paper, who was now busy scribbling away. Cecily smiled brightly for the photograph, clinging tightly to her boyfriend's arm. She was thinking all the while that life could not get much better than this. Her feelings for Cian were stronger than ever. She knew that she loved him – with all of her heart.

As they entered the Great Hall, Cecily felt overwhelmed. She did not know where to look first. As she spun around, she noticed that a stage had been erected just behind her in the large bay window area of the Great Hall, with microphones, speakers and lots of instruments on stands, waiting patiently to be brought to life by their maestros. Through the crowd to her right, she could make out a bar area, where bar tenders dressed in white tuxedos and black bow ties were serving elaborate looking cocktails over ice, with sparklers illuminating brilliantly beside brightly coloured cocktail umbrellas. A large Art Deco mirror had been hung behind the bar and in its reflection, she saw that the opposite side of the Great Hall boasted another bar with a matching Art Deco mirror. However, this bar was being dressed by waiters and waitresses with large silver cake stands and vintage china tea sets. Cecily knew, because Cian had told her, that this was the dessert bar. Through the huge double door, behind the dessert bar, was the dining room. She caught a glimpse of large circular tables dressed with white linen and extravagant, yet elegant, floral displays. As her eyes wandered back into the Great Hall, she noticed that the guests had turned to look at her and Cian as they entered. Cecily suddenly felt very self-conscious. As she looked down to check her dress, she saw that the lights emulated by the crystal chandeliers above her head, were dancing like fairies all over the black silk of her dress.

The couple made their way through the building crowd, Cecily clinging tightly to Cian's arm. Across the room, stood just beneath the balcony, Cecily spotted her friends and she forgot that she felt self-conscious and instead she was feeling instant excitement. She did not realise how much she had missed them. She was now in front of Cian, pulling him by the arm in a hurry to get to her friends. However, when she bounded over, only Kaden and Elisabeth seemed pleased to see her. Kaden was as kind and generous as always and was really warm and welcoming to Cian. Elisabeth was very complimentary about Cecily's dress. She thought how nice it was to see Kaden and Elisabeth together. Cecily pushed her way over to Fen and Sol and gathered Fen up in a big hug, wishing her, "Happy birthday," as she did so. Fen and Sol were pleasant enough, but Cecily felt that the atmosphere was a bit strained and so the longer she stood with them, the more awkward it became. Jedd simply nodded in her direction, although as he did, his eyes caught Cian's and Jedd quickly looked away. Cecily thought how strange this was. Did they already know one another? She was about to ask Cian this very question when there was an announcement from up above them on the balcony.

Dinner was to be served in thirty minutes and so Cian ushered Cecily over to the bar and got her a rather large, orange-coloured cocktail. If Fen, Sol and Jedd were not ready to talk to her yet, then so be it. She had Cian, although not for long it seemed. After he handed her the drink, he said he had to go and sort out some party business. He kissed her on the cheek and was gone. So Cecily reluctantly made her way back over to her friends and stood with Kaden and Elisabeth until it was time for dinner. She really tried to focus on the conversation, but she could not help looking round the Great Hall for Cian. She was missing him.

***

It was not long until there was a second announcement from the balcony above. This time it was Lady Bramble.

"Thank you, everyone!" she said as the din softened. "It gives me great pleasure to announce that dinner is now served! Please make your way into the dining room."

And so the crowd obediently shuffled to dinner, checking the two big boards on either side of the doorway to see where their table was located.

The tables were large and round, each seating eight people. The magnificent floral displays that Cecily had seen on her way into the party had now been removed to make space. The six friends and Cian were sat together on one table, leaving a spare seat, which was sat upon at various points through dinner by people stopping to say 'Hello' on their way to the toilet. So far, it had been occupied by Acantha, Millie Poole and Dawn and Cherry, who kept giving Elisabeth dirty looks as she was accompanying Kaden. Instead, the two girls turned their flirty attention to Jedd, although he was completely uninterested.

The starter came and went and the mood at the table had still not improved. It was not supposed to be like this. They were supposed to be having fun. So, with a couple of cocktails down her neck, Cecily attempted to lighten the mood with some funny anecdotes and a few bad jokes. However, only Elisabeth seemed to be enjoying the Cecily show. Everyone else seemed preoccupied and Fen and Sol were talking quietly amongst themselves. Worse still, Cian kept leaving the table between courses to sort yet more 'party business'. Cecily decided to give up. If they did not want to have a good time, that was their problem. She absent-mindedly picked at a bread roll while waiting for the dessert bar to open.

***

As dinner drew to a close, Cecily's mood had completely blackened. Two hours in the dining room had seemed like an eternity and she was glad that they were now being heralded back into the Great Hall, where the big band was set up, ready to whisk the dancing party goers into a frenzy. Cecily was hoping this would lift her friends' moods. Everywhere else she looked, people were having a great time. Tonight, the guests would be partaking in real dances, such as the Quickstep, the Foxtrot, the Tango and the Waltz and dance instructors were dotted around the Great Hall ready to give tips and impromptu lessons. Cecily could not wait to dance with Cian, but once more he guided her through the crowd to the bar and got her a cocktail. He apologised again as he said that he had to go and speak to his uncle about something. With that, he disappeared.

Drink in hand, she surveyed the room from the confines of the bar space. Fen and Sol were dancing nearby, as were Kaden and Elisabeth. However, she could not see Jedd anywhere and to her surprise, she felt relief. She was beginning to feel really sorry for herself as she tucked into her third cocktail of the evening. Everyone else was quite literally having a ball, except for her, who was deserted again. But she was not to be alone for long. Seeing her by herself, Justin Long, the kitchen porter, lumbered over and asked her to dance. Cecily accepted graciously. She may as well; Cian was nowhere to be seen. For such a large chap, Justin was surprisingly light on his feet. As Justin twirled her round, Cecily saw Lord Bramble ascending the grand staircase and she found herself wondering what the aristocrat and his nephew had to talk about. So far, this evening was certainly not turning out to be the fairy tale she had hoped for.

***

Kaden had remained vigilant up until now. He had spent all night watching everyone, looking for any indication he had missed something, but so far, he had seen nothing to be suspicious about. He did feel a bit bad for Fen. It was her birthday, but the gang were not having much fun. Jedd was more or less ignoring everyone, Kaden himself had certainly been preoccupied and although Cecily had made various attempts at lightening the mood, she had failed and so she now appeared to be sulking. However, Fen seemed oblivious to all of these happenings as she only had eyes for Sol.

As Kaden and Elisabeth danced their way around the Great Hall, Kaden noticed that the guests seemed to be having a fantastic time. People were talking and smiling and jovial laughter could be heard above the music. This did not look like a place where something dreadful was about to happen. Maybe on this occasion, he was over-thinking things. Maybe he had become paranoid. After all, the dreams, their warning signal, had ceased. If there had been imminent danger, maybe it was no more.

As the foxtrot came to an end, Elisabeth announced that she was going to the ladies' room, so Kaden told her he would wait for her at the bar. After he had ordered his drink, he turned to survey the room. He saw that Fen and Sol were close by, dancing a slow waltz together and gazing into each other's eyes. He could not see Jedd anywhere and come to think of it, he had not seen him since they had re-entered the Great Hall after dinner. He would not be surprised to find he had actually left for the evening. As for Cecily, Kaden was surprised to see her dancing with Justin Long, the kitchen porter. Once again, Kaden found his eyes darting from face to face to see if he could locate Cian, but he could not. He had not really had an opportunity to speak to Cian yet as he had been so busy with the party and rarely at Cecily's side, so he felt it would be unfair of him to judge Cian, but there was something about him. Not only did Kaden find something familiar about Cian, but when they shook hands earlier, there was something in his eyes and something smug about his attitude. But Kaden thought once more that he must be imagining things. If Cecily liked him, then he must trust her judgement.

Kaden had come to the conclusion that on this occasion, his paranoia had got the better of him and he was looking for signs that simply were not there. He decided that he was going to relax from now on and let his friends make their own decisions. He could not control everything all of the time. And with that last thought, he felt relief.

***

Even though everyone seemed a bit quiet tonight, Elisabeth was having a great time. She had felt a bit shy at first, but they were

101

all being so nice to her, even the formidable character that was Jedd. Although he seemed to be ignoring everyone else, he was courteous to her. She was sure she would become firm friends with them all as she got to know them better, as was her positive outlook. Elisabeth thought that Cecily was lovely, so bubbly and kind. She looked stunning tonight in her beautiful handmade dress. Elisabeth even felt a bit envious, but not in a malicious way. She admired Cecily and she looked fabulous together with Cian. That was what Elisabeth wanted and a fleeting thought passed through her head that maybe she and the glorious Kaden Quinn would get together. They had been dancing all night.

Elisabeth adjusted her long, raven curly hair in the mirror and refreshed her pink lip gloss, secretly hoping it would be kissed off by the end of the evening. She was in a bathroom in one of the bedrooms on the first floor. The queue downstairs for the toilet had been enormous and she was dying, so she had crept up the back staircase and used the en suite in one of the manor's seven bedrooms. As this room was fairly small compared to the other bedrooms, it was not frequently used. One of the chambermaids had told her this when they were chatting in the gift shop when she first arrived. The bathroom had two doors so it could be used by the bedrooms on either side of it. As she was about to leave the bathroom, she heard raised voices coming from the bedroom next door. Elisabeth stealthily snuck out of the bathroom, checking as she left that it was in the same condition as she had found it. She quietly closed the door and repeated the same actions on her way out of the bedroom. She tiptoed along the landing to the next door, even though that by going in this direction, she was moving further away from the back staircase.

Once outside the door, she could definitely hear voices coming from inside, muffles liberating themselves through the small gap at the bottom of the door. Elisabeth looked around warily to see if she was alone and when she was satisfied that she indeed was alone in the corridor, she lightly pressed her ear against the door.

"I do not think we should put any more lives at risk! There is no need!"

Lord Bramble's voice was getting louder with every word and he clearly sounded agitated.

"S-s-sir... if I may," stuttered a second voice, which Elisabeth recognised but could not quite place. "Maybe we could lure the five sacrifices up here while the other guests leave the party? I could be responsible for that. Then we could take them out to the clearing for the ritual."

Ritual? Elisabeth knew that she was overhearing a conversation that she should not. Her instinct was telling her to run, yet her feet were glued to the floor. She was suddenly feeling very hot, little beads of perspiration escaping from her temples.

From inside the room, a third voice began to speak, one that sent a cold shiver down Elisabeth's spine.

"Let me make it perfectly clear, I am in charge of this situation, not either of you, and I alone will decide what happens. This is not a democracy. You have played your roles well until this point, but remember, you are my servants. Do not give me reason to..." he paused, "end your, well let's say, your performance."

An evil cackle rang out chilling Elisabeth to the core. Even though the third voice was irritated, there was an eerie calm about it and an element of control.

And then she saw them out of the corner of her eye. She stumbled backwards as the shadows moved towards her and in doing so, she dropped her handbag to the floor with a loud thud. All of a sudden, it was like a fog had lifted. It was all coming back to her, memories of past lives flooding her head. She had to warn the others. As she turned to flee, she realised she was surrounded. The black mass was rising from the darkened corners, growling and snarling at her, daring her to move. Then the door to the bedroom flew open. Inside, she saw Lord Bramble and Jedd, with the one person in the world she did not wish to see. As he glided towards her on a sea of shadows, his wickedly calm voice spoke out of the void beyond his black hood.

"Apprehend her."

***

Kaden was feeling a little bit squiffy after one too many cocktails. It seemed like he had been waiting ages for Elisabeth to return from the bathroom, so he decided to go and look for her. As he battled his way through the dancing crowd in the Great Hall, he knew that his senses were certainly dulled. As he reached the ladies' toilet, which was situated by the drawing room, he assessed the huge line. He could not see Elisabeth anywhere. At the front of the queue, he spotted Dawn and Cherry. He ambled over to them and asked if they would nip into the toilets to see if Elisabeth there. The girls looked at each other for a split second with disgruntled looks on their faces, as if to question why he was looking for another girl, when the two of them were stood there.

However, as both of them had a mammoth crush on Kaden, their disappointment soon turned into clamouring affability. They rushed off giggling into the toilets and when they returned, they appeared overly pleased to deliver the news that Elisabeth was nowhere in sight. Kaden was slightly questioning whether he should believe the girls or not (knowing their true intentions towards him), but Kaden figured that if Elisabeth had been in the toilets, she would have been finished and out in the time he had been stood there. He thanked the girls sweetly and as he walked away, Cherry's excitable high-pitched voice reminded him where he could find her if he wanted to dance later.

Kaden headed for the drawing room, which housed the gift shop. When he got there, the door was locked; therefore, there was no access to the parlour either, as the only door to the parlour was inside the drawing room. He pushed his way back through the throng of people in the Great Hall, with slightly more urgency than before, scouring the party for Elisabeth. She was not waiting for him at the cocktail bar, so he made his way towards the dining room to see if she was perhaps sat down, resting her feet. It did cross his mind that he was possibly over-reacting and she had simply had enough and gone home. He pulled his phone out of his pocket to check for a missed call or message, but nothing. As he neared the entrance to the dining room, he saw Cecily talking to Fen and Sol. They were all laughing and looked to be having a good time. At least that was something as they had barely spoken all night. As he approached, Cecily saw him coming.

"Kaden!" she shouted. "Come here, you've got to listen to this! Go on Sol, tell him!"

Evidently, they had also had one cocktail too many as they could not stop giggling.

"Listen," he interrupted. "Have you seen Elisabeth?"

"Not for ages," replied Fen. "Why, is everything OK? You look rather pale."

"I don't know. I can't find her anywhere. She went to the toilet ages ago and hasn't come back. Maybe she has had enough and gone home, but she hasn't called or messaged to tell me."

The others could tell from Kaden's demeanour that he was worried.

"I haven't seen Jedd for a while either," shouted Cecily, straining to be heard over the music.

"Well they must be somewhere," said Sol, checking his phone. "Let's all go and have a look round together. We'll find them."

As they forced their way through the swaying couples, Kaden noticed that those closest to the grand staircase had stopped waltzing and were looking up at the balcony. As he followed their gaze, he was aware that the band had stopped playing too. Bit by bit, the joviality in the room was being replaced by low murmurs, which informed him that the rest of the party was catching up. A sinking feeling emerged in the pit of his stomach as he saw Lord Bramble on the balcony, overlooking the party below. He was as white as a sheet and he was shaking, although he was clearly attempting to hide his distress. Walking along the landing to join Lord Bramble was Cian, closely followed by Jedd, who had a tight grip on Elisabeth's arm. Elisabeth's appearance was dishevelled to say the least and she was frantically searching the crowd below, her eyes darting back and forth. Her eyes finally found Kaden's and the look on her face communicated what Kaden had been dreading.

"Oh no!" he whispered to himself. He should have listened to his gut instinct after all.

Kaden was staring up at the balcony helplessly, wondering what on earth he was going to do next. He had to get Elisabeth down from there. As muddled thoughts ran through his head, he felt Cecily nudge him in the small of his back.

"What is going on?" she hissed quietly, for the crowds around them were now practically silent.

"Trouble," replied Kaden.

"What is Cian doing up there with Jedd and Elisabeth?"

"I'm not sure," Kaden hissed back.

"Well, why is it trouble? Honestly Kaden, if you know something and you're not telling me…"

Cecily was interrupted by the trembling voice of Lord Bramble, for no matter how hard he tried to mask his anxiety, it was not working and he had lost all composure.

"I'm so sorry everyone, if I could just have your attention please." He paused while the room fell still. "I'm afraid that this party is over."

Chapter Fourteen

The crowd were stunned into silence for what seemed like an eternity. Cecily wondered if like her, they all thought it was an elaborate joke or prank; part of the evening's entertainment. But then she saw Elisabeth, white as a sheet, trying her best to stifle looming sobs, while Jedd, a man that she had known almost all her life, held Elisabeth's arm so tightly that Cecily could visibly see the blood building in her arm where he was preventing her circulation. She was aware that Jedd and she had not always seen eye to eye, but she knew him, didn't she? What was he doing? He liked to put on his hard man act, it was part of his bravado, but to hurt someone?

Cecily's horrified gaze came to rest on Cian and she felt like her heart had been pierced with a shard of glass. Her stomach was turning revolutions and she felt that she could be sick at any moment. The Cian she had fallen in love with was not the man standing on the balcony guarding his uncle. His face wore a cold detachment, all of the laughter gone from his eyes. It was like his soul had been separated from his body; the shell was there but the essence gone. What was happening? She was willing Cian to look at her, just to give her a nod and reassure her that everything was OK. However, her intuition told her this would not happen, his polar glare fixed steadily on his uncle.

The party stood silent, waiting with bated breath for Lord Bramble to enlighten them all. The aristocrat visibly took a large intake of air. He looked directly at his wife and children, although he was clearly addressing the whole room.

"Run!" he bellowed with all his might.

Kaden was already one step ahead of the multitudes. He grabbed Cecily's hand and the two of them, with Fen and Sol close behind, began to make a beeline for the exit. However, Cecily was not quite ready to leave yet and she was struggling to escape from Kaden's firm grasp.

"We can't leave them!" Cecily was trying with all her might to scream above the din of the room. "We have to go back for Cian, Elisabeth and Jedd!"

"There is nothing we can do for them at the moment, Cec. You have to trust me. We have got to leave."

Even though Kaden's tone was commanding as he spoke to her over his shoulder while still heading for the door, Cecily began to protest again. She could not face leaving them behind. Kaden's patience was fraying. "We've got leave NOW!"

This outburst from Kaden alerted Cecily as to the urgency of the situation as she was not used to hearing Kaden raise his voice; in fact, she did not think she had ever heard him get truly angry before. As the four friends neared the exit, they encountered a jam because of the volume of villagers trying to escape the doomed festivities, not even yet understanding what they were running from.

Cecily stole a look back at the balcony, just in time to see her beloved Cian slit Lord Bramble's throat from ear to ear. Elisabeth was screaming and Jedd's face was aghast, yet still he retained his grip on Elisabeth's arm and remained rooted to the spot on the balcony beside the murderous Cian. Cian, who did not seem fazed by the monstrous act of killing his uncle in cold blood, was now murmuring under his breath. He was moving his hands in an upward motion, as if trying to pull something out from the ground beneath him. An even wider pit of dread opened up in Cecily's stomach as she heard the familiar sound of snarling and shrieking coming from the shadows around her.

By now, the Great Hall was in complete chaos and the dark stench of evil drenched the atmosphere. The guests were hysterical as the people around them, their friends and family, were cut down like they were paper. The beasts were rising from the shadows, their jaws snapping from beneath like Great White sharks preying on unsuspecting seals at the surface of the ocean. She looked around at her friends to see if they were witnessing the same atrocities as she was, seeking clarification that she had not slipped into one of her nightmares. Her friends, however, had shifted into what could only be described as survival mode, doing whatever it took to escape this waking nightmare. Fen and Sol had managed to get in front of Kaden and Cecily. As bodies around the room were falling, victims of the shadows, Fen and Sol began to scramble their way to the door using a pure agility that Cecily had never seen before. Kaden was dragging Cecily along behind Fen and Sol in the channel they were creating.

Just as she reached the door, she turned one last time. A quick survey of the room in her remaining seconds at the Bramble Hall Golden Hollywood Summer Party, that had turned into a living hell, revealed the folk of Bramblegate in a blind panic, most covered in blood, clothes torn, in a state of disbelief and confusion as the company around them were being taken. She looked to the balcony and saw her beloved Cian staring directly at her, wearing a huge grin. As she was pulled from the Great Hall, there was just enough time to see Cian disappear and be replaced by a tall, dark figure in a long, black, hooded cloak, riding on a sea of black shadows.

***

Cecily was not sure how long she had been screaming for. It was only when they were running through the woods outside Bramble Hall that she was aware of her own cries. The passage of time was a blur for Cecily. She remained locked in her own head, playing out the events she had just witnessed: the arrival of Lord Bramble, Cian, Jedd and Elisabeth on the balcony, Jedd stoically gripping a sobbing Elisabeth, Cian's cold, unfeeling detachment, Lord Bramble's pale, shaking frame. Then the anarchy as everyone tried to leave, Cian severing his uncle's throat, Jedd and Elisabeth's horrified faces, people, her friends, being sliced down like ears of corn, blood and frenzy, the beasts of her nightmares in the shadows and that thing that Cian had turned into as they were leaving. What was she saying? Cian had changed into something? It was madness, utter lunacy! And she knew the change was meant for her. Her heart broke again as she remembered the sadistic smile directed at her before his metamorphosis took place. The pandemonium was still ringing in her ears.

The small group of friends had come to a stop. Kaden, Fen and Sol were talking to Cecily, but they seemed so far away from her. She wanted to answer them, but she just could not. She wanted to lie down, go to sleep and just forget about everything that had happened. However, Kaden was now shaking her by the shoulders quite forcibly. This brought her back to reality for long enough to understand what was being said to her. Or so she thought.

"Come on, Cec! Shut this place down!" Kaden was speaking with the same urgency he had earlier. "He can't perform the ritual with only two of us."

Ritual? What was Kaden talking about? Nonsense! Was this all a joke? Why were Fen and Sol agreeing with him, telling her to hurry? She looked at her surroundings for the first time since they had stopped. They were in the clearing, deep in the middle of the woods, where the old oak tree stumps formed a circle. Cecily stared into space. She wanted to talk, to answer their questions, to ask why. Why were they there? Why were they talking about a ritual and what on earth had just happened? What about Jedd and Elisabeth? They needed help. They must go back for them. She wanted to scream, but she had no voice left. She was locked inside her own head with the disturbing aftermath of recent events. She heard Fen speak.

"She's in shock. Look at her!" Fen walked over to Cecily and felt the temperature of her skin. "She is cold and clammy. We need to get her somewhere safe. She needs to lie down and warm up."

"The cottage," replied Kaden. "I can keep us safe there for a few hours."

She did not know if it was the alcohol, the effects of what she had just seen or the mention of home, but Cecily vomited everywhere.

"We need to go," said Sol, quietly.

Things once again became a blur for Cecily as she was dragged home by the others. As they were deep in the wood and far from the path, she kept tripping over the roots and undergrowth of the barely trodden nature, her legs failing her time and time again. She thought about how her beautiful, perfect dress was ruined, just like her beautiful, perfect life of the past few months was now also ruined.

They arrived at the cottage and bounded through the front door. Purdey was there on the other side to greet them. She looked straight through Kaden, Fen and Sol and began to question Cecily. Where was Cian? Why was she in such a state? What had happened to her dress? Had she been drinking? However, Purdey's questions were not registering with Cecily as her brain was far too full. They were simply bouncing off her, although she vaguely wondered why her mother was so concerned. Cecily was not entirely sure what happened next and in her current state, she could well have been imagining things. There was a pale blue, bright light and all of a sudden Purdey's questions stopped and she announced that she was going to bed.

Fen guided Cecily, Kaden and Sol upstairs to Cecily's room, sat Cecily on the bed and put a blanket around her shoulders. She then went to Cecily's little bathroom, poured a glass of water and made Cecily sip it slowly. Fen sat on one side of Cecily and Sol on the other, like sentinels on guard duty. Kaden did not sit. He was pacing the room, muttering to himself the whole while. Cecily wanted to ask him what he was doing and more importantly, ask him to stop. She wanted to ask what all of this meant, but she was still incapable of speaking. She heard Fen, Sol and Kaden talking in far off voices about things she did not understand. Then Kaden turned into a huge, bright ball of light and disappeared. That was the final straw for Cecily and she remembered nothing else.

Chapter Fifteen

It was a long time since Kaden had been here. His surroundings held nothing but a frosty blue glow. He did not see or hear them arrive, but he sensed them. Without warning, he was surrounded by six bright balls of light, just like himself in appearance, only different in other ways. Their essence was older, wiser somehow, only he did not know this for sure.

"Hello, brother." One of the balls of light greeted Kaden.

"Hello, Masters. I am afraid that I am not here with good news."

"We know, we see all young one."

This comment shook Kaden and it took him an extra heartbeat to answer.

"You saw everything? Were you aware he is back in our midst? That he was getting close to her? That one of our own has joined him?"

"Yes, young one."

Kaden felt his emotions rush to the surface. He knew this was a human trait he had acquired after so long on Earth.

"Why didn't you warn me? We could have stopped him, prevented the loss of all those lives."

The Masters spoke one at a time.

"We sent you signs."

"The dreams."

"The girl who is returned to you."

"That is all we were meant to do."

"We had our orders."

"We were not supposed to give you explicit warning, but let

events play out."

"Have you not learned to trust the Universe and its plan after all this time?"

"What is meant to be will be."

Their voices had a hypnotic musicality about them and they almost sang their responses in tune with one another, one starting before the other had finished, like a beautiful song.

Kaden spoke quietly. "I had a feeling but I did not act on it. I was afraid to come without solid evidence. I thought you would summon me." He felt dejection and failure; mortal feelings.

"Human failure is inevitable, but necessary."

"The Lord was supposed to agree to give up the gate and hand the guardians over to the dark one."

"That was his destiny."

"There has to be a balance between good and evil on Earth."

"Good cannot prevail all of the time, but nor must evil."

"Celestial forces are at work."

"The Universe must keep the balance."

Kaden could feel a ball of fire growing in his belly, a belly that was nothing more than light in its present state.

"What is the point then? What is the purpose of the guardians if not to prevent evil from rising? How can we protect if we are not informed?" He knew that his anger would not get him the answers he sought. He had to remain calm, even though his frustration was mounting.

"In every age, there are those who battle evil," replied one of the Masters.

"Be as you are, as nature intended."

"Think about the bigger picture."

"The Light will guide you."

"Go forth, Light Doer."

"What will be, will be."

As the Wise Ones were finishing their communication, their essences were fading, their words becoming more and more distant.

"Wait! What does Dasrus have planned? I need to know! I have to prepare!"

But their sweet musical tones sang no more and Kaden's pleas fell on deaf ears.

***

He waited a while in that place, trying to find meaning in their cryptic messages. One thing he was sure of, he must try and get a handle on his human sentiments, after all, he was not human, but a Light Doer, a spirit guide. However, after spending so long in a mortal casing, surrounded by humans, his spirit was bound to adopt some of their characteristics, in particular, emotions. Right now he was feeling guilty. He had let everyone down: his friends, the people of Bramblegate and especially those who had lost their lives. Trust in the Universe, the Higher Power. What will be, will be. Not if he had anything to do with it. At that moment, Kaden was finding it a challenge to accept what the Wise Ones had told him. He was having a difficult time placing his faith in something that may or may not support him in the job he had to do. His version of fate or destiny was that good prevailed. They were the guardians; the Cerbereans. He would certainly be as nature intended and battle evil until the bitter end. That was his job. But what was he going to tell the others? He was none the wiser as to Dasrus's plans. They would just have to figure it out by themselves.

Chapter Sixteen

They arrived at the clearing in the wood where the six ancient oak tree stumps sat in a protective circle. Elisabeth sensed the others had been there, but the area remained unprotected. This worried Elisabeth deeply. Why had they not protected the gateway? She did not like this one bit. Something had gone wrong.

She stole a sideways glance at Jedd. He too knew that something had gone wrong. She could see it in his eyes. In fact, his whole body was screaming that something had gone wrong. He looked on the verge of speaking, but he was holding back. She wondered what was stopping him. Fear? He was sweating, eyes wide and full of terror, like a rabbit caught in the headlights of a car. But what was he afraid of? The evil demon that was pacing around the outer circle of the tree stumps? The wrath of the Light due to his defection? Or the unparalleled betrayal of his fellow guardians, his friends?

Elisabeth considered for a moment how long she had known Jedd for, not just in this lifetime, but also in the others. She reflected on all they had been through together, all the evil they had battled in their roles as protectors. Jedd had barely looked at her since she was discovered outside the bedroom at Bramble Hall, let alone spoken to her. He knew what he had done. She was dying to talk to him, to discover why he was doing this. Why the betrayal? What was in it for him? She wanted to talk him out of it, make him see sense. Convince him to escape with her and get back to the others so they could work out how to stop Dasrus. But most of all, she wanted to tell him how much his treachery had hurt. Deep down, Elisabeth thought she may know the reason for his deception. However, she wanted him to admit it, say it out loud so she could tell him how ridiculous he was being.

At least the physical pain had subsided and she was thankful for small mercies. Jedd had relinquished his grip on her and she could now walk freely. Well, as freely as one could with bound wrists. Elisabeth knew that she must keep up her pretence of pain and anguish. She did not want to give anything away, just in case they had not realised she had remembered everything. Just as Jedd refused to look directly at her, she would not look directly at him, but for a different reason. She hoped that the reason he would not look at her was because he was ashamed of what he had done. She, however, did not want to give herself away by looking in his eyes, as she knew she would not be able to hide her hurt and disgust.

Initially, the shock of all her memories flooding back was too overwhelming. She was over that shock now and in warrior mode. For the moment though, she would continue the charade of whimpering and sobbing to throw them off her track. She was not scared of Jedd or of the dark entity that stood before her, now inside the sacred circle of oak, the gateway, not meant to let things in but to keep them out. His agents stood guard over them, some lurking in the shadows of the wood, watching, ready to pounce should she step a foot wrong. Others were in their place at his feet, ready to do his bidding. She could smell their acrid breath and hear their low growling and snarling; foul creatures from beneath. If only she could access her sword.

He spoke in his calm, yet sinister manner. "The gateway remains unprotected."

"Yes, my Lord," answered Jedd, "although I sense they have been here."

"You sense they have been here?" Dasrus remained passive, yet his servants' voices began to rumble louder. "Maybe the Light thinks it is not too late for you?" He turned and from beneath his hood his oddly glimmering eyes were set upon Jedd.

"N… n… no, my Lord," he stuttered. "I serve only you."

"You have seen what happens to people who betray me."

Jedd unconsciously looked down at his white shirt, covered in blood spatter from the recently deceased Lord Bramble. "I will not betray you."

Elisabeth recognised this resolve and the return of his bravado, feeling that he was lost to them.

"Can you sense them now?"

"No, I feel nothing."

Elisabeth knew he was telling the truth because she could not sense them either.

"What about you, raven one? I offer you the same bargain as our brave boy here. Join me and you will be rewarded handsomely."

Elisabeth continued her masquerade by not replying to Dasrus, but by simply looking at the floor and weeping quietly. Dasrus left the circle and rode on his sea of black to stand right in front of Elisabeth. As he spoke his speech was measured.

"I know that you remembered what you were earlier in this lifetime. I know that is why you were sent away. It is also clear to me that the other guardians have been reactivated, otherwise why come directly here? So, if the others have been reactivated, then so have you." He raised his voice and drew himself up to his full height which sent his agents into a frenzy of snarling and growling. "Do not lie to me, Cerberean! Drop the act!"

Elisabeth immediately stopped her crying and with a straight, yet slightly wet face, she too drew herself up to her full height and looked directly into the abyss beyond the hood.

"I will never join you!" She shot an acerbic look at Jedd who was now puce with anger. "I will die before I let you open that doorway! I am a Cerberean, a warrior of Light and guardian of the gateway. Protector of Earth and humanity."

As she recited her oath, her temper got the better of her and she launched herself at Dasrus, even though her hands were tightly bound behind her back. Luckily for Elisabeth, it was Jedd and not the beasts that anticipated her move. He pounced on her and pinned her down with his weight which rendered her unable to move. While Elisabeth's fiasco unfolded, Dasrus laughed hysterically.

"Very well, Cerberean. You will die and it is your death, your death and the death of the other Cerbereans that will open the gateway. By the time you return, Dark will have engulfed the Earth."

Elisabeth wanted to tell him that his plan would never work, that he would never open the gateway, but Jedd had winded her badly.

"It was Fate that led you to follow your curiosity and eavesdrop at the bedroom door. Destiny brought you to me. I already possess two of the Cerbereans; four more and I have myself a doorway. My time is now!"

As he turned to walk away, his gloating and neurotic laughing stopped abruptly.

"I know where they are. It seems another traitor has come good."

Dasrus's evil cackle ricocheted off the trees as they headed out of the clearing and into the wood towards the dell, Elisabeth, Jedd's prisoner once more, surrounded by hungry, salivating shadow beasts.

Chapter Seventeen

Kaden was still a ball of light as he arrived back at the cottage. As he was materialising in the bedroom, he could see Cecily lying down on the bed and Fen and Sol talking quietly to each other, probably so as not to wake Cecily, but they also had a lot of important things to discuss themselves. As humans in this lifetime, they had been attracted to one another and had come together. However, as Cerbereans, and warriors, their relationship was forbidden. They should have only one thing on their minds and that was protecting the gateway. He did not worry about Fen and Sol as they were fiercely loyal to the Light; however, mistakes had been made before, but he did not want to dwell on that at this time. To Kaden, it seemed a shame as he knew their true feelings. He had known them through many lifetimes.

That was why Kaden never got involved romantically. He did not have the luxury of forgetting like the others. He too was a Cerberean, only he was also an agent of the Light; a Light Doer. He was a connection between the Light and its warriors on Earth. You would have thought that the Higher Power might have come up with a more suitable title for a celestial being such as himself, like 'ambassador' or 'emissary', but 'doer' was sufficient. It simply meant that he gets things done. It was his job to remember everything, to keep a record in times of peace and to look for signs of imminent danger. That is why on this occasion, he felt that he had not lived up to his job title. He should have been more proactive. If he had, a lot more people would be alive. They would have Elisabeth and he could have prepared everyone slowly. They may even still have Jedd. According to his Masters, 'What will be, will be.' He did not like relying on destiny alone.

He startled Fen and Sol as he returned to his human form, seemingly appearing out of nowhere.

"How is she?" Kaden asked with genuine concern.

Sol replied. "She hasn't woken up yet."

"She just sort of passed out," Fen added.

Kaden turned to look out of the window. His protective barrier was glowing icy blue around the cottage, invisible to all but Kaden, shielding them from evil discovering their location. It was also concealing them from Elisabeth and Jedd. He just could not risk it.

"Kaden?" Cecily must have heard his voice as she was beginning to come around. She sat up with a sudden start.

"What... what is happening? Please tell me that I've had another one of my nightmares and we haven't actually been to the party yet?"

She had broken out into a cold sweat and panic laced her words. Fen and Sol wore empathetic looks on their faces and Kaden let out a deep sigh.

"You still don't remember then?"

"Remember what exactly? Are you trying to tell me that everything I have just witnessed really happened? Jedd kidnapping Elisabeth? Cian killing Lord Bramble? Those monsters, those things from my nightmares, eating the villagers? It was like a scene from a horror movie. How did we get out alive when others didn't? Cian changed, he..."

She started sobbing loudly. Her shock had certainly passed and the reality of what had happened was sinking in, even though she still refused to believe it. Kaden felt sorry for her human self.

"We know, Cec. We know what he is and what he changed into." Kaden tried to soothe her with his words. "I am so sorry, but he has deceived you from the very beginning."

Cecily was now crying uncontrollably, inhaling massive gulps of air. She would have to quieten down a bit or there was every chance that Purdey may reappear. Fen rubbed her back in a pacifying manner, trying desperately to calm her down, as both her and Sol offered words of comfort. Cecily was obviously deeply in love with Cian. That was the one thing Kaden wished she had not remembered.

It was some minutes before Cecily regained control of herself. Kaden knew her well and so he was ready for the barrage of questions that followed.

"Why did you take me to the clearing in the wood? What did you mean when you told me 'to shut the place down'?" She looked at Fen and Sol. "Why were you all talking about a ritual?"

Kaden took a deep breath. "Cecily, the clearing in the wood, the six ancient tree stumps to be precise, is a gateway, erm, that is, a kind of portal, to the Realm of Dark."

Saying it out loud to someone who did not understand sounded ludicrous, even to him. Cecily looked like she had just been slapped in the face.

"What, you mean Hell?" Cecily scoffed.

"Well, I suppose some would call it that, yes."

"Don't be ridiculous! I hardly think now is the time to be joking around."

Kaden stole a sideways glance at Fen and Sol. "Cecily, I think it is time to tell you a story."

Cecily said nothing, but sat on the end of her bed wearing a defiant look on her face, as if daring her three friends to pull the wool over her eyes by playing some highly-wrought trick.

Kaden began. "The Realm of Dark exists, Cec, whether you remember or not. To balance out the Dark is the Realm of Light. Earth is the in-between place separating the two realms and this plane is neither light nor dark."

"I can't believe what I am hearing," spat Cecily. "You are telling me that Heaven and Hell actually exist?"

Kaden turned to look out of the window. He knew she would

find it hard to believe him, but he had to continue as he needed her to remember and he was hoping that he may be able to stir some memories by starting with the basics.

"Not Heaven and Hell in the sense that religion portrays, simply light and dark. From the first moment of consciousness, the Realm of Light has existed. The Realm of Light is filled with spirits who want to help people. The Light wants to preserve Earth and show humans the error of their ways, make them choose the Light. The Realm of Light acts as guardian and protector of Earth and the human race."

"So, there is a God," Cecily chipped in sarcastically.

Kaden chuckled. "There are many gods, Cec, but there is a Higher Power, even above them. Everyone is accountable to the Universe."

"What about the Dark?" Kaden could tell that Cecily was alarmed, especially after everything she had seen that evening, but she was trying to put on a brave face. "Are there gods there too?"

"Of course. As there are spirits of Light, so are there spirits of Dark. Everything in the Realm of Light is mirrored in the Realm of Dark. That is how a natural balance is achieved. The Realm of Dark has existed since the very first evil deed, which happened shortly after consciousness. It contains all true evil. Unlike the spirits of Light, the spirits of Dark want evil and darkness to dominate the Earth and humanity. The agents of the Dark are a law unto themselves, battling one another for ultimate power. They spread chaos and destruction wherever they go. They want to get rid of the Realm of Light because it is the only thing that stands in their way. The Earth plane is fair game for both realms. The Dark tries to take over, the Light tries to keep the Dark at bay and so the battle goes on. The Light relies on humans to do the right thing and make the right choices. And that is what we call 'Reality'."

Kaden, who had been keeping watch on the woods below,

now turned to look at Cecily, hoping that he had triggered some well-buried thoughts. However, her face was blank as she stared into nothingness. Kaden, Fen and Sol left her that way, letting her digest what they had just revealed.

After a few minutes, Cecily began to laugh in a vehement fashion. When she had composed herself, she said, "I get it now! Cian originally wanted to hold a murder mystery party. Is that what happened? Oh my, you guys really got me! I think I'm going to be disturbed for life! Let's go back up to Bramble Hall and tell him I have worked it out!"

Kaden returned to his look out at the window. He felt more helpless than ever. They needed Cecily at full strength.

"After everything you have witnessed tonight, are you not convinced that we are telling you the truth?" He let out a deep sigh.

It was Sol's turn to try. "Cec, you have to get it into your head that Cian is not Cian. Cian does not exist and he is certainly not the nephew of Lord Bramble. He is nothing more than a murderous demon who has tricked you into loving him. Everything you shared was fake. Cec, you have to try and remember!"

Cecily choked up again. "So my nightmares are real? Those monsters in the shadows... exist?"

Kaden was not sure how much more of Reality she could take tonight, but he needed her to remember.

"They are not nightmares, they are echoes of the past, events that really happened. The dreams are designed to wake you up. They are a warning sign that danger is coming. I'm afraid those monsters are indeed real. Agents of the Dark, always hungry and always watching."

"Are they watching us now?"

"They cannot enter the cottage just now as my enchantment is protecting it."

Kaden wholly expected Cecily to break down again. Instead

she asked quietly, "And what of the ritual? You still haven't told me about that."

"We do not know exactly what Dasrus has planned, but one thing is for sure, he is trying to open the gateway. That is the only thing the ritual is used for. The Wise Ones told me that it was Lord Bramble's destiny to hand over the guardians. Thankfully, he had the courage to blow the plan at the last minute, otherwise we all would have been trapped inside Bramble Hall. As it stands, he has two Cerbereans, one by choice and one against her will. It is crucial he doesn't get us too as he needs all of us to perform the ritual."

"Cerbereans?" questioned Cecily.

"Yes," replied Kaden. "That is what we are. Warriors of Light and guardians of the gateway. Protectors of Earth and humanity."

Cecily looked very uncomfortable, but she continued to ask her questions.

"What will happen if he captures all six of us?"

"He will kill us and use our blood to open the gateway. If that happens, Dark will be released on Earth," said Fen, matter-of-factly.

"Oh," replied Cecily. She paused before she went on. "You asked me to shut it down. Why?"

"Because you have the power, Cecily, you just have to remember it. You are our leader on Earth and the Cerbereans follow you. You have the magic to stop Dasrus from entering the clearing in the first place."

The room fell silent. Moments later, the only sentence Cecily could muster was, "Is that his name? Dasrus?"

Fen held her hand tightly. "Yes."

Kaden waited in the silence that followed for Cecily to ask him the most obvious question, 'Who am I?' but she did not and he imagined that this was because she was on information overload and would rather not know or had not thought to ask. Instead, she got up off the bed, grabbed some clothes from the back of her chair and went to her small bathroom to change out of her ripped gown. As Kaden looked out over the cottage garden to the dark wood beyond, he thought carefully about their next move. Cecily was still out of action. He had to get her somewhere safe and help her get her memory back. They would have to worry about Jedd and Elisabeth later. Their main aim at the moment was keeping Dasrus from opening the gateway, which ultimately meant keeping the four of them out of Dasrus's way. He knew just the place and it would serve him for both priorities. However, there was still one thing they had to take care of before they left. As he was pondering this thought, he caught a glimpse of rustling foliage at the edge of the wood and he knew what was there before he saw them.

Fen had sensed it too and she gasped loudly, "He's here!" as Sol rose to his feet. "Does he know we are here or is he guessing? Your shield is supposed to be protecting us. He is here too soon!"

It dawned on Kaden why they had been discovered so quickly. As he put the puzzle pieces together, he realised how very naïve he had been. As he spoke, he did so with regret.

"There was already an evil presence here when we arrived tonight."

Chapter Eighteen

Cecily felt she could react one of two ways. She could flee her home and run into the deep, dark night, never to return again and think for the rest of her days that her friends were madder than she was. Or, she could stay and listen to them. They were her best friends and they loved her. Why would they lie to her? Just because she could not remember. Maybe all she needed was a little faith. After all, she had seen some horrific and unnatural things, with her own eyes. Not only that night, but previously in the store at Bramble Hall. All this talk of Light and Dark, Cerbereans, magic and an existence that she needed to remember was mind boggling, but her gut told her to trust her friends. And now, on returning from the bathroom, she discovered that this Dasrus, the one who had deceived her, was outside her home. Worse still, if she were to believe her friends, they were all in serious danger. Yet she could not move. She remained sat down on the edge of her bed, frozen to the spot.

The bedroom door flying open made her jump out of her skin. It hit the wall with such a force that the others, who had been looking out of the window, spun around to see what was coming through it. To Cecily's joint relief and dismay, it was only Purdey. She felt a momentary pang of guilt that she had not even considered that Purdey was still in the house and that she may fall victim to the murderous demon that had just arrived outside. But again, Kaden seemed to know something she did not.

"How could you? Your own daughter?"

Cecily was very confused. Kaden spoke with such venom. She really was not used to seeing this angry side of him.

"It's all over now," spat Purdey just as viciously. "You were foolish to think your trickery would work on me for long, Cerberean. Dasrus is here and this sorry tale is at an end. Eighteen long years I've waited for this moment."

Cecily thought how ridiculous she must look, sat dumbstruck on the edge of her bed, with her mouth hanging down to the floor. She certainly did not recognise this version of her mother either.

"She's your own flesh and blood! Why betray her to him when you know what he will do to her... and the rest of the human race?"

Kaden was now furious and Cecily swore that his eyes were glowing a pale, ice blue. However, like Fen and Sol, she could not look at Kaden for long as she was staring in disbelief at Purdey.

"She's no flesh and blood of mine!" Purdey gave an obligatory nod in Cecily's direction, but did not look at her. "The Lord approached me shortly after her birth and told me what she is. He convinced her father and me to move out here to Bramblegate and said this is where she was meant to be. He offered rewards beyond our wildest dreams just to be guardians to her until after her eighteenth birthday. He showed me what would be mine. After I found out about her, it was so difficult to love her. Over the past few years, I've barely been able to look at her. It is only because I know what is owing to me that I've stuck around at all."

You could almost see the pound signs in Purdey's eyes. Cecily knew there was no love lost between her and her mum, but she was still her mother after all. Surely, she did not mean these things she was saying?

"Mum, what are you talking about?" Cecily did not mean for the question to sound as whiny as it did.

"What I said!" she snapped. "You are no daughter of mine. You are simply borrowing that body until it grows old and tired and you can get your hands on another one."

"I... I don't understand," replied a befuddled Cecily.

"You are weak, just like your father. If you were strong, you wouldn't be in this position now, just like your father would still be alive if he were strong. All I had to do was browbeat you both and keep you downtrodden to stop you from fulfilling your destiny. With a little help from Dasrus, of course." Her eyes lit up as she mentioned her master's name.

"And what of her father?" asked Kaden.

"He was spineless!" screamed Purdey. "He never wanted to agree to the bargain in the first place and so he spent the rest of his days with his head in a book, trying to find a way to stop Dasrus or a way to awaken Cecily early. Professor was his guise. He dedicated his life to protecting that little trickster!" Again, she indicated that she was referring to Cecily with a nod of her head. "What a waste!"

"You killed him, didn't you?" dared Kaden.

"Yes, I killed him! It was easy though. Like I said, he was weak." She looked at her daughter properly for the first time. "Oh, how I have enjoyed seeing you struggle with grief and nightmares ever since!" She let out a wicked chortle.

Cecily had no words and she certainly did not have any tears left. As she listened to her mother's speech, she knew deep down that every word was true. It all made sense now. She had known all along that her mother despised her. Cecily felt anger, not for herself, but for her father. Purdey murdered her father, the one shining light in her life and the one person who made her feel safe. She felt hatred burn throughout her body. She could not let Purdey get away with this.

But before Cecily could think any more, she heard familiar growling and snarling sounds emerging from the shadows. The acrid breath made her feel faint and dizzy, as the shadows cast by furniture began to ripple. Out of the darkness of her little bathroom, she saw a black mass gathering, eyes glowing.

"Now the torture of having to pretend this is my daughter is at an end. It is time to collect what is due to me and start living my life."

Kaden jerked his head round to look out of the window for the hundredth time that night. "The shield has gone!" he said, urgently.

As soon as Kaden uttered these words, Cecily knew that Dasrus was on his way. She could not explain it, but she could somehow feel him. He would not hurt her, surely? All they had shared together over the past few months. She was sure he loved her. But then Sol's words resounded in her head, "… he is nothing more than a murderous demon… he tricked you into loving him… everything you shared was fake…" Was she in denial? She was about to find out as standing at Purdey's side was Dasrus and Purdey looked like she had just won the lottery.

Cecily heard the sound of metal unsheathing, coupled with a bright, flash of light and she turned to look at Kaden, Fen and Sol, who, to her surprise, were now holding very large, very shiny swords. As Cecily was wondering where the hell they had pulled them from, her bedroom lights went out and she could only watch as her friends clashed with the pellucid, salivating beasts in the middle of her room. All Cecily could do was take her feet off the floor, sidle back up towards her headboard and bunch her knees up to her chin. She did not mind admitting she was terrified as her friends were doing battle with the shadows, swiping their blades left and right, moving with such agility as she had never seen. It was like a beautiful dance, graceful yet altogether violent; such a paradox.

She turned to look at her mother and Dasrus, hoping that they would both come to their senses and stop this. . However, they were simply laughing and jeering, enjoying the revelry. It felt like an age to Cecily, but it must have only been a few minutes. The three warriors were being overpowered by the growing black mass and the monsters were backing them into a corner. They were not at full strength; Jedd had gone, Elisabeth was captured, and she could not remember. Dasrus must have been preparing for this moment.

From the door, he shouted his command, "Enough!" and the shadows began to retreat from whence they came with a low snivel and growl. She looked once more at Purdey who was practically rubbing her hands with glee. Dasrus began muttering under his breath again, just as she had seen him do at Bramble Hall. He pointed a finger at Fen. Momentarily, she appeared stunned and then, as if made of jelly, she collapsed to the floor in a heap.

"No!" Cecily heard herself screaming. What had he done to her? Before she had time to think, Dasrus had done the same to Sol and then Kaden. They did not stand a chance, it happened so quickly. And now it was Cecily's turn. Dasrus pointed his finger at her, but wait, did he hesitate? A poker hot pain seared through her body, quickly making its way to her brain and not for the first time that day, Cecily slipped into blackness.

Chapter Nineteen

Purdey felt very smug as she turned to face her Lord and Master. For eighteen long years she had been in his service and tonight, finally, they both had what they wanted. She revelled in her glory as the inanimate bodies of her daughter and her friends were taken away by an expanse of shadowy misery, growling and snarling as they went.

"My Lord," began Purdey, bowing her head slightly as she spoke. "I kept her from finding out the truth and I stopped her meddling father from finding a way to destroy you. Now it is time to claim my reward."

Ever since Dasrus had approached Purdey all those years ago and showed her the life she could have in exchange for her cooperation, she had yearned for it.

"Yes, you have done well," spoke Dasrus in his eerily calm manner. "The Cerbereans are now my prisoners and her treacherous father is dead. You have been a faithful servant and kept me well informed…" Dasrus paused before he went on and as much as Purdey worshipped her master, she felt uncomfortable as those unnatural, glimmering eyes fixed upon her from beneath his hood. He continued "… however, you have also been a terrible mother."

Purdey threw her head back and let out an involuntary laugh. "You didn't expect me to grow close to her? Ever since our pact, she has been nothing but a burden. Now the truth is out in the open, it is nothing but a relief."

Dasrus turned away from Purdey and glided slowly, deep in thought, towards the window on his rippling sea of black.

"You certainly belong to the Dark, Purdey Stalks, I'll give you that," he pondered out loud. "You shall get your reward."

Purdey felt utterly euphoric. "At last, I get to spend an eternity with my Lord and Master!" she cried.

"It is true, Purdey, you will live forever." Dasrus began to mutter something under his breath. "But certainly not with me," he added, savagely.

Purdey feared that this situation was not exactly going her way and she began to plead her case urgently as if defending herself in a court of law.

"But, Master, you offered me an eternity with you!"

Dasrus continued mumbling his spell.

"You offered me a life I could never imagine, riches beyond my wildest dreams!"

Dasrus was concentrating hard as Purdey tried to defend herself. She continued to speak, although she knew it was futile, her words falling on deaf ears. When Dasrus had finished, it seemed like he had heard everything she had said.

"That is all well and good," he replied, "but don't you know, Purdey dear, you should never make a deal with the Devil."

Dasrus extended his arm towards Purdey, which she imagined was the final part of the spell that sealed her fate, for her soul belonged to him. She had signed it over many years before. She felt intolerable pain as Dasrus began to rip her soul from her body. However, her soul did not leave as one whole entity, it was dragged from her in pieces, and now, on the verge of death, Purdey understood that her soul was broken due to the wicked life she had led. As each fraction left her body, the hideous deeds she had committed flashed before her eyes. As the final smithereen of her shattered soul left her body, her consciousness joined the other fragments as they whooshed around Cecily's bedroom. From above, she saw the hell beasts devouring her still warm flesh. The fragments of her soul, now reunited, took a downward turn through Cecily's bedroom floor. In quick succession, the pieces travelled through the living room floor and down into the earth to goodness knows where. All the while, Dasrus's evil laugh was resounding in her consciousness. This was her reward.

Chapter 20

"Come on, Kaden!" A four-year-old Elisabeth was tearing around the school playground, her raven curls billowing in the late autumnal breeze. She looked behind her and saw a weary Kaden chasing her at some distance.

"I am!" he shouted back, exhausted. "You are running too fast!"

"Well we can't slow down," she roared over her shoulder, as she ran as fast as her chubby little legs would carry her. "We've got to be faster, get better. We must practise!"

"Practise what?" yelled back an exasperated Kaden. "I'm tired! I'm going inside to have my milk!"

Elisabeth stopped running and saw Kaden making his way to the door. She managed to catch up with him as he was about to enter the classroom. She stood defiantly in front of him.

"Stop!" she yelled in his face. "We must be ready for when he returns! It is our job to protect the world!" Elisabeth felt very passionate about what she was doing in the playground. She knew it was important, but she did not understand why and she felt annoyed with Kaden for not taking it seriously.

"I don't want to play anymore!" Kaden stamped his foot in a petulant manner. "I want to go and have my milk! Move!" He pushed past Elisabeth in an attempt to gain access to the door. Although she momentarily stumbled, she remained steadfast and would not let Kaden past.

"It is not a game! It is real!" she bellowed. Instinct told Elisabeth what she needed to do. Without hesitation, she reached

back behind her head to the top of her back. She grabbed hold of something that although invisible to the naked eye, was physical. With all her might, she unsheathed her sword, the sharp blade making a slicing sound as it left its casing, the afternoon sun reflecting in its mirror-like finish. The mighty blade was almost as big as she was. Kaden's eyes were wide with horror.

"Put it away!" he screamed.

Elisabeth awoke but kept her eyes shut tight. As her memories came flooding back, she realised that must have been the moment that Kaden decided she should leave Bramblegate. As a child in this lifetime, she had remembered everything and it was dangerous to have a child running around with all of that knowledge and power. She understood his decision. She must have been deactivated and her stimuli, that is, her surroundings and her friends, removed.

She slowly opened her eyes and tried to see into the darkness, but the pitch black formed an insurmountable wall before her eyes. She inwardly cringed as yet another memory came back to her; the fact that she'd had a crush on Kaden Quinn as a human in this lifetime. She'd secretly hoped it would develop into more. How could she think or want that? She was so embarrassed and hoped no one else had noticed.

As her eyes began to adjust, she heard a sharp intake of air and then a familiar voice followed.

"Where am I? What is going on? Kaden?"

It was good to hear Cecily's voice, although she wished it was not so panicky. It did not reassure Elisabeth to hear her leader in this state.

"I'm here." A contrasting voice of calm emerged from the obscurity.

"I take it you don't remember then, Cec?"

"Elisabeth?" Cecily and Kaden urgently asked at the same time.

"Yes, I'm here," sighed Elisabeth, almost like she had given up.

"Fen? Sol?" Kaden was now trying to locate the others.

"Here," said Sol with about the same amount of enthusiasm as Elisabeth.

Fen drew the air in through her teeth and let out a small, "Ouch."

Sol quickly responded to the sound, "Are you OK, Fen?"

"Yes, I'm fine," she replied. "Just a cut, I think."

"Is anyone else injured?" asked Kaden to the pitch black.

"No, I don't think so," said Sol.

"Nope," said Elisabeth.

"I'm not hurt, but I'm scared and I have a headache," grumbled Cecily. "Where the hell are we?" She let out a small sob. "It is so dark. I can't even see my hand in front of my face. Kaden, where are you? Are you near?"

Elisabeth thought that Cecily must be very scared, as she was warbling.

"We are in cells," chipped in Elisabeth before Kaden could speak. "Each of us in our own separate prison."

"How can you tell?" asked Sol. "It is so dark in here, I daren't get up and walk around."

"I was awake when we arrived."

"Awake?" questioned Kaden. "Do you know where we are?"

Elisabeth paused. She was not sure whether to tell them. She knew where they were and as a result of this knowledge, she could smell the misery and despair in the air, feel it seeping into every pore. She could taste the hopelessness of their situation on the tip of her tongue. But she knew that if there was even a remote chance of them escaping this hellish place, she had to tell them.

"We are in some kind of holding place between Earth and the Realm of Dark."

Sol was the first to jump on her remark. "Impossible! All of the entrances to the Dark are sealed."

"Well that's not strictly true," interjected Fen, "because

Dasrus found a way out."

Kaden was next to speak. "Elisabeth said we are in a holding place between realms, so we are not actually in the Realm of Dark, which would make sense; nothing can enter the Dark and nothing can get out. Dasrus is very powerful and has obviously found a way out, but can he get back in again?" You could almost hear Kaden's brain ticking over as he quickly slotted the pieces of the jigsaw together in his mind. "Why bring us to a less secure holding place if he could take us to the Realm of Dark and to his dungeons? He has almost everything he needs for the ritual and this ritual is too important to him to risk losing the key to it. He finally has all six of us. I mean, what are the chances? Something doesn't quite add up."

Sol grunted in agreement.

"Well we are definitely close to the Dark," murmured Elisabeth. "My powers are not working down here."

"It's the first thing I tried," replied Sol.

"Me too," said Fen. "I have nothing."

"I'm afraid that I seem to be out of commission as well." Kaden sounded despondent. Elisabeth knew that this was out of character for him as he was always so positive. In moments of despair, Kaden brought hope. However, with Cecily down and with no memory, Kaden was by far the most powerful and if he could not muster any magic, they were in trouble. Cecily stirred Elisabeth from her musings. She had obviously been listening hard and pondering a few things herself.

"If we are close to the Realm of Dark, does that mean those things, those shadows, will come back? I used to dream about them." She began whimpering again. "You told me they are agents of the Dark, but what are they?"

Elisabeth felt for Cecily. All she had witnessed must be overwhelming for her, but saying that, there was no point in lying to her.

"They are dark souls, Cec. They have existed since the very

first evil deed, just like the Realm of Dark. They are an ancient beast."

"Dark souls? Are you telling me those things were once human?" Cecily could not hide her disgust.

"Every human soul is born new." It was now Sol's turn to explain things to Cecily. Elisabeth thought how it was like handling a small child. "Every human soul has the chance to pass to the Light or Dark depending on their earthly deeds. The essence of the Light and Dark has the capability to possess any soul. However, it is ultimately the choice of the human which way they turn."

"As I explained earlier, Cec," Kaden added, "the Earth plane is fair game for both realms."

"So, every human who chooses the Dark turns into one of those things?"

Elisabeth could visualise the revulsion on her face. "No, they are 'special'," she quipped sarcastically. "They climbed the ladder of success. Most human souls who choose the Dark spend an eternity in torment after being tricked by demons."

"How do we kill them?" Cecily's survival instinct had obviously kicked in.

"We can't!" explained Fen. "They are immortal. All we can do is lock them away, which until now, we thought we had done."

"But I saw you fighting them."

"We can fight them," continued Kaden. "Our swords are equipped to deal with them. They strike the shadows as if they were a physical mass and this temporarily disperses them. We can also use our magic to keep them at bay, but all these measures are not a remedy for the problem. As Fen said, the best method we have for stopping them is to lock them away.

"Are they here now? You said they are always watching, always hungry. How can I defend myself? I'm in this cell all alone!" Cecily sounded on the verge of hysteria.

"They are not here now," said Elisabeth in the most reassuring voice she could manage. "There is nowhere for them to hide in this blackness. They live in the shadows around the light and they are good at hiding, but this is their ideal environment. They have no reason to hide here. We would know if they were here. We would be able to smell them."

"Oh my, I have so many questions! I don't know where to begin!" Cecily sounded exhausted and she was probably having a hard time believing her friends. It was a testament to Cecily's faith in them, which was a good sign at least. She was relying on them to make sense of her experiences.

"I have questions too, Kaden," said Sol. "What happened when you went to see the Wise Ones?"

"You've been home?" interrupted Elisabeth, excitedly. This was the first time she had felt joyous since her memory had returned.

"No, not home, just on an information-seeking mission."

"Well, what did they say?" It was now Elisabeth needing clarification urgently and not Cecily.

"Now is not the time for questions. We do not know who is listening." Kaden, wise as always. "We need to figure out how to get out of here. We have two critical missions to complete and both need immediate attention. Elisabeth, what do you remember about getting here?"

"I'm sorry, but I was unconscious for most of the journey here," said Elisabeth, matter-of-factly. "Jedd's your man, Dasrus's new stooge. As we arrived at the dell earlier tonight, Jedd knocked me out good and proper. There was nothing I could do; my hands were bound." Elisabeth added the last remark in an attempt at excusing herself for becoming incapacitated by Jedd. "When I woke up, I was being carried by Jedd. I kept my eyes shut tight and I listened to see if I could gather any intelligence. They did not say much though, just that we were on our way to this holding place and Dasrus said he almost had everything he needed. Jedd didn't say anything at all except, 'Yes, Master'".

Elisabeth mimicked his snivelling tone. "The first time I realised the rest of you were there was when Jedd accidentally tipped me onto my side. I dared to peek and I saw the beasts carrying your comatose forms. Wherever we were walking, the ground underfoot was rough. Jedd stumbled, which is how he came to lose his grip on me. He soon righted me, so I didn't want to open my eyes in case I got knocked out again. I have no idea where we are, only that we descended a lot of stairs."

The cells once more fell silent as she finished speaking, except for the continual rhythmic drip of a single droplet of water, somewhere within the confines of the prison.

Eventually, Kaden whispered from the darkness, "It's OK, Elisabeth, we'll figure it out. Hopefully the Light will send help. What's meant to be, will be."

Chapter 21

Jedd had been crouched in a damp corner of his cell ever since he had brought his fellow Cerbereans to this miserable place. He too was captured. However, the others did not know he was there as it all happened during the commotion of getting everyone in their cages. Dasrus said nothing when he locked Jedd away, he just fixed those unnatural eyes on him, daring him to say something. Jedd knew his time was up. He knew he had to die as part of the ritual so he was not surprised at all that he had been imprisoned with the others. He had served his purpose. There was no point in arguing.

Now he was locked up, having betrayed his friends and allies to the Dark, he'd had time for reflection, especially as the others were still unconscious. They would all die as part of the ritual; however, the others would be reborn. He, most likely, would not. His soul no longer belonged to the Light. It now belonged to Dasrus and to the Dark. He had made a deal. Dasrus had shown him everything he could possess if only he deceived his friends, but the most appealing thing to Jedd was not the riches, but not having to feel the pain any more. Although after witnessing what had happened to Purdey, he realised he probably had an eternity of torture ahead of him. He should never have made his bargain. He willingly handed over his soul, even sought out the Dark. And why? Because he had become bitter over time and because he was jealous. These human emotions had got the better of him and now he would pay for an eternity. He should have trusted Kaden and told him he remembered. Kaden would have helped him for sure.

But at the time, the thought of being away from her crippled him. What if he could never remember again what he felt? In hindsight, that would have been for the best. His hate and his rage at those feelings not being reciprocated had eaten him up and he had made a massive mistake. Cerbereans cannot be together anyway. His thoughts wandered to Fen and Sol and he was curious as to how they were doing. They were always drawn to each other unconsciously and every time they were reactivated, they had to break things off, hide their feelings and become the true warriors they were. They were strong and loyal to the Light. This shamed Jedd. He was disgusted with himself. Instead of being brave, instead of acting like a warrior, he had taken the coward's way out. He should have asked for help. In the dank cell, the darkness taunted him for his actions. What had he done? His plan had not worked as Cecily still did not remember and the others did not understand why he had turned his back on them.

As he sat there with nothing but time to kill, he tried to anticipate Dasrus's next move. The truth was that Dasrus had told him nothing of his intentions. He was on a strictly need to know basis and as a result, he was completely useless. Jedd contemplated why Dasrus was waiting. He had everything he needed for the ritual, the six guardians and permission from Lord Bramble, human protector of the gateway, yet Dasrus had mentioned needing one last thing. Whatever that thing was, Jedd was now grateful for it as it would give him the opportunity to do the right thing. This was entirely his fault. If he had not approached the Dark, the wheels would not have been set in motion. He gave Dasrus his opportunity and now many people were dead and he and his fellow Cerbereans were in this prison awaiting death. He had to try and fix things. His calling to the Light was at its strongest now that the others had been reactivated. He was a part of something huge. He had found himself lost along the way though and his rage and bitterness had caused no end of trouble. He needed the chance to redeem himself.

Jedd waited for what seemed like an age for his friends to awaken and when they did, he listened carefully to their whispered conversation. He heard the terror in Cecily's voice. Obviously, she was having a hard time coming to terms with everything, especially as she could not remember anything. He tried to put himself in her shoes, but he just imagined he would think everyone was nuts. He had to respect her for trying and his heart went out to her for more reasons than one. Jedd thought how angry she would be with him after the argument in Bramblegate. He had said a lot of nasty things to her that night, fuelled by his will to lash out and hurt her and to top it off, ever since that night he had avoided her.

Kaden, Fen and Sol were stoic as always; true warriors. However, Elisabeth was also very angry with him and he did not blame her one bit. The way he had treated her had been despicable. He had kidnapped her, bound her, kept her as his prisoner and finally knocked her out cold. He wondered if she would ever be able to forgive him as this was not how you treated a friend. He had betrayed them all badly. Would any of them be able to forgive him and give him a second chance? He needed them to look into his heart, to see how sorry he was.

Jedd waited for the most opportune moment to speak. He did not want to interrupt them, firstly because deep down, he wanted to gauge their feelings towards him and secondly, because he was their only chance of escape. He knew this, so part of him wanted them to feel despair and hopelessness so that he would be welcomed back into the fold. Although he knew it would take more than pulling off an escape from this dungeon for them to trust him again.

When his friends' conversation had been exhausted, he took his chance to announce his presence.

"I still have my powers," he said in the most timid, unthreatening, apologetic tone possible.

"Jedd?"

Kaden was the first to speak, quickly followed by Elisabeth who added imperatively, "Don't trust him!"

He saw that one coming.

"I know what you are thinking," said Jedd, carefully. "I'm so sorry, more sorry than any of you know. I've made a huge mistake. I just want to put things right and come back to the Light."

"Why should we trust you?" spat Elisabeth. "You've betrayed all of us. You engineered this whole situation from start to finish!"

"I know and I was wrong. I was bitter and angry."

"Why, Jedd? Why have you done this?" Fen sounded wounded.

"I never forgot. I was born again this time with all of my memories and I felt so alone. Human emotions ate me up inside and I turned to Dasrus."

"Why didn't you tell me, Jedd? We are friends!" The shock in Kaden's voice was evident, but Jedd was pleased to hear that he spoke about their friendship in the present tense and not the past. "I could have deactivated you, like I did Elisabeth."

"What?" chorused Fen and Sol.

"You were both reborn with memories? Activated?" questioned Sol, trying to understand what Kaden and Jedd were talking about.

"Yes. Elisabeth drew her sword in the school playground. I deactivated her and sent her away until she was needed again, just to be sure she would not accidentally reactivate again," explained Kaden.

"I didn't know about Elisabeth. I will never be able to truly explain the reasons for what I did. I regretted it the moment I started. I'm going to put things right. I'll get us out of here and then I'll do whatever it takes for you to trust me again."

"That's all very well, Jedd, but you are a Cerberean," pointed out Kaden.

"I know," said Jedd, regretfully. "I've broken my oath."

"I'm afraid it will not be up to us how you remedy this situation or even if you can."

"That is a chance I've got to take, for my own peace of mind, if anything."

Also for the sake of his soul, but he decided not to tell them just yet that it belonged to Dasrus.

"Coward!" screamed Elisabeth.

"Elisabeth," reproached Kaden, his manner calm. "If there is a chance for us to get out of here, we must take it. We've work to do. Think about how long we've known Jedd for."

"I think we should give Jedd another chance," offered Sol. "Everyone makes mistakes."

"Me too," Fen agreed. "Being in human form for so long you start to adopt some mortal traits. We've all done it." Fen paused and Jedd could imagine her blushes. "I believe we should give him the opportunity to redeem himself."

"Well, I too am in favour of giving Jedd the chance of redemption. It is for the Light to judge him and not his fellow Cerbereans."

Jedd knew that Kaden would offer him the scope to prove himself. His heart was warmed by his friends' confidence in him. Then the voice he had truly wanted to hear from spoke through the darkness.

"I'm afraid I agree with Elisabeth. He has deceived us all and I don't know if I can forgive him yet, let alone trust him. He was supposed to be my friend, in fact, a friend to us all."

This condemnation spiked Jedd through the heart, but what did he expect? He had treated her appallingly and as she was still human, she would not be able to rise above it and control her emotions. He would have to prove himself and when her memories came back, she would remember his previous loyalty like the others did. However, it was Elisabeth he needed to convince. Did she see something in him the others did not? She was so mad with him, understandably, but she too would have to control those dangerous human emotions. He was speaking from experience. Or maybe she had already mastered her feelings and was demonstrating her deadly warrior instincts.

After a few moments, Elisabeth spoke.

"One wrong move, Jedd, and I will rip your throat out myself." Her quiet menacing tone was bordering psychotic. He did not want to be on the wrong side of her.

Kaden sprang into action. "Jedd, you said you still have your powers?"

"Yes, I didn't think to try until you all said you did not have yours. Turns out mine are working fine!"

"Dasrus must have blocked our powers. Why would Dasrus make the effort to intercept all our powers, yet leave you with yours?" pondered Kaden.

"Maybe in all the commotion, he forgot. I didn't know I was going to be locked up here until we arrived and then he simply shoved me in this cage and left without so much as a word."

"Dasrus did not forget," replied Kaden. "He is not stupid. He has done it on purpose. I buy the fact that we are in this less secure holding cell because he cannot return to the Dark, but I do not believe he would forget to block one set of powers, not after all of his hard work to get us here."

"It's a trap," said Elisabeth, matter-of-factly.

"Yes, that was my first thought," mused Kaden, "and the obvious answer. Or maybe he is testing Jedd's loyalty. Has Dasrus confided in you, Jedd? Do you have any information?"

"No, he has told me nothing. At first, I could not understand the delay in performing the ritual. I mean, he has everything he needs. But then, shortly before we got here, like Elisabeth already said, he mentioned needing one more thing to complete the ritual."

It went quiet again and Jedd could hear his own heart

thumping in his chest. If anyone could figure it out, Kaden could.

"It's a trap. Jedd's right, Dasrus needs one more element to complete the ritual and he needs us to lead him to it. We need to leave right away. We cannot risk him obtaining it by himself and returning here to imprison us for real. Our first mission just became critical."

"So, we are going to walk straight into his trap instead?" questioned Cecily. "Do you have a death wish, because I don't. Let's just get out of here and disappear. He can't perform the ritual at all without us."

"He knows we won't run though. We are Cerbereans, protectors of the human race and we have sworn an oath. We can't let him manipulate the final piece of the puzzle."

"Are you saying the missing part is human?" Sol sounded quizzical.

"Yes, I believe it is."

"OK, so we go and rescue this person, walk straight into Dasrus's trap and give him everything he needs to complete the ritual, all tied up with a pretty bow on top?" said Cecily, sarcastically. "Have you forgotten that Dasrus defeated us badly only a few hours ago?"

"There are five of us this time, Cec. We are stronger." Jedd knew that Fen was trying to put Cecily's mind at ease.

"Providing Jedd fights with us," snapped Elisabeth.

"Look, I have a plan to get what we need and escape quickly, but if the plan is going to work, we have got to start trusting each other."

"Elisabeth, I am sorry!" Jedd implored. "I will prove to you that I am back. I won't let you down again."

Jedd felt his apology from the bottom of his heart, but Elisabeth said nothing. In addition, Cecily was still unconvinced of the plan.

"I think the whole thing sounds crazy. We should run."

"I know you don't understand yet, Cec," explained Sol, "but

you have to trust Kaden."

Jedd heard Cecily breathe a deep sigh. She will be mortified that she suggested bolting when her memories come back.

"Let's go then," she muttered without zeal.

"Your heard the lady, Jedd!" shouted Kaden.

Jedd reached over his shoulders with both hands and felt the ice cool hilt of his sword as he grasped it. As he unsheathed his sword, the slicing sound of the sharp blade filled him with power and a bright white light erupted from behind him. With one clean swipe he was able to slice through the thick and heavy lock and chains like a knife through butter. As the door to the cage sprang open, Jedd leapt outside it, feeling more alive and more powerful than ever. He was back.

Chapter 22

Jedd effortlessly removed the chains from the other cells with his supernatural sword. At least that is what Cecily presumed it to be; it was certainly not of the world that she knew. As she heard Jedd slice through the chains of her prison door, she darted forward to feel for the exit. She had not realised while sat in her small jail, as the dark was impenetrable, but the cell door was old-fashioned, like a dungeon, made up of thick metal bars, the heavy chains wrapped around them. *So easy for Jedd to access,* she thought to herself. Even once outside her cell door, the darkness enveloped her still; there seemed no escape from this wretchedness. The gloom and anguish of this cold, obscure place filled her head. She felt her brain soaking up the hopelessness, its receptors feeding the same feeling to her heart. She could barely see something if she was stood right on top of it. How were they supposed to feel their way out of this place? Just as she felt the desperation begin to pull her under and the panic rise in her stomach, she heard Kaden, unflappable as ever.

"Right, let's get out of here!"

They walked in single file, Jedd up front as he still had his powers, closely followed by Kaden with Elisabeth, Fen and Sol bringing up the rear. Cecily was sandwiched between Kaden and Elisabeth. Jedd knew which direction they had come in from as he had not been blindfolded, so he led them slowly and carefully along a cool and slimy wall. Again, Cecily found herself thinking how easy it was for them to escape, having Jedd with them at full power, knowing the way out. The wall felt disgusting and Cecily kept squealing and recoiling at the different textures she was experiencing, trying not to think about what they were. It was as if she were a contestant in one of those Japanese game shows where they blindfold you and then make you stick your hands into various containers of goodness knows what and you have to guess what it is. She wanted a hot shower.

They eventually came to a stop.

"What is it?" Sol whispered loudly from the back of the line.

"Stairs," said Jedd in an equally exaggerated hushed voice. "I'm sure we came down these stairs. There are a lot of them, so be prepared."

However, nothing could have prepared Cecily for the ascent. Not only was it tough, it was never ending. She started out strong and determined as she wanted to get out as soon as possible to escape the oppressive atmosphere. Her lungs were begging for some fresh air. However, as time ebbed away, she became more breathless and tired and the muscles in her calves burned as they headed for what she hoped was the surface. The more exhausted she became, the clumsier she got. The stairwell was narrow and the steps were uneven. Plus, she still could not see anything, so she found that she stumbled easily, which made Elisabeth fall over her, then Fen over Elisabeth and Sol over Fen, causing a domino effect. Elisabeth kept helping Cecily to her feet, but she felt Elisabeth's annoyance. Jedd and Kaden also had to slow their pace on account of her.

It was all right for them, they were superhuman warriors. She was just plain old Cecily Stalks. If only she could get her memory back. What was she thinking? She did not know who or what she would be if she remembered. Maybe she would not like herself? Maybe she was preventing herself from recalling, somehow protecting herself? She did not think that her yelps and shrieks were helping matters either, every time she fell or came across something in the dark she did not quite like the feel of. *Well, they will just have to bear with me and be patient,* she thought defiantly. She was trying her best. And so her ordeal continued as she climbed and climbed. The only reason she was moving at all was due to sheer will power. She did not want to appear weak in the eyes of the others. If her friends were struggling like she was, then they showed no sign of it. They were completely stoic, whereas Cecily was fighting back the sobs. She could not think about where she was or what she was doing, because if she did, she felt hysteria setting in, then her mouth watered and bile rose. She could vomit at any moment. Just when she thought she could take no more, Jedd spoke excitedly.

"Light! I can see light!"

"Are you sure?" answered Kaden.

"Of course I'm sure! It's been pitch black and now I can see light... around a doorway!"

Jedd was right. The top of the narrow stairwell opened up into a small passage and a couple of metres away, the outline of the door was highlighted by chinks of light. Jedd ran the short distance and began pushing, but he could not shift it. Kaden and Sol joined him, yet the three of them could not budge the door either. However, with the power of Elisabeth and Fen added to the force behind the door, the five of them managed to slowly push the heavy door open.

The brightness showed the door to be made of rock. With a last burst of energy, Cecily made her way out of the depressing, soul-sucking dungeon. She bent forwards, hands on knees and took in a deep breath of fresh air. However, the air up there was anything but fresh; it was putrid. Cecily vomited noisily in a corner. She could hear Kaden and Jedd discussing her current state.

"It is too much for her," said Kaden, sounding genuinely concerned.

"It is not that much further. We can help her." Jedd was being overly confident as usual. At least they did not want to leave her there.

When she had finished emptying her already hollow stomach,

she stood up and looked at her surroundings. She did not like what she saw. Above the surface of the dungeon, it was marginally lighter than down below, although Cecily could not see where this light source was coming from as the sky was grey with thick clouds. In the distance, Cecily could hear the rumble of thunder while sizable forks of lightening crackled over vast mountains. She looked to either side of her and saw the same drab and ashen rocky terrain as far as the eye could see. Behind her lay nothing but a craggy wall belonging to yet another mountain, whose depths she had just dragged herself out of.

Cecily dared not breathe in, not only because she was afraid the rotten stench would make her heave again, but because a fine red dust floated in the air. She looked down at her sweatshirt and jeans and saw that the powder had settled on her clothes. When she shook her head, it drifted down onto her shoulders. She looked around and noticed the rocks were also covered by a fine layer of this red sand-like dust. It gave the grey atmosphere around them an eerie crimson hue, almost like a beautiful sunset, only without the beauty or the sun. The temperature in this ugly place was very warm, so she took off her jumper leaving herself in a t-shirt, although she was already regretting its white colour. She wrapped the top around her mouth and nose to prevent herself from breathing in too much of the dust. It seemed the others had the same idea.

Luckily, Cecily had changed at home, but the others were still in their evening wear from the party. This did not seem to faze them though. Elisabeth and Fen were ripping bits of material from their already torn dresses. Kaden, Jedd and Sol had discarded their dinner jackets and were tearing at them easily. The girls had taken off their party shoes before the climb. It seemed that bare feet did not bother them in the slightest. She looked at her friends in their odd combination of ruined evening wear against the backdrop of this scarlet granite desert. Why were they not complaining? Did they feel no pain? Cecily was the only one dressed halfway appropriately for this adventure in jeans, a t-shirt and trainers and she felt ill-prepared. Not only that, she hurt all over. Her friends really were warriors. And they were truly in this nothing space, this forlorn place between realms.

When they were all ready, they set off walking. At least they had no more climbing to do as they appeared to be in a valley that was fairly flat, surrounded by craggy peaks on all sides. The terrain was very treacherous under foot and true to form, Cecily spent much of her time stumbling, going over on her ankles and falling to her knees, but she was grateful for small miracles and thankfully, she did not have to climb a mountain. She knew she was slowing the others down again. She watched them as they walked in front of her. They were so agile and nimble. They seemed to float above the rocks, just skimming their surface. Cecily was drained. She looked back to see how far they had come and it was not far at all. Over the ground, she saw where she had made footprints on the lightly dusted surface. Some of the footprints were elongated where she had dragged her weary limbs. No one was chatty and so their trek was silent.

After a while, Fen said to Kaden, "We still haven't got our powers back. What if Dasrus attacks us here where he knows we have nothing to draw on?"

"There is no point in attacking us here. He requires us to lead him directly to what he needs to complete the ritual. That is what this whole elaborate scheme of his has been about."

Cecily felt she had something new to worry about. "What if you don't get your powers back when we get to the other side? He'll kill us when he's finished with us."

Kaden was as calm as ever. "Dasrus can stifle our powers in a place such as this where we are close to his realm, but he cannot take our magic away. Even he is not that mighty. We draw our power from nature. If you look around, there is not much in the way of natural life around here."

Kaden was right. Even though the thunder roared in the

distance and the leaden clouds rolled in the sky above them, there was no sign of water anywhere, no trees or plants, just hard rock.

"We probably could draw some magic from the rocks, which is why Dasrus has used his magic to stifle our powers while we are here. Once we get back to the Earth plane, especially Bramblegate, we will be back to full capacity. Dasrus knows this and he will be ready."

"Does anyone else think that this plan of Dasrus's is a bit elaborate?" questioned Sol. "I mean, why go to all this trouble? He had us right where he wanted us. We were weak and outnumbered. Why didn't he just force us to give him what he needs?"

"Maybe it is a test for Jedd," replied Fen. "This whole situation is geared towards Jedd betraying Dasrus and setting us free so we can lead him to the final piece of the puzzle. He was counting on Jedd betraying him for this plan to work."

"He must know him well," retorted Elisabeth, sarcastically.

"It just doesn't make sense," continued Sol, ignoring the comment. "Did he not think that we would work out his motive?"

"He made it too easy for us to escape," chipped in Cecily. "Telling Jedd he still needed something to complete the ritual, leaving him with his powers, those pathetic chains holding our cell doors locked and leaving Jedd without a blindfold on the way in so he could lead us straight out of here."

"Like I said, elaborate," replied Sol.

"We can't presume to know what Dasrus is up to. It may well be a test for Jedd. All we know is that he needs one last thing to open the gateway and I know what it is," argued Kaden. "Where Dasrus is concerned, let's assume the worst."

"It's bound to be an ambush," said Jedd.

"Do you know that for sure?" Elisabeth jumped on his comment, still not trusting him.

"No! It's obvious though, isn't it?"

Kaden intervened, "One step at a time. Like I said, I've a plan to get us in and out."

"Well at least we still have our strength," added Elisabeth. "He cannot take away our fighting spirit."

The group once more fell silent. They had a lot to think about. Cecily was having a tough enough time in this place. She did not know if she could handle what Dasrus had to offer when they eventually got home. She began hatching her own plan to run away. She could not go home, especially after all Purdey had revealed. She imagined charging through the front door, packing what she needed and telling her so-called mother exactly what she thought of her. Now she'd had time to digest what Purdey had said to her, she too had a lot of things she wanted to say. Then she never wanted to see that murderer's face again. She was not bothered that Purdey hated her. She was more upset for her beloved father.

She had thought her plan through, now she wondered how she was going to execute it. Was she going to make a dash for it as soon as they arrived home? She somehow doubted the others would let her leave and they had supernatural powers, so she was no match for them. She could try and sneak off when they were otherwise engaged, but she thought it would not take them long to realise she was missing. Also, by that time, they might be with Dasrus and those hell beasts might come after her or worse still, Dasrus. What if the others got angry with her for trying to leave and so refused to protect her? If she did make it home, what if Purdey stood in her way? She also had to pack some things. In the end, she concluded that making a run for it was probably not wise, so it seemed she would be facing Dasrus with her friends, whether she liked it or not.

Cecily was so busy mulling over her problems that at first, she did not realise Jedd had dropped back from the front of the group and was now walking next to Cecily, matching her pace. She felt that the uncomfortable atmosphere between them was palpable; however, she was not going to be the first to speak. She felt like she had nothing to say to him. So they continued walking in awkward silence. After a while, Cecily forgot he was there. She was concentrating on her footing, whilst rambling over the rugged landscape. The last thing she wanted was a sprained ankle, which would make her even more of a burden to the others. Also, she was still very much embroiled in her own problems, so when Jedd spoke, it made her jump.

"I am truly sorry, Cec. I never meant to hurt you. I know that I said some awful things to you and let you down. I will make it up to you."

He sounded genuine enough, but she did not know quite know what to say to him. She felt they had never seen eye to eye. He had been mean to her for as long as she could remember. It was too soon and she felt that at the moment, she would rather conserve her energy than talk to him.

When she did not answer, he continued. "I was so lost and I did some horrible things. But I've realised the error of my ways. I'll prove I am back with the Light. I don't want to end up like Purdey…" He stopped mid-sentence. Well that definitely sparked her interest.

"What do you know about my mother?" she asked rather flatly.

Jedd seemed to carefully consider his response before speaking.

"I'm sorry, Cec. She didn't make it. Dasrus…" Jedd was unable to finish his sentence.

"How?" Cecily enquired, simply.

"How?" echoed Jedd.

"Yes, how? Stabbed, shot, hung, smothered, choked? How?" Cecily could feel her anger building, but she did not know to whom her anger was directed.

"Well, magic I guess," offered Jedd. "He ripped her soul from her body."

Jedd carefully explained to Cecily exactly what he had

witnessed and carried on talking even when he saw her wincing. He explained how the soul had left her body in pieces, how it had whirled around the room like a mini-hurricane and how it had taken a downward turn and had disappeared into the ground.

Cecily remained impassive. "Her body?"

"Eaten by the shadow beasts."

Cecily fell quiet again and did not speak for a long time. Now it seemed she had to get her head around the death of her mother. Jedd walked beside her for a while, also in silence. Eventually, Kaden called Jedd back to the front to help them retrace the route, although Cecily was so lost in thought, she did not notice his absence. While they trekked tirelessly, Cecily forgot her exhaustion as she tried to pinpoint her feelings about the news she had just received.

Her mother was dead, killed in the most atrocious, inhumane and unbelievable way. To top it off, Jedd had actually witnessed her soul go into the ground; therefore, it was unlikely she had gone towards the Light. She was dead. Cecily would never see her mother again. Purdey was out of her life. She kept repeating these mantras to herself in an attempt to stir some emotion.

She thought back to when she found her father swinging by his neck in the back garden. She remembered calmly calling the ambulance, following this with a call to her mother. She denied the reality of what was happening, hid from the facts surrounding her father's suicide and blocked out words of sympathy from well-wishers. She remembered sitting in the doctor's surgery with her mother. The doctor explained that this denial was a temporary response to the pain. When her pain finally re-emerged and it did not take long, she remembered with agony the anger she had felt.

Now, with the death of her mother, it was like she had missed the first stage of grief and gone straight to the second stage of anger. Why did she feel such fury towards her mother? She would never see her again. Is that not what she wanted? Was this rage down to the fact that she felt the pain of her mother leaving her? Because they had departed on such bad terms and because Cecily had not had the opportunity to say all she wanted to Purdey? She'd had so much she wanted to say to her mother, none of it pleasant and now she would never get the chance. This thought made her all the angrier. Deep down, Cecily knew the reason for her outrage and that was because her last hope for revenge had gone; revenge for her father's murder by her own mother's hand. How could she do that to him? How could she do that to her?

At that moment, Cecily realised her mother had meant every word she had said to Cecily and now that had sunk in, Cecily just wanted to lash out at her, only now it would never happen because Purdey was dead, killed by Dasrus. She had not thought to ask Jedd if he knew why Dasrus had ended her, but she guessed it was because she had served her purpose. Now she would be paying for her wicked deeds. Cecily did not feel like weeping for her mother's soul, she did not feel as if she wanted to cry out in pain or at the injustice of losing both parents so young. She just felt anger, anger that her mother would not die by her own hand.

Shocked by her feelings, Cecily was glad to be awakened from her thoughts by Kaden shouting, "It's there! I see it!"

The others had climbed up to a ridge ahead of her to get a better vantage point.

"How do you know that is the right door?" enquired Fen.

"Is that the door you came through?" Kaden asked Jedd, pointing off into the distance.

"Absolutely!" replied Jedd, with the utmost certainty. "I've retraced the route exactly."

"Then that is the door we must exit from," said Kaden.

Cecily could see Kaden pointing in the opposite direction to where they had originally been looking.

"Are you sure that is the right door?" questioned Sol. "We don't want to end up somewhere other than Bramblegate."

"If Jedd is certain that he came through that door, then we

must leave through this one," said Kaden, arms and palms extended as he explained. "As you know, portal doors come in pairs, one entrance and one exit."He was so confident that he seemed to placate the group.

Cecily decided it was time to join her friends and so she scrambled up the ridge. As she reached the top, she saw a door on top of the mountain ahead of her. She was surprised to see it was just a regular door. Not attached to walls or a frame, just a normal door, stood alone on top of a mountain. Her eyes followed the horizon to see if she could see the other door, the entrance to this realm. Sure enough, the adjacent mountain had another solitary door perched on top of it.

Now they had reached the edge of the valley, they had some climbing to do to get to the top of the mountain. The fatigue overwhelmed Cecily as she digested the enormity of the task ahead. Cecily spoke for the first time since Jedd had revealed her mother's death and as a result, her throat was tight and her voice cracked.

"I can't do it," she croaked. "I can't climb that mountain."

Before anyone else had the chance to speak, Jedd stepped forward.

"I'll carry her."

"Great," said Elisabeth, icily. "At least that means she won't slow us down."

This comment burned Cecily. What was her problem? She tried to attract Elisabeth's attention, but Elisabeth would not look at her. She knew Cecily was still human, she could not help it. Jedd swept up Cecily like she was a pile of feathers. As he did so, he displaced the red dust that had been gathering on her as she walked and as the dust rose in a cloud, it made her sneeze. Cecily and Jedd giggled at the tiny mouse-like squeak that liberated itself from Cecily's nose and as they did, Elisabeth shot them a glacial look. Cecily once again found herself wondering what she had done to Elisabeth, but she decided to make an effort not to think about it. She felt she could think no more.

They made good time, even though the path to the door was a tough climb. Her friends clambered over the rocks lightly and swiftly. They appeared to find footholds where there were none. As they scaled the mountain further up, Jedd needed to use both of his hands, so he transferred Cecily to his back, where she clung onto his neck for dear life. Cecily was glad of this as Elisabeth was travelling behind them and now she did not have to endure the unpleasantness of trying to avoid her stare. Her friends were fast. She realised Elisabeth was right, she had been slowing them down.

There was a small flat landing on top of the mountain on which the door was precariously perched. Jedd carefully put Cecily down and her friends neared the door to check it out. Cecily hung back for a minute and decided to look down. As she did, she found her stomach in her mouth. She had never been afraid of heights, but they were a long way up. Cecily turned her attention to the door. It was just an average black door and as she had seen from the bottom of the mountain, it stood alone, unattached. It seemed as though if you were to open it and walk through, you would fall down the other side of the mountain. As Cecily got closer, she saw the others were pinching their noses and pulling faces. The black colour of the door was in fact a slimy mould. It was dripping from the door and dissipating as it hit the rocks with a loud hiss. The door seemed to contract as if it was breathing and as it did, it expelled the most repulsive, fetid smell. The door seemed to be rotten to the core.

As Kaden reached for the handle, Elisabeth shouted, "No!" and batted his hand away. "Jedd should go first. We still don't know what is waiting for us on the other side."

Jedd simply shrugged and took hold of the door handle. As he did, the mouldy putrid slime covered his hand like a thick black tar. The handle turned easily; however, Jedd had to apply a lot of pressure in order to push it open. He shoved the door with his shoulder and as he did so, his left side became covered in the horrid sludge. As he stepped away from the open door, the ooze dissipated once more.

"Why is it so difficult to open the door?" enquired Cecily, peering through.

"It's a portal to another realm, Cec," explained Kaden. "The physics are different."

Cecily, who was expecting to see Bramblegate, saw nothing. Whatever was on the other side of that door was white in colour and opaque. She could not see through it. Jedd went to step through the door, but Elisabeth stopped him.

"Wait, I'll come with you. If the coast is clear, I will send Jedd back to tell you," she said to the others.

"It's probably best if the four of us go together," suggested Sol, referring to himself, Fen, Jedd and Elisabeth, "just in case there is an ambush. I'll come back and tell you if everything is OK," he said to Kaden.

And so the four of them disappeared through the door, first Sol, closely followed by Fen, Jedd and Elisabeth, all engulfed by the thick, non-transparent material.

As soon as the four Cerbereans had departed, Kaden offered his condolences to Cecily.

"I'm so sorry about Purdey, Cec. I know you two had your problems but she was still your mum."

Cecily dared not speak. She did not want to reveal her true feelings towards her mother. Problems? That was definitely an understatement. So she simply smiled at Kaden instead. Even in this bleak place between realms, Kaden could still make her smile. She remembered why they were friends. The white substance through the doorway began to move and shift, revealing Sol.

"Let's go!" he said, before disappearing once more.

"Hold my hand and don't let go," Kaden told Cecily.

"OK," she replied, full of trepidation as to where this portal was going to lead her. As Kaden pulled her through the gateway, she took one last look at the foreboding rocky landscape and in her heart, wished for the beauty of Bramblegate.

Chapter 23

Cecily did not know what to think as she passed through the portal. She had to push hard through a thick, white, opaque, gel-like substance which appeared to stick in between every orifice. She held on tight to Kaden's hand, fearing that if she lost it, she would be congealed in this gelatinous substance forever. It seemed to take them quite a while to push their way through, although in reality, it was probably only a minute or two. She was just beginning to feel claustrophobic, like the gel might suffocate her, when she felt fresh air on her face and immense relief. However, this feeling did not last as then she was falling. Before she knew what had happened, she had hit the ground in a crumpled heap. She looked around and saw that Kaden had landed skilfully on his feet in the same crouching position as that of a big cat ready to pounce. All eyes were now on Cecily as she was patting herself down, not only to check if she was alright, but also to see if the sticky substance she had just passed through had left its mark. Miraculously, she was bone dry and when she looked up, so seemed her friends. Unfortunately, they could not disguise their amusement.

"What happened?" questioned Cecily, who had not yet managed to pick herself up off the floor.

"The portal exit is there," laughed Sol pointing upwards.

However, when Cecily looked up, she could see nothing. Fen must have seen by the look on Cecily's face that she did not understand, so she kindly explained.

"The portal exit is just there, Cec, in the air beside that tree."

Fen was pointing upwards, just as Sol had done.

"I can't see anything!" said a puzzled Cecily.

"You are not meant to see it. We wouldn't want just anyone to happen upon it, it would cause too many questions."

"But why can't I see it?" asked Cecily, matter-of-factly, thinking of the door she had just passed through in the other realm.

"It's just a tear, a small rip in the fabric of our atmosphere. You will only see it if something pushes out of it," explained Fen.

"Ah, OK," said Cecily, not altogether sure she understood exactly what they were talking about. "And what was that sticky stuff?"

"The sticky stuff is the gel that holds the realms together. Disgusting, isn't it?"

Cecily agreed with Fen as she hauled herself to her feet.

"I wonder why portal doors come in pairs?" she pondered. "I mean, doors open from both sides. It seems silly to have separate doorways to the same place."

Kaden was quick to respond to her musings. "Most people aren't even aware other realms exist, Cec. We can't have revolving doors between them, it's unsafe. Think of the entrances and exits like one-way streets."

Cecily said nothing. She was so tired. She wondered if the others were getting sick of having to explain things to her. At least she could supply their entertainment. Kaden quickly reminded them of the situation.

"We need to go," he said, soberly.

"Where are we going?" enquired Elisabeth.

"Let's not discuss it here," replied Kaden. "We don't know who is listening. Has everyone got their powers back?"

Cecily watched as Fen, Sol and Elisabeth reached behind them to grab the hilts of their invisible swords, well, invisible until they needed to use them. Then they appeared out of nowhere, big and powerful accompanied by bright, white light. When they all smiled, Cecily took it they were back at full strength. Sol even flexed his muscles for good measure. When she turned to look at Kaden and Jedd, Jedd was sliding his sword back in place and Kaden's hands were glowing an icy blue. Cecily still found it difficult to accept her childhood friends as they were now.

"Right, let's go," said Kaden, leading the way through the trees.

Cecily knew they were in Bramblegate Woods. She would have recognised them anywhere, although at the moment, she was a bit disorientated and she wondered in which direction they were heading. The others were light and nimble, dancing over exposed tree roots and shrubbery. It was a beautiful warm, sunny day and Cecily felt she would rather be enjoying the woods; however, she had to make a real effort with her footing and watch it carefully. She thought that just by herself, she sounded like a herd of elephants. As well as trying to be light on her feet, she was also attempting to look from side to side for any imminent signs of danger in the form of those dreadful shadow beasts she so despised, but she was sure the others had undertaken that task as once again, she was sandwiched between her friends just in case they were ambushed.

They must have come through the portal in the north of the woods, as now they had arrived at the gravel track that led from Bramblegate down into the dell. Instead of taking the path, they crossed it carefully back into the protection of the woods again. Cecily knew they were heading down into the dell, only she did not want to ask why. The thought of seeing her childhood home made her sick to the stomach. It was the location of so much pain in recent years that she now knew was caused by Purdey and the cottage was also the scene of her horrific downfall. She tried to put it to the back of her mind and concentrate on her footing as they continued the walk down into the dell. She was again very aware of how much she must be slowing the others down.

When they got to the dell, they entered behind Kaden's

cottage. Cecily's thoughts wandered to Kaden's stepfather and she wondered if he was OK. Kaden, however, did not even give his childhood home a second glance and he carried on walking in the direction of the Fanes' cottage. Both Cecily and Kaden knew the Fanes well as they had all shared the dell over the years. No one else tended to go down there unless it was purposely to visit one of its residents.

Cecily was surprised when the group made their way around the back of the Fanes', through the picket fence and into the small, well-kept garden. Kaden strode up to the back door and knocked. After a minute or two, the door creaked open, seemingly of its own accord, revealing no one to be stood there. Suddenly, Mr Fane appeared from above, dropping to the floor whilst coming out of a very spritely back flip, making Cecily jump out of her skin. She was so surprised at what she had just witnessed, she could not speak. She was thinking where he could have come from and the only answer she could come up with was that he had been clinging to the top of the door frame.

Before she had more time to consider Mr Fane, she heard a click behind her and a voice saying, "Don't move an inch." The group slowly turned their heads to see who was threatening them and Cecily could hardly believe her eyes. There stood Mrs Fane, holding a crossbow poised with a very sharp arrow, pointing directly at them. Mrs Fane must have gone out of the front door and around the back to surprise them. As Cecily turned back to look at Mr Fane, she realised that he too was holding a crossbow and arrow that had them marked. Cecily automatically raised her hands to show she posed no threat and looking at the others, she saw that they had done the same.

"Identify yourselves!" said Mr Fane, sharply. "Careful now," he added as Kaden stepped forward.

"My name is Stellan."

Cecily was puzzled as to why Kaden was using this strange name.

"Show me!" said Mr Fane in the same sharp tone.

Although Kaden's back was facing Cecily, she could see the ice blue glow emanating from his person.

Mr Fane maintained his emotionless face and simply said, "Next!" One by one her friends stepped forward, introducing themselves by names Cecily had not heard before. Fen introduced herself as Amira, while Elisabeth said she was Toril. Sol said his name was Breccan and Jedd, Inigo. But this peculiar system of identification did not stop there. After they had said their names, each of her warrior friends reached behind their heads to the top of their backs, where the hilts of their swords could be found and Cecily heard the unmistakable sound of sizzling flesh. Cecily managed to peer over Fen's shoulder as she was standing close to her. What she saw was that the sword had made a brand on the palm of her hand which disappeared as quickly as it had made its mark. Cecily tried to see what the brand was, but it disappeared in an instant.

When all of her friends had undergone the same process and identified themselves satisfactorily, it was Cecily's turn. She looked helplessly at Kaden, who simply nodded his head in suggestion that she should step forward. Cecily found herself stood in front of Mr Fane, looking down the arrow of his cross bow.

"Well, what are you waiting for?" said Mr Fane, impatiently.

"My name is… Cecily Stalks," ventured Cecily, hesitantly.

Mr Fane immediately looked to Kaden. "She doesn't remember?" Kaden simply frowned and shook his head.

Mr Fane began to fire a series of questions at Cecily, whilst shining an unusually bright torch in her eyes that he had just acquired from the kitchen table.

"Where did I use to take you in the summer holidays?"

"You used to take me to work with you if Mum and Dad were busy."

"Where?"

"Well, the gardens at Bramble Hall, of course!" She was looking incredulously at Kaden.

"What was your father's middle name?"

"John."

"Named after who?"

"His Uncle John. He was my dad's favourite," she added.

"What was the last thing your father said to you?"

This question caught Cecily off guard and she had to think for a moment. She had to return to memories that were painful.

"To beware of the dark. To beware of the dark and always trust in the light."

It was like a penny had dropped and she was sure the realisation was clear on her face.

"He was trying to warn me! Did he know he was…" she hesitated, "… going to die?"

"Aye, lass," replied Mr Fane in his broad Lancashire accent. "He had an idea. I saw him on the afternoon of that terrible day. He told me his fears and what you'd talked about. Of course, I had no idea it would happen so soon…"

Mr Fane's voice trailed off and there was sadness in his eyes as he looked at Cecily. He turned to the others and said, "You'd better come in."

"Thanks, Abram…" began Kaden.

"Use some of that magic of yours to ensure we are not being overheard, lad," he interrupted.

Kaden obliging began to murmur and wave his hands around, which were glowing their pale, icy blue colour. Cecily presumed he was shielding the cottage.

When Mr Fane was again satisfied, he made his way into the living room, beckoning everyone to follow him. He shouted back in the direction of the kitchen, "Verena, put the kettle on!"

"Yes, dear!" called back Mrs Fane obediently.

Kaden continued, "We need your help, Abram. We need to know what has been happening while we've been gone."

"Gone? I thought you might have been lying low, but gone?"

"Yes, gone, Abram. I'll explain in a moment. What date is it?"

"The eighth of June, lad," replied a puzzled Mr Fane.

Kaden breathed a sigh of relief.

"Well at least that is one piece of good news," he said to his companions. "The passage of time seems to be the same between realms as here on the Earth plane. That means we have not lost too much time. We've only been gone a day."

Cecily was really confused. "What do you mean, the passage of time is the same? Should it be different?"

"In the Realm of Dark, time goes much slower than here on Earth," explained Kaden. "I suppose more time to fit in all that torture and pain. That is the point of it."

Cecily flinched at the mention of torture and pain as that was what Purdey must now be experiencing. Kaden gave her an apologetic look and carried on.

"In the Realm of Light, time goes really fast. One human lifetime is but the blink of an eye to those in the Light."

Cecily accepted what Kaden said by nodding her head. She found she was now accepting the weird things her friends told her as the everyday norm.

"Between realms you say, lad? I would like to know more about that!" piped up Mr Fane.

Kaden explained to Mr and Mrs Fane all that had happened from the balcony at the party, to their defeat and capture and finally about how they escaped. Cecily noticed how kind Kaden was about Jedd's deception, never blaming or fully implicating him in any way.

"So that is the story of our adventure," Kaden concluded. "Now we need to know what is happening here. Have you been watching?"

"Well that is our job, young Kaden!" said Mrs Fane in consternation, as if Kaden was implying that they were not doing what they were supposed to be doing.

Cecily felt that she had another question to ask about their job, but she realised that now was not the time.

"We didn't go to the party of course," began Mr Fane. "We are too old for all that now, but like you, we had a feeling something was off. We weren't surprised when we heard the commotion coming from Bramble Hall, especially on the night of the village party. It reminded me of last time..." Mr Fane's words again trailed off and he appeared to be somewhere else. Mrs Fane brought him back to the present.

"The screams were so loud that we could hear them down here in the dell, a mile away!"

Mr Fane continued. "We got our things and headed straight up there. We kept to the trees and saw the last of the guests escaping down the driveway to the village. We made our way up to the house and had a look through the windows of the Great Hall. We saw bodies lying everywhere, being devoured by those disgusting shadow beasts. Then we saw him, Dasrus, bold as brass and true to his natural form, coming down the staircase with the two young Cerbereans there (he pointed at Jedd and Elisabeth for good measure). We hid in the grounds of the manor for a long time. After Dasrus had gone, the shadow beasts took their time in feeding on their victims; very upsetting knowing that nothing could be done for them. They were long dead. Let's just hope their souls passed to the Light.

Eventually those hell monsters melted into the shadows. Verena and I waited a little while longer to make sure they weren't coming back. We were severely outnumbered. When we were pretty sure they had gone for good, we entered Bramble Hall through one of the windows in the dining room that had been left open. It was eerily silent. As you'd expect, there were no bodies to be seen. Those bottom feeder cretins eat more than flesh. They guzzle bone too. And clothes don't seem to bother them either. We poked around the dining room and Great Hall. All we saw was blood spatter on walls and bits of shredded clothing. The furniture was upturned and it was full of broken things, like crockery, glasses, mirrors, ornaments and such. It looked like a burglary gone wrong. However, not a body to be seen, just bloodstains, evidence of a heinous crime.

The parlour and drawing room were locked. We looked through the windows on our way out and they appeared untouched. We had a look around upstairs but there was no evidence anything had happened there. It looked like most of the guests tried to escape out of the front door or windows downstairs, rather than hiding in the building."

"I don't blame them," said Kaden, interrupting Mr Fane's account. "I wanted to be as far away as possible from Bramble Hall too. We were among the first to get out and even then, the crowd was bottlenecked at the main entrance. We should have stayed to help."

"You'd have stood no chance, lad. The amount of those things in there pitted against three of you, whilst you were trying to protect Cecily? You did the right thing. As it was, Dasrus and his agents caught up with you anyway."

Kaden shrugged his shoulders and Mr Fane continued to recount his tale.

"We had a poke around the kitchen, but there was no one about. As far as we could tell, the place was empty."

"What about the chapel?" asked Kaden.

"The door was unlocked so we had a quick look round, but as Abram said, the place was deserted," replied Mrs Fane. "Not a soul in sight, so we made our way home. It was coming up dawn before we left."

"What about yesterday? Did you go up to the village?" questioned Kaden.

"No, we didn't. Thought it best to stay away. We didn't want people to think we were sticking our noses in. As soon as we got home yesterday morning, we alerted the authorities and they dealt with the fall out."

"The authorities?" queried Cecily. "What on earth are they going to do about this? They aren't a match for Dasrus and his hell beasts and even if they were, who is going to believe what actually happened at Bramble Hall? How can we explain a massacre with a load of missing people, yet no bodies?" She looked round imploringly at her friends in an attempt to rally some support.

"Not human authorities," said Kaden, quietly. She got the impression that he was trying not to appear patronising. "Agents of the Light. I suppose the best way to describe them are as angels. That's who humans think they are."

"Angels?" Cecily took a moment. "What can they do? If I were regular Joe Bloggs at that party and I'd witnessed either my mother, wife, sister or daughter cut down and eaten by one of those monsters and I was lucky enough to escape, the first thing I'd have done was call the police. I would have wanted help, back-up, an explanation as to what was happening. The police would never believe what regular Joe Bloggs and the rest of the people said they saw. Sure, they could test DNA from the blood spatter, but they would never find the bodies because they have been eaten by demons. Then the police would think the villagers were conspiring. The murders would be pinned on innocent people!" Cecily was aware that she was running away with herself, but she had thought about this. "And how am I going to explain my mother's death?"

Cecily saw Mr Fane look to Kaden for confirmation of Cecily's last question and she saw him slightly nod his head in affirmation. Mrs Fane handed Cecily a cup of tea.

"Now I've put a bit of sugar in there for you, love, so it is nice and sweet. It will calm you down," she said, soothingly.

Cecily thanked Mrs Fane. She knew everyone was now looking at her, probably annoyed at her stupidity, but she did not care. How could they explain this away?

"Cecily, the agents of Light are what we call a purification team."

"Purification? Sounds like a religious ritual!"

"Well, I suppose it is sort of a ritual. Whenever the Dark strikes, there is chaos. It falls to the Light to clean up their mess and that is what the Purification Unit does."

"How?" Cecily enquired.

"Well in this instance some of the team will have gone immediately to the police and the rest to the families of the victims. They don't lie to people, Cecily, in fact they will have been very open about what happened. They will tell them that there are some things out there that they just can't explain, some things that most people will never experience, but just because they haven't come across them before, it doesn't mean they don't exist. They will counsel those left behind, explain that their souls have passed to the Light and how one day, they will be reunited. They are messengers of hope, Cec."

"And those who have lost their loved ones in such unnatural circumstances just accept what these agents say?"

"Well no, they are assisted to put it behind them."

"You mean their memories are magically wiped?"

"No, Cec. We are not the bad guys. These people will always be somehow aware of what happened and what they were a part of. But let's just say they accept it faster than it would ordinarily take and they don't ever discuss it with anyone. The Purification Unit helps them to put their pain behind them."

"So, they are brainwashed?"

"Well yes, I suppose, kind of, but in a good way. Humans are only on Earth for a short period of time. The Light does not want them to suffer due to unnatural causes."

"So why can't they do that for everyone who experiences loss?"

"Not all loss is supernatural, Cec. Loss is a fact of life and most have to learn to deal with it in their own way."

"And what if their loved one's soul has not passed to the

Light?"

"The Purification Unit doesn't lie. Most humans are aware if someone they love has chosen a path of darkness."

"So, what about the police?"

"Well the same really. The police and ranking officers are met with and told the truth, the same as the victims' families. There is no point in investigating an incident when they already know what has happened. They are always aware of what happened, but again they are helped to deal with it, understand what happened and put it behind them. And so, the case is closed."

"What if someone decides to re-open the case or a family decides to openly discuss what happened?"

"An agent will be assigned to the case so if anyone feels the need to revisit the incident, the parties involved, whether family or the law, will be reminded why it should not be discussed. We remind them to let sleeping dogs lie."

"Sounds like removing free will to me."

"The Light never takes anyone's free will, Cecily. At times though it acts how it sees fit. It helps take pain away in supernatural situations out of their control. It answers their questions so they are not left wondering why. They can continue their lives without burden, a burden that was placed on them by the continuing battle between Light and Dark."

Cecily had nothing further to say on the matter. Every time she asked a question, it created five more.

"I know it is hard, Cec, a lot of information to process which you can't understand while you are still human. Things will be clear when you get your memory back."

"What if I don't want my memory back?"

"You have to want it," said Kaden, simply. "We need you."

"Just to let you know, love," chipped in Mrs Fane, "the agents called this morning just before you arrived. Purification was a success. They've told everyone to stay away from Bramble Hall for the time being. I think they are going up there shortly to clean it up."

"Verena, could you call them and tell them to hold off for the time being?" asked Kaden. "We need to go there first."

"Of course, Kaden dear," replied Mrs Fane. She then disappeared to make the mysterious call and Cecily found herself wondering how such as call was made.

"So where do we go from here?" asked Jedd. "What's up at Bramble Hall?"

Kaden explained his theory to Mr Fane about Dasrus needing one final piece of the jigsaw in order to complete the ritual and how Dasrus was expecting the Cerbereans to lead him to it. Then he would have everything he needed in the one place.

"Well, it wouldn't be the first time he's tried to open the gateway. That's why we have guardians. There's only one reason for Dasrus to be on the Earth plane and that is to bring darkness and corrupt souls."

Halfway through the conversation, Mrs Fane had re-entered the room and she was busy topping up everyone's tea cups. She placed a plate of hot buttered crumpets in the middle of the table, which were gratefully received.

"Hopefully, what we need is in the organ loft above the chapel at Bramble Hall," said Kaden.

"But you said it was a person?" queried Sol.

"It is a person," replied Kaden cryptically. "Centuries ago, when the Bramble family agreed to be human protectors for the gateway in the woods, they only agreed on the condition that they would have a place of safety to flee to if anything went wrong and they needed to go into hiding. Somewhere the Dark and the demons would be unable to detect them. There is a large priest hole in the floor of the organ loft that is protected by the very strong magic of the Universe itself. It is drilled into every Bramble whose current responsibility it is for the gateway that there is a safe place where only the Light can find them. Only the protector and his immediate family ever know about it. As years pass between incidents, it becomes the stuff of legend, but they still take it seriously and rightly so."

"So how do you know about it?" asked Cecily.

"I helped find the location of the safe place within the house. I am the keeper of records, Cec. I have never told anyone about it and it is a well-guarded secret within the Bramble family. My guess is that Dasrus thought Lord Bramble disposable and in his anger at the early warning, he killed Lord Bramble, thus cancelling the contract and rendering his blood useless. I think Dasrus intended that there be no survivors from the party, after all, his demons have waited a long time to feed and they have been loyal to him. The party was probably their reward. I think that Dasrus was hasty in ending Lord Bramble's life because he had another little lord in the making right there; his son, Oscar. As soon as Lord Bramble died, Oscar became the new lord and it would be much easier for Dasrus to manipulate Oscar and his mother. I am hoping that Lord Bramble told his wife about the priest hole and at his warning, they fled there. I am hoping they are waiting in safety for us to rescue them."

"If Dasrus's intention is to perform the ritual and open the gateway, then his plan is risky," pointed out Mr Fane. "He had you all right where he wanted you, yet he let you escape. Why didn't he force you to tell him where the little heir is?"

"We did think about that, but it would have done no good. We can withstand torture all night and in any case, the others didn't know about my theory and the priest hole, and I would never give up the location of the safe place. He needed us to think we'd escaped so we can lead him straight to Oscar. He knows our first priority is to secure the gateway."

"I see where you are coming from, lad, but something doesn't sit well with me. It seems that this plan relied an awful lot on young Jedd betraying Dasrus."

"I think that was Dasrus's plan all along, to use Jedd. He must know we wouldn't turn our back on a fellow Cerberean."

177

"Mmm," murmured Mr Fane, as if he did not really agree. "Are you expecting an ambush at Bramble Hall then?"

"Yep," said Kaden, "we need to get in and out quickly. Once I've got Lady Bramble and the children, we need to get them to a place of safety and fortunately, I can tie this in with our next priority, which is helping Cecily get her memory and powers back. She can then shut down the gateway and Dasrus's plan will be foiled. We just have to figure out a way of returning him and his minions to the Realm of Dark and keeping them there. Lady Bramble and the children can then return to Bramble Hall and hopefully, Bramblegate can return to some kind of normality."

"So, what's the plan?" asked Sol.

"Well for one, we need to stick together as a group. We don't want to get separated."

"We've got to keep Cec safe too," added Jedd.

Cecily saw Elisabeth roll her eyes. What was her problem?

As the others began to discuss battle tactics and formations, Mr Fane beckoned Cecily to one side with a nod of his head.

"I was truly sorry about your father, lass. He was a good man, one of a kind."

"I know. I miss him desperately. It's been hard."

Cecily thought to herself how she could have used the Purification Unit after her father's death, only her mother killed her father. Nothing supernatural about that.

"You were the apple of his eye you know, Cecily. Everything he did was for you. You are the reason he was so good at his job. He used to write science fiction before you came along and your mother made that deal. He was so much better at mythology and folklore."

"He loved it."

"Yes, he did. Sometimes we find joy in the darkest of places."

"And now Purdey is dead too. It happened just after we were captured." Cecily felt the need to say this even though it had already been mentioned. She filled Mr Fane in on what Jedd had witnessed. She noticed that his face did not change at all as she recounted what happened, but then again, she found it difficult to show any emotion where Purdey was concerned.

"Well I can't say I'm surprised, lass, although I am sorry for your loss. Your mother was a bad egg, out for herself. She didn't deserve you and your dad. She sure will be paying for it now though, if that is any consolation." Then he added, "But of course she was still your mother," just in case he had caused offence.

"Whatever she gets she deserves."

Mr Fane's tone then softened somewhat and he said, "I know it hurts now, but when you get your memory back, you'll see the bigger picture. You are a very special young lady, Cecily Stalks, and you have an important job to do."

Cecily returned Mr Fane's smile, although she could not imagine ever seeing the bigger picture or the point of all this pain and death.

"Why did you shine that torch in my eyes, Mr Fane?" she asked.

"Call me Abram, please," said Mr Fane. "I had to check it was you in there and demons don't like bright lights."

"Oh right!" said Cecily, thinking she would remember that fact.

"One more thing," added Mr Fane. "Watch out for young Jedd. I never did think much of traitors."

Cecily was digesting Mr Fane's last comment when Kaden announced it was time to leave.

"Hang on, love," said Mrs Fane. "I'll just get my things."

"Are you coming with us?" challenged Kaden.

"Well of course we are, lad!" said Mr Fane. "We are Watchers. We'll keep a look out while you go inside and fetch what's left of the Bramble family."

The group waited while Mr and Mrs Fane secured their lethal cross bows and arrows to their backs. The unusual party of young and old then set out for Bramble Hall, not quite knowing for sure what awaited them when they got there.

Chapter 24

The group decided not to take the path through the woods up to
Bramble Hall. Kaden thought it best to stick to the cover of the
trees and the friends were in full agreement. They carefully made
their way through the trees, but Cecily found that she jumped at
every sound and every time she did, her voice let out little sounds
of fright. She really was trying to be brave, just as hard as she
was trying to be quiet, but the harder she tried, the more noise
she seemed to make, earning her disapproving looks from
Elisabeth. Cecily was expecting an ambush at any minute, even
though just before leaving the Fanes', Kaden had assured her that
Dasrus and his beasts would not appear until they had the little
Lord Bramble. Mr and Mrs Fane demonstrated the same agility
as her companions. Every now and then, the pair would separate
and disappear. Further along the track, they would reappear from
trees, which they had just been up to see if they could spot any
signs of danger around them. Cecily was amazed and she
wondered why she had never seen this side of them before.

They emerged from the dense woodland near the top of the
gravel driveway that wound up to the manor. The avenue of oak
trees was only a few hundred yards away from where they now
stood. Kaden gestured the group to gather around him and then
he said, "From this point on, we are going to be very exposed as
we won't have the protection of the woodland, but we've got no
choice. It's the only way we can reach the entrance to the chapel."

"Let's go for it!" said Sol, who seemed rather pumped.

"Verena and I will stay hidden and patrol. We'll keep a look
out for Dasrus and the shadows. Any sign of danger and we'll
come and assist."

"No!" objected Kaden. "If you see Dasrus come into the chapel, do nothing. We'll deal with it inside. However, if you see Dasrus leave the chapel with little Lord Bramble and his family, you must inform the Light as a matter of urgency. Please do not try and help us, just watch."

"Whatever you say, lad," agreed Mr Fane, although he did not seem pleased with the situation.

"Right everyone, ready?"

Her companions nodded. Cecily thought to herself how strong they looked. Mr and Mrs Fane wished them luck and headed back off into the trees, while the six friends made their way to the avenue of oaks and the large gardens that lay before Bramble Hall.

Cecily could feel the adrenaline pumping around her body, although she knew it was driven by fear rather than excitement. She could feel every bone in her body shaking through terror. Anxiety and panic lay in her stomach, waiting to erupt at the mere sight of Dasrus and his abominable shadows. How she was placing one foot in front of the other she did not know. It took all she had not to turn and run for the cover of the trees.

They made it to the top of the avenue without incident, moving slowly from tree to tree, three Cerbereans flanking either side of the driveway in an attempt to make them less conspicuous and more difficult for them to be captured altogether. Cecily remained with Kaden and Jedd while Sol, Fen and Elisabeth treaded the far side. As they reached the top of the avenue, Kaden signalled for the others to rejoin them. He pointed to the chapel, which sat on the far left of the house. The only way to reach it directly was to go straight across the large lawn at the front of the house. Cecily glanced over to the main doors of the manor that had been the scene of so much turmoil only two nights earlier. The great heavy doors were now closed and Cecily found herself wondering who had closed them, if it was Mr and Mrs Fane or perhaps someone else. As she looked around at the house and the grounds, she found that everything here reminded her of Cian and happier times. How she longed to be back there, wonderfully oblivious to whom her beloved Cian really was.

When she turned back to her friends, she noticed that Fen and Sol had already started making their way across the lawn, looking all around them for any threats lying in wait and trying to keep as low as possible, which was ridiculous really because they were on display for anyone in the house or surrounding grounds to see. The rest of the group followed suit and Cecily found herself having to jog to keep up with them. Within a minute or two, they had made it to the left part of the house and the chapel door. Kaden had his hand on the ringed black iron door handle getting ready to enter, signalling everyone to be ready just in case there was a welcome party on the other side of the door.

As Kaden was about to open the door, the group heard a deep throaty growl coming from around the side of the chapel. The friends looked at each other and immediately formed a wall in the direction of the sound. Jedd grabbed Cecily and held her close behind him, which she found very uncomfortable indeed. The warriors were poised, hands resting on the hilts of their swords at the top of their backs ready to draw. A few seconds later, the source of the deep throaty growl rounded the corner. The source was Acantha Sims.

As soon as Acantha laid eyes on the Cerbereans, a huge smile spread across her face, but this was not her usual smile, it was a distorted, evil smile. As she walked towards them, Cecily noticed that her footsteps were unnatural, forced somehow, as if it took a massive effort to drag one foot in front of the other. Her arms were outstretched, ready to grab onto the first thing that came into her path and she continued the snarling and growling as she went. As she came closer, Cecily realised that although it was clearly Acantha, her face was different. It was hideous, full of pure malevolence and her eyes were empty. She had some thick gunk drooling down her chin.

The Cerbereans drew their swords.

"What should we do, Kaden?" said Elisabeth urgently, as Acantha lurched forward and was now trying to sink her teeth into Sol.

He was holding his sword in one hand and holding Acantha by the neck with his other hand, keeping her at arm's length, all the while being covered in that awful slobber.

"Oh my, poor Acantha!" half-sobbed Cecily, but Acantha did not seem to be too concerned as her wicked smile prevailed.

"What is wrong with her?"

"Possession."

"Possessed by what?"

"A demon, probably a shadow beast."

"Can they do that? I didn't know that could do that!" Cecily felt panic on a whole new level.

"Erm, guys?" said Sol. "I'm getting covered here, what should I do?" This distraction really did not seem to faze him.

"Well we can't kill her. That won't kill the demon and there's every chance that when the beast leaves her, she'll be OK, so we don't want to murder her."

"What do you mean, a chance she'll be OK?" asked Cecily, who could not take her eyes off Acantha.

"Well, possessions don't always have a happy ending, Cec. Sometimes the demon consumes their prey from within."

"You mean it eats them?"

"Yes, Cec." Cecily thought she was going to be sick. "And we can't just let her go as she might report straight to Dasrus."

"A torch!" shouted Cecily, enthusiastically. "Mr Fane said demons don't like bright lights!"

"True, but we don't have a torch."

As Cecily and Kaden were having their conversation, Jedd stepped forward and knocked Acantha on the head with the hilt of his sword. She was out cold.

"Thank you, Jedd," said Sol, glaring at Kaden and Cecily.

"Eewww!" Fen winced as a bit of whatever Sol was shaking from his arm and hand landed on her.

"Sorry, Fen," he said, sheepishly.

"We can't leave her out here," said Kaden. "Someone might see her."

Fen, Elisabeth and Jedd obliged by dragging the lifeless body of Acantha to a bush growing at the side of the chapel. They ensured that she was well hidden by arranging the foliage around her.

"Why would one of those demons possess her, Kaden?" Cecily was repulsed.

"Who knows what their motivation is," he said. "Sometimes possession gives them a voice, sometimes they do it for sport. The agents of the Dark are pure evil. Don't worry about Acantha just yet, she might be ok. We'll get Verena to inform the Purification Unit. They will try and help her."

Cecily hoped he was right.

Having temporarily disposed of Acantha and the thing she was hosting, the group entered the chapel with trepidation. However, no one jumped out at them, there was no attack or ambush, in fact it was still and strangely quiet.

Kaden whispered, "There's time yet, be on your guard."

The area inside was large for a chapel. It was more like a small church. Cecily looked up at the high sloped ceiling and beams which formed the pointed roof. It was ornately decorated with statues, paintings and other Christian iconography. It had a stone floor with a rich red plush carpet flowing down the middle of the aisle, held in place by a gold runner. Cecily counted ten rows of pews either side of the aisle and as they progressed towards the front of the chapel and the organ loft, the warriors checked left and right to ensure that nothing was hiding between the ornately carved benches. Cecily tried to forget about what might be waiting for them and instead tried to focus on the exquisite stained glass windows which ran along the wall on one side. The sunlight that shone through the windows cast bright and colourful patterns on the opposite wall. Four magnificent pillars made of cold-looking marble held the structure in place. Cecily thought how stunning this building was, definitely a match for the house it was attached to. She tried to imagine the chapel full of people on a happier occasion, such as a wedding or a christening. Even though it was a warm June day outside, the chapel was draughty and little cold shivers kept running down Cecily's spine, causing her to shudder. At the front of the chapel, to the right-hand side of the altar, Cecily could see the shiny metal tubes of the organ. Below the tubes was a door which Cecily presumed must lead up to the organ loft and they were now making their way towards the door. It seemed like her distraction technique of thinking about other things was working as she felt much calmer.

Kaden went first through the door to the organ loft, the others looking out towards the back of the chapel for any movement. When Kaden was sure the organ loft was safe, he gestured for the others to join him. Behind the door to the organ loft, there was nothing but a flight of stairs. *Nowhere to hide* thought Cecily to herself. When everyone was in the organ loft and the door at the bottom of the stairs was closed, Kaden whipped aside the rug that was lying over the floor, exposing bare, rough floorboards. Kaden began murmuring and waving his hands over the floorboards, his eyes closed the whole time. When he had finished, he opened his eyes and stood back. A rectangular shape in the floorboards began to glow an icy blue. It revealed itself to be a hatch which opened itself up outwardly.

"Quick, inside!" whispered Kaden.

Fen and Sol jumped inside the space first and then they helped Cecily down, followed by Elisabeth, Jedd and finally Kaden, who closed the hatch and seemed to seal it, as once again it shone a pale blue.

"Lady Bramble?" asked Kaden to the room. "We're here to help."

As Kaden did not get a response, he started to search the small room. Small though it was, it was still big enough to house three camp beds on one side of the room. Another camp bed stood unmade and folded against the wall in the space where it would ordinarily lie. At the other end of the room was a small kitchenette with cooking facilities, a sink and a small fridge. The wall by the kitchenette was occupied by a long, metal shelving unit that stood floor to ceiling and Cecily noticed it was filled with lots of cans and dried food products. There was enough to survive on for quite a while and Cecily thought how this would not be a bad place to come in the event of a nuclear war. Small lamps lit the room which Cecily noticed were plugged into electrical sockets, so the hideout also had a power supply. The room was L-shaped and as Cecily looked at the space beyond the beds, she noticed a bookcase filled with books and another door, which Kaden was now knocking on. Someone had been to this room recently as there was evidence of it being lived in. The beds folded down and made up, pots in the sink and the lights on. On one of the rugs that covered the floor, a jigsaw had been started. There must be someone here.

Kaden was now opening the door, the others crowding round to see if anyone was in there. It was simply a small bathroom with a toilet, sink and bath around which a shower curtain was drawn. Kaden moved forward and pulled the shower curtain back. It revealed Lady Bramble and her two children, Oscar and Delilah, one child sat either side of their mother, their eyes closed and heads down with protective arms around them, shielding them from the horror about to be shown to them with the removal of the shower curtain. Lady Bramble's eyes were shut tight too and she let out a scream as they were unveiled. Fen winced, probably afraid they would be heard.

Kaden immediately tried to calm her down. "Lady Bramble, it's me, Kaden Quinn. We're here to help. We are sent from the Light."

The look of relief on her face was undeniable.

"Oh, thank God," she cried. "Children, it's ok, we are saved!" Then when she looked at her rescue party, she added, "Although I thought they might have sent someone older."

The three of them got up and as they did so, a knife fell from Lady Bramble's knee.

"I don't know what use that would have been," she sighed.

Although Lady Bramble was quite obviously relieved, the children were still unsure. They did not speak or even look at their Cerberean saviours, but remained close to their mother's side, hugging her tightly.

"We are going to take you to an even more secure location with us, Lady Bramble. You are aware of the danger you are in?"

"Of course I'm aware," she said, sourly. "I was warned of what might happen before I married into the family, but who believes that a bloody demon is going to come after your husband and ask him to sign over his rights as protector of a gateway to Hell and give his blood so it can be opened. It sounds a bit far-fetched, doesn't it?" she added, sarcastically. "If he wasn't already dead, I'd kill him again. Why did he agree to work with that demon? I'm so stupid. I should have known that there was something wrong when he reminded me how to get into this room and to stock it up, just in case. He told me we didn't know what terrorists were capable of these days. The poor children, having to witness their father die like that. And now the responsibility of all that human protector crap has fallen to Oscar. He's only ten! How can I protect him, both of them? My poor stupid husband!"

Lady Bramble started sobbing loudly.

As Kaden tried to console her, Elisabeth whispered, "Won't someone hear us?"

"No," replied Kaden. "As long as the hatch is sealed this room is invisible to both sight and sound. Neither human being nor supernatural being can see it. The magic protecting this room if very powerful. You can only get in if you are a Bramble or if you know the spell, like me. Of course, you have to know the room exists first."

"Speaking of spells," said Sol, "can you not place a protective shield around the chapel to stop Dasrus and his agents from finding us and getting in?"

"There's no point. Dasrus has come back more powerful than ever. If he wants to get in, he will. I may as well conserve my magic for getting us to where we need to go."

"And where is that exactly?" asked Cecily.

"The two most important things at this time are getting both the Brambles and us to safety so that Dasrus can't perform the ritual, and helping you to get your memory back. We need you at full strength, Cec. We can't defeat Dasrus unless you are."

"Oh right," said Cecily, too tired to argue. She really did not think she was capable of beating Dasrus, if fact, she was sure they had the wrong person.

"So where are we going?"

"I'm taking us back in time. I'm taking us back to a certain point in history which I hope will jog your memory. Also, there is little chance of Dasrus finding us there. Even if he realises what we've done, it would take him too long to try and find us as we could be anywhere."

"Right," replied Cecily, slowly, "and how does time travel work?"

"Haven't you learned to trust me by now, Cecily Stalks?" laughed Kaden. He turned to the Lady Bramble who appeared to be in as much shock as Cecily at the prospect of travelling back in time. "Is that all right with you, Lady Bramble? It's only temporary until we can get Cecily's memory back and figure out a way of stopping Dasrus."

"As long as my children will be safe, I am in agreement."

"They will be. It's far safer than being here at the moment and you can't stay in this panic room forever."

"Sounds good," said Fen, cheerily. "How are we going to get

there?"

"A spell," said Kaden.

"Great, let's go then!" Cecily noticed how Sol was always so eager.

"I can't from here. I need to draw my power from nature. I've got to take nine of us back in time. There is not enough natural energy in here for me to do that. The woods will serve me best."

"You're telling me we've got to go back out there?" said Elisabeth. "That is asking for trouble, Kaden. We will probably be walking straight into a trap. And goodness knows how many of those zombie things there are out there."

Lady Bramble and her children gasped loudly.

"Look, it will be OK. We can make it." Kaden was as positive as ever, although Cecily was not filled with the same confidence as him. "Right, let's go. Same plan as before, stick together. Ready?"

Kaden squeezed past the others and left the bathroom where they had all been stood. Everyone followed him to the hatch. Kaden murmured his spell and when he had finished, he silently gave a count of three, using only his fingers. The hatch opened outwardly as it had on their way in and Kaden jumped up, grabbed the edge of the hatch and hoisted himself up into the organ loft. After a few seconds, he indicated that the coast was clear. Fen and Elisabeth jumped up to join him while Jedd and Sol remained to lift everyone else out of the safe room. Cecily went through the hatch next, lifted by Jedd, again feeling uncomfortable at being in such close proximity to him.

As Cecily pulled herself to her feet, she heard Lady Bramble say, "We have ladders, you know." And so to Cecily's dismay, everyone else was able to remove themselves from the room with the help of the ladders. Kaden once more sealed the hatch and then led the way down the stairs into the chapel.

All was quiet with no demons in sight and they made it to the main door of the chapel, again without incident, the warriors carefully checking every nook and cranny as they went. Once they were all assembled at the door, Kaden said, "Right, we don't know what is waiting for us on the other side of this door. Cerbereans, are you ready?" They all nodded. Kaden gradually opened the door bit by bit. He must not have seen anything as he ventured out alone to investigate further. A minute later, he was back. "I don't see anyone. Although Acantha has gone. Be on your guard."

"Acantha?" quizzed Lady Bramble.

"I'll explain later," replied Kaden, respectfully.

The party, now larger than it was on the way into the grounds of Bramble Hall, made it across the lawn safely with no hint of the presence of the Dark. When they reached the old oak avenue, Cecily saw her friends look at each other incredulously. They swiftly made their way to the bottom of the avenue, wanting to take advantage of their good fortune. Once at the end of the avenue, they dived into the woods beyond where an equally baffled Mr and Mrs Fane were waiting for them.

"Did you see anything?" asked Kaden, urgently.

"Only Ms Sims," replied Mr Fane. "What's wrong with her?"

"Possession."

"Aye, we thought as much," Mr Fane said turning to Mrs Fane. "Nothing else out of the ordinary though, lad."

Mr Fane turned his attention to Lady Bramble. He removed his cap and made a short bow.

"Good day, Lady Bramble." He nodded in the direction of the children, "Master, Miss. We are so sorry to hear of your loss. If there is anything we can do."

Mrs Fane curtseyed at them all.

"Thank you, Mr and Mrs Fane," replied Lady Bramble. "I didn't know that you were a part of... erm... this."

"Yes ma'am, always," replied Mr Fane with a smile.

Cecily thought how very old-fashioned and respectful they seemed towards the Brambles and then she remembered that the

Brambles had once been Mr Fane's 'reverent' employer, but then this made her think of Acantha's lectures and how she too held them in high regard. This upset Cecily because Acantha was now possessed.

Mr Fane turned his attention back to Kaden. "So, what happened to the ambush?"

"I've no idea," answered Kaden, "but we are not out of the woods yet, so to speak."

"What now then, lad?"

"I'm going to get us all to safety and then we have got to try and help Cec get her memory back. Only when Cecily is back at full strength can we think about how to deal with Dasrus."

"Yes, I agree," said Mr Fane. "Where will you go?"

"I won't tell you, Abram, just in case agents come knocking."

"I understand, lad."

Cecily suddenly felt extremely afraid for the Fanes.

"Hopefully, we won't be gone for long though. Verena, can you inform the Purification Unit that we've finished at the manor? They can do what they like there now. Also, that there is a possession there?"

"Of course, dear. Now you all be careful and we'll see you when you get back." Mrs Fane smiled kindly at the group.

"Abram, Verena, thanks for everything. Take care, both of you." Kaden offered his hand to them, but the old couple ignored this and grabbed him in a warm embrace. Kaden blushed and walked over to a tiny clearing in the trees.

"Now then," he instructed his companions, "when I turn into a ball of light, walk into me, like a doorway."

The Cerbereans nodded and Lady Bramble looked confused. Cecily was sure the children were still in shock as they had not yet spoken. Why were odd things surprising Cecily less and less? She thought how only a few months earlier, she had cursed the predictability of her life and the predictability of Bramblegate. She thought of all she had been through in the past couple of months and all she had discovered. Her world had been turned upside down and she longed for nothing more than predictability. The phrase, 'Be careful what you wish for', came to mind.

Cecily watched Kaden carefully. His legs stood apart from one another and his hands and arms were outstretched, pointing towards the ground. He was once again murmuring under his breath with such concentration, like she had seen him do before and like she had seen Dasrus do. He was omitting a wonderful light and she thought how handsome he looked; tall, muscular and golden. She had always thought him angelic and now she knew why.

All of a sudden, the bright, golden illumination turned into a pale, icy blue ball of light with a burst and Kaden was gone.

"Hurry!" said Jedd.

One by one they stepped into the ball of light that was Kaden. As she went, she silently said farewell to Bramblegate as the Cecily Stalks she was now, for she might well come back someone different altogether.

Mr Fane winked at her and said, "Try hard now, lass. Make your dad proud."

She simply nodded and then took a leap, yet again into the unknown, wondering where this doorway would lead her.

Chapter 25

"Are we still in Bramblegate?" asked a puzzled Cecily.

She wondered if her journey through the portal had frazzled her brain. As soon as she had stepped into the ball of light that was Kaden, a lot of whirling and twirling had started to happen. She imagined it was a bit like being in a washing machine on spin. The portal had spat her out and once more she was in a twisted heap on the floor, looking up at her friends and the Brambles, although it looked as though Lady Bramble and her children had been in a similar predicament seconds earlier, as they were brushing debris from the wood floor off their clothes. Cecily was still dizzy as she pulled herself to her feet.

Kaden, who was now the walking, talking, humanoid version of himself again, simply grinned and said, "You're absolutely right! We are still in Bramblegate! The question is when?" he added knowingly, tapping the side of his nose to indicate he had some inside information.

Cecily looked around. Everything was exactly the same here as it was from where they had just come. The only way she could tell it was different was because of the fine drizzle that was falling from a greying sky. A minute ago, it had been a glorious June day. And of course, the absence of the Fanes gave it away.

Along with her children, Lady Bramble now seemed to be in shock also. She stood staring at the floor, mouth opened slightly, clinging tightly to her children.

"We should really get changed," said Fen, looking down at her ripped evening gown and lack of shoes. "We are not really dressed for the weather here."

Elisabeth, Jedd and Sol muttered in agreement.

"We'll go and find some clothes up at Bramble Hall. I'm sure they will have something for us to wear. We'll take Lady Bramble and the children with us. They could probably do with some familiarity round about now."

Fen looked at the family with sad eyes. As they headed off in the direction of Bramble Hall, Cecily could hear Fen comforting Lady Bramble and the children. This was more like the Fen that Cecily knew. She had temporarily dropped her guard; the tough warrior was momentarily gone and her caring side shone through. Cecily thought how Sol must have been glad about this. Cecily noticed that they had seemed uncharacteristically distant from one another since they were reactivated.

"Come on," said Kaden, snapping her out of her thoughts. "We're going this way!"

"Wait!" replied Cecily, rather urgently. "Where are we going? Will they be ok? What if Dasrus and the shadows attack them at Bramble Hall?"

"They'll be fine, Cec," said Kaden, earnestly. "Honestly, you really don't have to worry here. We are all safe in this place. Even if Dasrus happens to work out what we've done, he has no way of knowing which date in the past we have returned to. It would take him a while to locate us and in any case, I don't plan on being here too long."

Cecily felt comforted by Kaden's assurances.

"So where are we going?"

"Well first of all, down to the dell. We'll stop there and get changed on our way to the village."

"The village? Why are we going there?" questioned Cecily.

"It's time for you to get your memory back."

Cecily was quiet on the walk down to the dell. In truth, she was nervous about what she may witness in this place and time. She was scared about what she might find out. Her thoughts drifted back to the Bramblegate she had just left and she wondered how people there were coping. Maybe thanks to the Purification Unit it was like nothing had happened. Perhaps they were carrying on with life as normal, minus some villagers, who were savaged by demons. She thought about Bramble Hall and wondered if the Dairy had reopened. Were Joan, Millie and John all right? They had all been at the party. Had Acantha been cured and was she now trotting about Bramble Hall in her navy-blue court shoes like she owned the place? Did anyone even miss Cecily or wonder where she had gone? Would they report her missing? Her experiences over the past few days were too much for Cecily to take. It was so surreal.

As they neared the dell, Cecily said to Kaden, "What if I don't want to remember? I just want to be me, no matter how good or bad my life turns out."

"Cecily, I promise you that when you get your memory back, your human life with all its worries will seem trivial. You will want to help the cause. It is what you are here for. You will get to be human again soon enough. Once we have sorted Dasrus and his demons out, you will be deactivated again."

"Until the next time."

"Yes, until the next time, but you won't remember any of these feelings. This time there has just been a ..." Kaden paused while he found the correct word, "... a hitch with your reactivation."

If she was born over and over again, just like Kaden had said, then Cecily found it troubling that she could not remember who she had been or what she had done or her feelings. Was she a different person every time she came back? How could she ever truly know herself?

As they entered the dell, it occurred to Cecily that she did not know who Mr and Mrs Fane really were either and this surprised her as she had spent a lot of time around them growing up, living in such close proximity. She decided to ask Kaden about the elderly couple.

"Mr and Mrs Fane are what we call Watchers. I have been with them for as long as I can remember. They retain their memory, like I do mine and they watch for pending danger. I suppose they are a bit like spies."

Cecily wondered how Dasrus and his demons had managed to infiltrate Bramblegate right under their noses, especially if they were spies on the look out for threats, but she felt this was disrespectful to the Fanes and Kaden, so she said nothing.

"What were those strange names that you all gave to Mr Fane at his house?"

"They aren't strange names, Cec," explained Kaden. "They are our real names. The names we were given by the Light when we came into being. Kaden is the name my mother in this lifetime gave me. Do you want to know your real name?"

"Erm, no thanks," she replied. "Cecily will do just fine." She felt she was already struggling with her identity without being given a different name too.

"Suit yourself," said Kaden.

"And what were those brands that appeared on their hands?"

"They are the warrior's mark. Each brand is unique to a certain sword, just as each sword is unique to the warrior. By showing the brand, they can prove who they are."

"But someone could just copy the brand and pretend to be that warrior," suggested Cecily, attempting to find holes in anything Kaden said.

"Ok, so what was Fen's brand? I saw you looking over her shoulder."

"Well I couldn't quite see... I don't know, I can't remember!"

"Exactly!" spewed a triumphant Kaden. "Very strong magic. You forget the brand as soon as you see it. It wouldn't matter anyway. No one could pretend to be a Cerberean. They would need the sword."

"What is the deal with those swords? Where on earth do they come from? Are they invisible?"

"No, not invisible. The swords are not on this plane. They are in the Realm of Light, only retrievable when the owner calls for it. Again, powerful magic."

"But someone could just steal it out of their hands while it is on this plane," said Cecily, impudently.

"Impossible!" replied Kaden. "Once a sword has left its owner's hand for whatever reason, it returns to the Light automatically."

"Let me guess? Magic!" said Cecily, sarcastically.

"You may mock me, Cecily Stalks, but you will see for yourself soon enough."

When Cecily found herself outside the cottage, she did a double take to check she was in the right place. It was very different from the home she knew. It was constructed from the same grey stone; however, the two windows at the front were tiny and the door was rounded and made of wood. The roof was thatched, so unlike her childhood home where the roof had red brick tiles and contained a dormer. There was no garden to speak of and it seemed the grassland surrounding the cottage was tended to by a couple of grazing cows. Kaden must have seen the shock on her face, because he tugged on her sleeve and gestured that they should go inside.

"Shouldn't we knock first?" asked Cecily as he began to open the door.

"Don't worry about it," said Kaden as he made his way inside.

Cecily followed him hesitantly and was even more surprised at what she saw inside. The cottage comprised of one room. She could almost sketch out the way the cottage had changed into the home she knew so well in the future. Due to the two tiny windows at the front of the house, the room was very dark. On one side of the room, there was a large open hearth with a cauldron hung above it and a roaring fire. As there was no chimney, the room was thick with smoke. In front of the fire sat a simple wooden table with benches on either side, upon which sat a loaf of bread, a knife, a jug and some wooden bowls. Opposite the fire on the other wall, there were some storage chests. Tools and pottery vessels were hung from hooks on the walls. Rushes covered the floor and in one of the far corners of the room, were what Cecily thought must have been beds, made of straw. Cecily thought how simple it was. The people who lived there must be very poor. There was a layer of soot on everything and underneath the heavy smoky atmosphere lay an insipid smell that Cecily could not identify.

"Who lives here?" she asked Kaden.

"It's not important," he replied, cryptically.

Kaden had darted over to the back corner of the room opposite the straw beds and he was now muttering and waving his hands in front of the wall. A block of stone removed itself and hovered in the air while Kaden reached inside the hole and pulled out various packages wrapped in cloth. He was checking the contents of each and when he found two parcels he was happy with, he set the stone to its rightful position with a wave of his hand. Kaden tossed Cecily one of the packages and said, "Here, get changed."

"I'm OK in my jeans and jumper, thanks," said Cecily, holding out the package back towards Kaden.

"Your clothes are not practical, Cec. Please get changed," insisted Kaden. He had acquired that tone of voice in which Cecily thought it best not to argue with him.

She walked over to the table and placed the package upon it. She unwrapped the cloth to see what clothes lay inside. To her horror, she found brown cotton trousers, a pale olive-green long sleeved top, a cropped brown, leather waistcoat with buckles down the front and studs up and down the seams and a matching brown leather belt. A gold arm cuff lay in between the fabrics and leathers for protection. As Cecily was holding up the cuff, trying to examine it in what little light was available, Kaden told her, "That is one of your favourites."

"Oh right!" said Cecily. She had to admit, it was beautiful, ornately decorated with golden flowers and precious stones for the petals.

Cecily quickly got changed and she discovered that the outfit was a good fit. The trousers were fitted, as was the top, although the material was quite thick and heavy and once she had the leather waistcoat on, she felt quite warm. Kaden was still rooting around the cottage. He too had changed into a similar garb of cotton and leather. As he handed Cecily a pair of socks and pair of long, brown leather boots, he looked her up and down and said, "Perfect!" very enthusiastically. "You are looking more like you!" he added with a wink.

Cecily tutted as she sat on one of the benches to pull the thick socks and long boots on. The boots came over her knee and they too had buckles down one side. The boots then folded over at the top and they were, of course, flat. *Practicality first,* she thought to herself sarcastically.

"I feel like an idiot," she said to Kaden when she was ready. "I would never wear these clothes."

"Trust me, you would!" said Kaden, laughing unsympathetically.

Cecily heaved a big sigh as Kaden said, "Come on, let's get something to eat before we go back out again. We've not eaten in a day or two. You must be starving, I know I am!"

Kaden began cutting large slices of bread from the loaf which lay on the table.

"Kaden, should you be doing that?" challenged Cecily. "That is not our bread to take. What if someone misses it?"

"Cecily, it's OK," replied Kaden, as he continued to cut the bread. "We are just observers here in this time and these events, this time, has already passed. Think of it as a live history lesson. We can touch things, feel things and learn things, but we can't be seen and nor can we change anything. This bread won't be missed as this day has already gone, already been lived. We are in a physical domain, but everything here is an echo of past events. So please, don't worry. We can eat the bread."

Cecily was not quite sure she understood Kaden's explanation, but she was starving and so she tucked into the slightly stale bread, being careful to cut the soot-covered crust from it first. She washed the frugal meal down with a few cups of water and thought it was the best meal she'd had in ages.

"So where are we going and what are we going to see there?" asked Cecily to Kaden, who was still eating.

Kaden took a drink of water before he answered.

"There is a war happening at this point in time, just outside the village in the fields and woodland."

"A war?" questioned Cecily. "Between whom?"

"The Light and the Dark, of course," replied Kaden. "We were a part of that war, Cecily, and we won. I'm hoping that if you can see yourself in action, see your true self, it might trigger reactivation."

Cecily said nothing. What more could she say? She could disagree violently and tell Kaden he was lying and yet here she stood, in her own home, hundreds of years earlier. Kaden must have read her mind.

"I know it's a lot to take in and probably hard to believe and I know I keep saying it will all become clear when your memory returns, but it really will. You have to have faith, Cec."

Cecily walked over to the storage chests and began opening each one of them to have a look inside.

"How do you do it, Kaden? How do you cope with remembering lifetime after lifetime? Do you not get tired of it?"

"It's my job. It's the way it's always been. I'm a Light Doer. I keep records of happenings on the Earth plane regarding the domain we protect and I'm here should the Dark attempt to return."

"Yes, but is it hard?" questioned Cecily, opening yet another chest.

"I've never known any different as I've never been

deactivated. When I'm not needed to fight, I try and enjoy life like the rest of you. There are many wonders, Cecily. Life is a gift."

"You always seemed more mature then me growing up. You were always right about everything. Now I know why!"

"As a child, I still have the same active mind, but I've become good at playing each role, I feel."

"It all makes sense now, how well you handled your mother's death and the way you handle your stepfather."

"It is sometimes difficult for me to engage fully in every day human stresses and their trials and tribulations. I am often able to see the bigger picture because I remember everything. I am able to be less selfish and less self-involved, although I realise I still have a part to play, for example, the loving son who has just lost his mother. My mother in this lifetime had an awful illness and although I tried my best to make her as comfortable as possible, she endured a lot of pain and suffering. When she died, she passed to the Light. That should be celebrated. She was relieved of her pain and suffering. As for my stepfather, he is on his own journey, yet to choose Light or Dark and so I must leave him to it."

"Kaden, did my father pass to the Light?" asked Cecily warily, somehow knowing the answer, but still afraid of Kaden's response.

"Of course he did, Cec. Your father was a good man."

Cecily breathed a sigh of relief.

Kaden continued. "Human emotions are a powerful thing. It is sometimes hard for the others as they live a true human existence, like you are now; dormant, sleeping until needed. Even though they are now reactivated, their emotions are still very real to them, as reactivation has only just happened. They have to battle them. Fen and Sol are having to try extremely hard as relationships between Cerbereans are forbidden."

"Oh wow! Poor Fen and Sol! I thought they had seemed a bit

distant from one another. I was also wondering how Fen was coping after all that happened on her birthday, what with the massacre at the party and getting captured. I would have been devastated if that had happened on my birthday."

Cecily was genuinely sincere, yet Kaden rolled his eyes.

"That is what I call a triviality. The birthday is not important, what happened is."

Cecily felt embarrassed and looked away sheepishly. She continued to rummage through the storage chests. She knew that Kaden was not trying to make her feel bad. She was still human after all.

"Jedd has also been experiencing the same battle. As he was not deactivated this time around, he has been wrestling with his emotions the whole time, which is what led him to betray us. Bitterness and anger are dangerous emotions. I feel them too and sometimes I have to check myself when I feel them getting the better of me. You will have to as well. Once we have been reactivated and we are Cerbereans again, it is not our job to feel. We have to see the bigger picture, put others before ourselves and get the job done. Although we look after each other, of course."

Cecily had now finished rooting through the storage chests and she returned to where Kaden was sat at the table. She slumped onto one of the benches.

"I'm just not like all of you, Kaden. I'm not mentally strong enough. None of you seem to feel pain and you never complain. That hike out of the dungeon to the portal was horrendous. And Fen and Elisabeth did it wearing no shoes! I'm just not good enough. I moan about everything!"

She buried her head in her arms, feeling exhausted and very sorry for herself. Kaden simply chuckled.

"That is part of their power as Cerbereans, Cec! Do you honestly think Fen and Elisabeth would have been able to do that without shoes had they not been reactivated? As warriors, they are strong both physically and mentally. They possess endurance and agility, courage and determination, they are disciplined and loyal with combat skills second to none. They are not afraid. Don't worry, you'll be the same once reactivated."

"Mmm," mumbled Cecily. "I just can't see it. Even the old Fanes are more supple than I am."

"Well, they do possess some warrior traits too. They have agility and endurance and as they are Light Workers, that is, servants of the Light, they instinctively possess courage and determination and are loyal by nature. They can defend themselves, but they are not warriors. They also remember, like me. They have to remember in order to do their jobs. They have to know what they are watching for. With a gateway to the Dark in Bramblegate, it is all hands on deck. Also, it saves me from losing my mind," he laughed, "knowing that I have the Fanes to discuss things with."

"Did my dad know what the Fanes are? Mr Fane mentioned that he'd had some discussions with my father."

"Yes, he did. He knew about the Fanes, but not about me. They were helping him with his research, well, let's say they were pointing him in the right direction."

Cecily sighed and she thought how brave her father was to confront this unseen world head on.

"What about your powers, Kaden? I've seen you do all these amazing things!"

"Well, I'm a Cerberean, so I have the same warrior traits as the other Cerbereans, as do you, but I also have magic, again, like you, Cec."

Cecily still felt sceptical about her herself. It was hard to hear that she was capable of all these things. It was like Kaden was talking about a different person.

"Why do you glow blue?" she asked rather bluntly.

"The colour of my magic is simply a manifestation of my personality. Blue symbolises trust, loyalty, wisdom, faith and truth. It represents calm."

Cecily was on the verge of asking more questions. There was still so much she needed to understand, but Kaden interrupted her flow and announced that they should leave.

Cecily dragged her tired body from the bench and turned to depart the dark, smoky atmosphere, when suddenly, the door flew open. To Cecily's dismay, her father barged in, buckling under the weight of the injured young man he was carrying. He balanced the youth on the edge of the table, supported by one knee and in one swipe, cleared the table of everything: the bread, knife, bowls and jug. He delicately laid the boy, who was not much younger than Cecily, on the table and immediately began tending to his wounds, speaking soft, comforting words all the while.

"Dad! Dad it's me! Cecily! Dad!"

She was even able to place her hand on his shoulder and shake, desperate to try and get his attention. Her attempts were futile though. Her father did not notice her and he carried on with his urgent business of helping the boy. Kaden gently guided Cecily towards the door.

"He can't hear or see you, Cec. Remember, these events are past. They have already happened."

"What is he doing here?" she asked, sick at the torture of her beloved father being right in front of her, yet being unable to speak to him.

"Souls from the Light can be reborn if they choose. Your father is a true Light Worker, always fighting for the cause, always willing to return to Earth to help."

Seeing her father treat the injured boy with such care, love and consideration made her love him all the more and she held hope that she might be able to speak to him again one day. That was how she felt now but she was worried she would not feel the same way once she was reactivated. She also wondered if her feelings towards her mother would change once she was able to see the bigger picture. Cecily's mind wandered back to the times when Purdey had smothered her after neglecting her for a period of time. Maybe she did sometimes feel guilty for the pact she had made and the way she treated her husband and her daughter. At that moment, she thought she would feel the same about Purdey forevermore.

"Come on, Cec, time to go," said Kaden mildly, disturbing Cecily's thoughts.

She found it extremely difficult to tear herself away from her father. She just had to keep reminding herself that he was not really there.

On the walk up to the village, Cecily felt frustrated and upset. She felt like it was a cruel trick, her father being so close, yet so far away. The beauty of the woods was exactly the same here as it was in the future, but even this did not lighten her spirits and the fine drizzle that was falling was dampening her mood further.

"He was your father in this lifetime too, you know," shared Kaden. "And that young man was your brother."

Once again, Cecily felt the familiar sensation of disbelief, but in a good way.

"What... what happens to them?" she stuttered. "Will they be OK?"

"They both survive this war and go on to lead healthy, happy lives. You need not worry."

Cecily felt overjoyed and relieved that he had been her father before and that at some point in the past, she'd had a brother.

"Do you ever forget anything? It must be hard to remember every single detail."

"Yes, I do forget some things, of course I do. But I am the record keeper. I can go and access them whenever I like if I want to check something."

"And where could you possibly keep generations of records? In your bedroom?" joked Cecily.

Kaden laughed along with her. "They are all kept in a place between the Earth plane and the Realm of Light, much like the place we were imprisoned in, only nothing like it! Same principle though. My records are kept in a library which I can visit at any time. I can also meet the Wise Ones there. They are my link to the Realm of Light."

"How do you get there?"

"Magic. It's one of the only spells I can perform during times of deactivation. I am only at full power when we are needed and then I am reactivated with everyone else. I have my memory and a couple of spells, that's it."

By now, they had reached the top of the gravel path, which was just dirt in this time, and they were in the heart of the village, only this was not a village that Cecily recognised. There was no road, just a mud track, worsened by the rain. She could see a church and a graveyard on the site of St Peter's and where the Bramble Arms usually stood, was a one storey building that simply said 'Tavern' above the door. Next to the tavern was a cluster of small cottages with thatched roofs, scattered around a tiny green which was covered in puddles and muddy patches. Where the school resided in modern day Bramblegate was a busy forge. Cecily could just see the blacksmith and a couple of other men moulding what seemed to be swords and other such weaponry. They looked very hot and bothered. There was no village store, but instead a large bakery. Cecily was pleased to see the familiar sight of Bramble Hall's gatehouse and on the small hill above the village, she could see the roof and chimneys of the manor house. Kaden must have seen that Cecily's face was aghast.

"There is also a market here, in times of peace. Most of the villagers farm the land during this period."

Cecily followed Kaden's eyes to the bottom end of what was usually the high street and the residential cul-de-sacs. There was nothing there but farmland, which Cecily suspected extended down into the valley, with grazing livestock upon the fields.

"*When* the hell are we?" she asked Kaden, warily.

"The Middle Ages," replied Kaden, nonchalantly. "This is medieval Bramblegate."

As they walked along what was normally the high street, Cecily tried desperately to take in all the sights and sounds. The village was bustling, the streets lined with injured men and boys, some crying out for help and others being tended to by their women. There was a distinct smell of body odour along the track, mixed with the smell of freshly baked bread from the bakery and charcoal smoke from the forge. Once they had left the hustle and bustle of the village, the sights and sounds were replaced by the low braying of animals and the stench of manure, as they made their way into the surrounding countryside.

Cecily and Kaden walked out of the village for quite a way before she heard the sounds of battle. They had passed the vantage point, the site on which the petrol station stood in modern day Bramblegate and they had even passed the isolated location of Jedd's present day home. As they approached the vast battlefield, Cecily experienced a sudden assault on her senses. Everything she could see, hear, taste and smell transported her back to the horror of her nightmares. She realised for the first time that what Kaden had told her about her dreams being echoes of the past, events that really happened, was completely true. This realisation forced Cecily to stop dead in her tracks. Feeling sick, she bent her head over and placed her hands on her knees.

"What's wrong?" asked Kaden, obviously concerned.

Cecily stayed bent over while she tried to compose herself, waiting for the nausea to pass. When her head had stopped spinning, she slowly stood up straight.

"You were right," she began solemnly. "My nightmares were flashbacks. I've been here before, in my dreams."

In a way, Cecily was relieved. At least she knew she was not crazy. However, this was now another thing she could add to the list of things to be angry at Purdey for, because she let her think herself mad.

"Oh my!"

As they neared the battle and as Cecily looked around, she did not know if she was more stunned about the bloody violence or about that fact that this was real. She had lived through it and later dreamt about it. It was hard for her to accept.

"This battle is exactly the same as the one in my nightmares. The cries of the people, the smell of the blood and sweat..." Cecily stopped talking abruptly. She averted her eyes to the edges of the battlefield and the tree line. Her suspicions were confirmed. "... and there they are. Those heinous shadow beasts. In my dreams, I could see them out of the corner of my eye and now I know why." She turned to Kaden, eyes filling up as once more she was on the verge of tears. "They were awful, Kaden. When the nightmares started getting worse, it was as if the shadows were still with me when I woke up. I never felt alone, like I was always being watched. Now it turns out that I probably was."

This all felt very surreal. Knowing what she knew now, she was afraid for that Cecily Stalks, that young, naïve teenager. However, stood here, amidst the battle, she did not feel as terrified as she once had.

"Well, finally," said Kaden, portraying his words in an exaggerated manner. "The amount of times I've tried to get you to talk about your nightmares over the last three years. I knew they were getting worse, but I had no way of knowing for sure."

"It's all my fault, isn't it? My dreams were the warning signal, weren't they? If I'd have told you about my nightmares, I could have prevented all this. I just did not want them to be real."

Cecily began to sob as guilt overcame her. Kaden was as kind as always and immediately set about comforting her.

"You mustn't beat yourself up, Cec. Everything happens for a reason. The way this whole episode has played out was pre-destined. There must be a reason why you are blocking reactivation, but why?"

Kaden seemed to drift off to another place as he was deep in thought. How she now wished she had confided in her best friend.

"Why didn't you just force me to tell you? said Cecily, interrupting Kaden's thought process. "You should have told me what was at stake!"

"The rules are very clear, Cec. I can't talk about suspected threats with those in deactivation. There must be proof and after I've got proof, I must then discuss it with the Wise Ones. There are processes. In any case, there were others signs. Elisabeth returning to Bramblegate, Jedd's strange behaviour, even the mysterious boyfriend that no one had met, so you mustn't beat yourself up. The dreams weren't the only clue. Looking back, it seems obvious that something was going to happen. Even though I suspected it, I had no proof."

They were now stood in the midst of the fighting. As Cecily looked around her, she could not see warriors with super powers fighting demons, only regular humans fighting one another.

"Kaden, what is happening here? Those look like normal human beings to me."

"They are normal humans, Cec. Remember how I told you that each human chooses Light or Dark? Well in times of war, this is what that choice looks like. Each human is a soldier fighting for what they believe in."

Cecily once more found herself lost for words. They were just normal people. They could be your next-door neighbour, your doctor or even your cousin.

As Cecily looked around, or rather, gawped at her surroundings, out of the corner of her eye, she saw a flash of green. As she turned around to see what it was, a streak of auburn whizzed past her. When whatever it was came to a stop, Cecily had to do a double take for the second time that day. It was her. It was Cecily Stalks. It was like looking in a mirror, apart from the hair. Instead of the short bob that she herself wore, this other version of her had very long, wavy hair. Kaden's eyes had followed Cecily's gaze and he was now looking at her, awaiting more questions.

"Why do I look exactly the same?"

"Because you are the same person?" answered Kaden, obviously puzzled.

"I don't know why, but I thought that each time we're reborn, we look different."

"Why would you think that? You've just seen your father back there who looks exactly the same. Our essence remains the same for all time. When we are reborn, our essence naturally moulds to our human exterior. We shine from the inside out. Our spirits always determine what we look like as humans."

"I also thought that as Cerbereans, as Warriors of Light, we are immortal. Why do our bodies have to die at all? I mean, this body," she said pointing to herself, "looks the same as that body," she said pointing to her other self. "Why do we have to go through the madness of being reborn over and over? Why can't we live like, erm, v… v... vampires?" she stuttered.

Kaden laughed at her perception of the matter.

"Bodies grow old and tired, Cec. They are not designed to keep going. Human beings generally get illnesses and things start to give up, especially as they get older. Being Warriors of Light, we are immortal. We have the ability to live forever and our immortal souls keep our human casings in better shape than most. For example, we don't get sick, but eventually, especially during times of deactivation, our bodies grow old and tired and die and we are then immediately reborn again. With the Cerbereans, that process happens at more or less the same time, so we are all reborn together. As for the act of the rebirth itself, you don't remember it anyway. Not until you are reactivated and then you have the immortal mind to cope with it."

"But what happens if we die during reactivation and we are still needed? Also, what happens if we are really old during reactivation?"

"We can't die under normal circumstances, Cec. We can't die from shot wounds or stab wounds or even most magical conditions. If we were old during reactivation, and we have been before, it doesn't matter. Look at the Fanes."

"Well, ok then. What if we are babies when reactivation happens? We wouldn't be able to walk and talk, let alone fight." Cecily paused for thought. "In any case, that would be just plain weird, warrior babies!"

"There are spells, Cec. The Universe is very powerful. It has never happened yet, but I imagine something like accelerated growth. Our souls are immortal and they carry us through in times of need."

"So, can Dasrus kill us?" asked Cecily, not sure if she wanted to know the answer.

"The only way we can die an unnatural death is through a magical ritual, like the one Dasrus wants to perform. In the event he did manage to complete the ritual, we would die, yet we would still be needed to fight. In these circumstances, there is a way to carry on."

Cecily looked worried. "What is it?"

"Our spirits can inhabit another human casing."

"You mean possession?"

"Yes, Cecily, but only for the good of all and only in desperate circumstances."

"Wow!" she said, gazing into space. At least Cecily knew what Purdey meant now when she accused her of borrowing a body until it becomes old and tired.

"The truth of the matter is that although our immortal souls can prolong life, our human bodies, the casings, are mortal and they can't last forever. I'm sorry to shatter your illusions, Cec, but vampires just don't exist!"

Cecily knew that Kaden was teasing her and she managed a half-smile. "So, are all human souls immortal?"

"Souls live forever in the Realm of Light or the Realm of Dark, whichever realm they choose as a human. In both realms, some souls choose to come back as humans to fight for their cause. In the Realm of Light, they are called Light Workers, in the Realm of Dark, Dark Workers; remember everything is mirrored in the two realms. Should souls decide to return to the Earth plane, they are human beings with no special powers and without immortality. They do not remember their life on the other side, nor do they remember previous lifetimes. They are soldiers fighting for what they believe in and they die for what they believe in."

"Like my father," said Cecily, sadly.

"Yes, like your father, Cec," replied Kaden, compassionately. She knew Kaden was aware of how much her father meant to her.

Cecily sighed deeply, while the chaos ensued around her. Nothing surprised her any more. How could it when she had journeyed back to the past and was currently witnessing a medieval battle first-hand, which she was a part of. She looked around and relocated what she thought of as her other self. She saw herself battling skilfully with a couple of adversaries, sword in one hand and green flashes discharging themselves from her other hand, which she presumed was her magic. Once these enemies had been dealt with, there was a lot of whirling and twirling around while she dispelled some shadows snapping at her heels with her weapon. She then spun around and prevented another attack on herself by hitting a foe on the head with the hilt of her sword. Next, the other Cecily plunged her sword into the heart of the unconscious being. Cecily winced and once more she felt vomit rise in her throat.

"I know it is hard to watch, Cec. No one enjoys killing someone. We have to do it for the greater good. I'm so sorry to have to put you through this, it's just I need to stir your memory."

"This is like another nightmare for me. I used to dream that I killed people with a sword. I mean, in my dream, it was actually me plunging the sword into bodies. I could feel the resistance of the blade as I drove it into the lifeless torsos. It is so hard to accept because I wasn't just dreaming, I've actually done those things, killed those people. I often thought that if my nightmares became any more vivid, then I would be able to piece them together and get the whole story. Well, here it is!" she exclaimed, her arms indicating the conflict around her. "I wish they had have just been nightmares."

She turned her back to Kaden because she felt her eyes well up. She continued watching the skilled warrior who wielded so much power, who looked exactly the same as her, who was supposed to be her. Cecily did not recognise anything about herself in this other person. She felt the time had come. She needed to know exactly who and what she was supposed to be. She turned back to Kaden who was smiling at her encouragingly. She thought he was probably expecting the question.

"Who am I, Kaden?" She closed her eyes and braced herself for Kaden's reply.

"You are a goddess, Cec. You are Mother Earth."

Chapter 26

Cecily could just not help herself and she burst out laughing with an explosive belly laugh. The pressure and the shock of the last few days must have finally got to her. When she realised that Kaden was not laughing along and he had a stern look on his face, she tried to compose herself. She felt like a naughty school girl being reprimanded by her teacher for being silly in class.

"It's true," said Kaden, a bit too seriously for Cecily's liking. "You'll see when you get your memory back and the sooner the better if you ask me. This is not a joke, Cecily."

A red mist descended on Cecily and she snapped. Shouting at Kaden, she said, "I am a human girl! Plain old Cecily Stalks from the small village of Bramblegate! That warrior is not me! I'm sorry, but you've got the wrong person!"

Cecily thought that her face must have been flaming as all her rage and anger at everything that had happened since her father's death erupted from her like boiling, bubbling lava from a volcano. It seemed Kaden had plenty of anger in equal measure as he now started to yell, which was uncharacteristic for him.

"Cecily Stalks, whether you like it or not, you are a goddess; the Earth Mother, Gaia, Mother Nature, Terra, Parvati, Mother Goddess or whatever other names the humans want to call you by. You are NOT a human! You are immortal! Your spirit is anchored inside a human casing, but your very essence is goddess!"

"Gods and goddesses belong in myths and stories. They live in the sky, not down here whiling their time away as humans, waiting around just in case they are needed!" screeched Cecily.

Their argument was becoming quite heated and she expected the battle surrounding them to stop at any minute and watch the proceedings.

"How would you know?" yelled Kaden. "You can't remember! Don't make a mockery of who you are! You are the heart of the Earth and the protector of this plane. The sooner you remember the better! You have a responsibility, Cec. You can't just pick and choose what you want to be. You are a servant of the Light. Look!" he barked, turning her round by her arm quite forcibly.

Cecily had to sidestep to avoid a collision with a duelling pair, the battle coming a bit too close for comfort.

"That is you. Look at your strength and agility. Look at your amazing combat skills; they are second to none. Look how you wield your magic. That is you, Cecily Stalks!"

Kaden's tone had now softened and as a result of this kindness, Cecily broke down, sobbing violently.

Through her tears, Cecily managed to say, "I can't cope with all of this! I'm just a normal girl who has lost her whole family and I've been thrown into this strange world I've no hope of ever understanding!" She began to pace up and down, throwing her arms around wildly in expression as she spoke. "I should have the worries of a normal eighteen-year-old, like my boyfriend dumping me, like I hate my job, like is anyone at home even missing me?" Her tears were once more convulsive as she added, "I should not be trying to work out how to be a goddess! I don't even know who I am anymore!"

It suddenly dawned on Cecily that her father had been preparing her for the truth about her identity all along, through the stories he told.

"Cec, this is the extremes of human emotion that I was telling you about. I know that right now it is hard to have perspective. You have been bombarded by this new world and with the reality of who you really are. Naturally, you are angry, but it will get better once your memory comes back. You will have a better handle on your mental state. And I promise, I will do everything I can to help you."

Cecily was still mildly weeping as she heard the familiar voices of Fen and Sol approach from behind her.

"Hi, you two!" she heard Sol say. "Right in the thick of all the action, I see! Gosh, I remember this battle like it was yesterday!"

As Cecily turned around to greet them, she immediately saw the concerned look on Fen's face.

"What happened? Are you OK, Cec?"

All Cecily could muster was a nod. She did not want to embarrass herself further with more violent sobbing.

"You've been crying! Kaden, what's wrong with her?"

Kaden looked at Cecily, giving her the opportunity to answer, but she turned away.

"Cec has just discovered her origin and she is finding it a bit hard to accept."

"Oh Cec," said Fen, walking over to her and placing a comforting arm around her shoulder. "You will be OK. As soon as your memory comes back, it will all make sense."

Cecily snapped once more. She knew she was taking out her frustrations on her friends.

"I'm sick of hearing that everything will become clear and that I will understand as soon as I remember. I already have a memory and a perfectly good one at that, thank you very much! I don't want to remember that!" And with a sharp nod of her head, she indicated warrior Cecily, who had just sliced a man's head off for nicking her arm with his sword.

"You have to stop fighting it, Cecily," said Sol, who had now joined the girls on Cecily's other side. "You are who you are."

"We've not experienced this before, that is, one of us remaining deactivated, so we don't really know what to do. You have to try, Cec. I promise you, that is you," said Fen, as she gestured towards the other Cecily. "Everything Kaden has told you is true. We need you, Cec. We need you to remember." Fen was pleading.

"Right, well at this moment, this is like having an out of body experience. I can see someone who looks like me, but I feel no connection to her whatsoever. I cannot imagine myself as that!" she spat, petulantly. "How will I even know when this reactivation happens? What will it feel like?" She wondered if the fear was evident in her voice and she felt vulnerable.

"Well, it's a bit like double vision," explained Sol. When reactivation occurs, it's like everything comes into clear focus again. The human life you have just been living feels like a dream as you remember everything you truly are and your real purpose. You feel the Light and embrace it; it is part of you. You feel strong and gain clarity. It is a wonderful thing and a privilege to be a warrior of Light."

"Does it hurt?"

"Not at all! It's empowering! You are you again! Let it in Cec, don't be afraid."

Sol slapped her on the back a little too enthusiastically, causing her to stumble.

"Where are Jedd, Elisabeth and the Brambles?" Kaden asked Sol.

"We left them at Bramble Hall. The kids seem to have come out of shock, but now they can't stop crying. The whole family is a mess. Thankfully, most of Bramble Hall's inhabitants from this time are out, probably fighting here, except for the odd person wandering about. It is frightening for the Brambles. It's a hard concept to understand. We all managed to change though," he added, pointing to his own attire for demonstration purposes, "and we ate a bit of food."

"Come on," said Kaden. "I think we've seen enough for today. Let's go back to Bramble Hall."

"But I haven't seen myself in action yet!" complained Sol. He was clearly disappointed.

217

Cecily tutted and stormed passed her three friends. She did not think that war and killing people should be something to be proud of. She walked slightly ahead of the others on the way back to Bramble Hall. They must have decided to give her some space as they did not try to speak to her again. The truth was that Cecily was no closer to remembering and in any case, she had not liked what she had seen. All the violence and gore had made her queasy. Not only that, but the battle was like a version of her nightmares and she felt it had set her back, seeing this place. What was Kaden thinking, bringing her here? Seeing her other self on the battlefield doing all those terrible things made her want to remember even less, so she decided she was going to do everything possible to keep her current memory intact. They would just have to stop Dasrus without her.

By the time they all got back to Bramble Hall, they were damp and muddy. The structure of this Bramble Hall was far smaller and far simpler that its counterpart in the future. The approach to the manor house was a mud track, much like the one in the village, only better maintained. It had a downstairs and an upstairs visible from the front of the building; however, the addition of the two wings must have happened later. As the friends entered through the heavy, wooden front door, Cecily looked both left and right. They were in the Great Hall, only it was one huge room with a roaring fire at either end. In subsequent years, each end of this hall would be partitioned off to make the dining room, parlour and the drawing room. The grand staircase still stood in the middle of the Great Hall, which Cecily hoped led to bedrooms, because she was exhausted. She thought how much more luxurious the manor was, even in medieval times, compared to the cottage. The windows were small, but they had glass in them; the house had chimneys, which meant that the atmosphere was not thick with smoke and rich tapestries made of wool lined the stone walls.

Cecily was glad of the blazing fires that now burned and she made her way to one end of the Great Hall, where Jedd and Elisabeth were watching over the Bramble family. Cecily pulled her long boots off and tossed them to one side, resolving to clean the mud from them later. She then sat herself by the fire in a beautifully upholstered chair with an oak frame and hoped that she would soon dry off. The Bramble family were all huddled together. Lady Bramble sat on a chair similar to Cecily's and the children sat on small stools at her side. They were dozing. Cecily had not even acknowledged Jedd and Elisabeth and they were now looking at her quizzically.

"Well?" asked Elisabeth. "Did it work? Do you have your memory back?"

"No, thankfully," replied Cecily, rather curtly.

At that moment, Kaden, Fen and Sol walked in and even though her back was to her five friends, she felt one of those looks pass between them. Cecily was exhausted. She had not slept for a couple of days. Pure adrenaline must have been carrying her through. But now, as she sat in the chair by the hot, smoky fire, she found it hard to keep her eyes open and so she stopped resisting and drifted off into a troubled sleep.

***

Cecily awoke to the sound of clattering plates and wooden benches scraping the floor. She had no idea how long she had been asleep for. As she craned her neck around the chair, rubbing the sleep from her eyes, she saw that everyone, including the Brambles, were up and about and preparing the ornately carved wooden table for dinner. She was not complaining as she had woken up famished. As she moved across the floor to where she had flung her boots, she felt the eyes of her friends boring into her back. She turned to look at them, boots in hand, to find them staring expectantly.

"Still me!" she said sarcastically and with disappointed looks,

219

they continued with their business.

"Do you need any help?" she called over to Elisabeth, who was placing a rather delicious looking pie onto the table.

"No, it's OK. You stay there," replied Elisabeth. Although she sounded sweet enough, Cecily could still detect resentment.

She found a shoe brush on the mantelpiece and so she sat down and drew her comfortable chair a bit closer to the fire, where she began brushing the mud from her boots into the hearth. The fire had died down somewhat, so she was more than comfortable to sit in such close proximity to it, although she still felt her face reddening from the warm charcoal.

About ten minutes later, Lady Bramble announced that dinner was served. They hungrily tucked into a hearty meal of pigeon pie and bread and cheese, with a choice of wine or water to wash it down with. Cecily opted for a goblet of wine. She did not want to get drunk, but she hoped the wine would send her off into a pleasant slumber. The conversation at the dinner table was stunted and it was Kaden who kept it going with small talk, although he was not really able to engage anyone. The mood was definitely solemn.

When her stomach was full, Cecily gave it a pat and said, "That was lovely! Where did you find the food?"

"In the kitchen," replied Kaden.

She was about to ask if it would be missed, but then she remembered that this day in history had already passed and so it would not matter.

"Well, thank you," said Cecily, not forgetting her manners.

Kaden and Fen gathered up the dirty plates and goblets and carried them away in the direction of what must have been the kitchen. As she had not contributed to the meal in any way, Cecily thought she had better help clean up and so she took the remains of the bread and cheese and followed Kaden and Fen to the kitchen. She went out of a doorway on the far side of the grand staircase and she had to balance the plates as she walked down the many stairs. The kitchen was obviously still in the basement.

As she came upon the kitchen door, she heard Fen and Kaden whispering and the door had been pushed to, probably to prevent anyone from listening in on their hushed conversation. Cecily stood close to the gap, but flat against the wall so they would not see her.

"Everyone is getting impatient," she heard Fen say in a whisper. "The others can't understand why reactivation hasn't happened yet."

"She just needs a bit of time," replied Kaden. "It will happen."

"We don't have time, Kaden! And it's miserable here! Yes, we are safe, but the Brambles want to go home and they desperately need a visit from the Purification Unit to help them with their grief. Also, there is the small matter of Dasrus. He needs to be stopped! We can't just while the time away here waiting for Cec to remember who she is. We don't have that luxury!"

"I'm sure it won't be long now," reasoned Kaden. "We can afford a day or two more here. Remember, she is still human at the moment. It has been hard on her, this revelation."

"I know," said Fen, "and I'm not trying to be unsympathetic. It's just she is no good to us as a human. If she hasn't reactivated by the morning, I think you should go and seek advice from the Wise Ones."

Cecily had heard enough. She charged into the kitchen, slammed the plates of leftover food onto the wooden bench and ran up the stairs. She could hear Kaden and Fen shouting apologies, begging her to come back so they could explain, but she did not stop until she had reached the landing on the first floor, where she hoped the bedrooms would be.

She walked to the very end of the landing and poked her head around the door that stood there. When she saw it was empty, she made her way inside. She saw a wardrobe and matching dressing table made of heavy, dark wood. In the centre of the room was a bed, with red curtains hanging around it. As she pulled back the curtains, she unsettled some dust which made her sneeze. She found the bed was made of the same dark wood as the wardrobe and dressing table. Cecily decided that she would not sleep in the bed, just in case any inhabitants of the medieval period decided to join her. Instead, she took the bedding and made herself a comfortable bed on the floor in the corner, out of the way.

She thought about the whispered conversation between Kaden and Fen and found herself getting annoyed again. No use to them as she was now? Obviously her friendship meant nothing. Tomorrow, she was going to demand that Kaden take her home and she was going to get as far away from Bramblegate as humanly possible. Maybe she would even go overseas. One thing she was sure of though, she was determined to remain plain old Cecily Stalks and if her friends did not like that, it was tough. They would have to figure out what to do about Dasrus by themselves.

Just as Cecily was about to settle down, there was a knock at the door. She contemplated ignoring it, but she feared that whoever was out there would persist. She walked over to the door, opened it marginally and peered through the gap. It was Jedd.

"Sorry to disturb you, Cec," he said rather jovially. "I've just come to see if you're all right," he continued as he muscled his way inside.

"I'm fine, thanks. In fact, I was just about to try and get some sleep, so if you wouldn't mind?" Cecily gestured to the door, but Jedd did not seem to notice.

"You know, it doesn't matter to me whether you remember or not. I still feel the same way about you."

"Erm, thanks Jedd… I think," she added as an afterthought, not knowing if that was a good or a bad thing.

"I see you for who you really are, whether that is Cecily Stalks or Gaea, Mother Earth. I see into your soul."

222

Cecily felt uncomfortable and quite intimated as his large bulky frame towered above her. His steely grey eyes bore into hers.

"I'm quite tired, Jedd. Can we talk about this tomorrow?"

However, Jedd did not seem to hear her. "Before our last deactivation, Cec, I told you things, important stuff. Only deactivation happened before you could give me an answer. When I was born again into this lifetime, I found that I was still activated. I remembered everything. It was torture for me as until you were reactivated, I would never know if you felt the same way. So I had to find a way to bring about reactivation and give us all a reason to become Cerbereans once more."

Cecily did not like where this was going. "Really Jedd, you don't have to explain yourself to me."

"I do, because you are the reason I have done what I've done. In this lifetime, you've shaped the person I am. I love you, Cecily and I'm sure that you feel the same way about me. That is what gave me the courage to confess my feelings before our last deactivation and why I betrayed you and the others, to force reactivation. Everything I've done is so we can be together."

Cecily was certainly not expecting that. It hit her like a bolt out of the blue and now she just wanted to get him out of the room. She felt nervous because she found Jedd unpredictable at the best times and right now, his eyes were wild.

"Wow, Jedd, I'm flattered. I obviously can't speak for, erm, Gaea, but as Cecily, I can honestly say that I don't... I mean, you are my friend. I love you like a brother."

She tried to put it as delicately as she could while still being honest, although in truth, she was not sure she even liked him anymore, let alone loved him like a brother. She was right to fear his unpredictability, as he went off like a firework.

"It's him, isn't it? Why do you always choose him? It's like you are drawn to him. I don't understand. What's he got that I haven't?"

Cecily just looked at Jedd and she imagined that she must have appeared somewhat befuddled. Was he really expecting her to answer that question? She could not remember anything and she had no clue what he was talking about.

"Answer me, Cecily! Why do you always pick Dasrus? You can never be with him!"

"Dasrus? Don't be ridiculous! I would never want to be with him!" But as soon as the words left her mouth, she realised that she had wanted to be with him. After all, Dasrus was Cian. "Anyway," she continued, "we are Cerbereans and I thought Cerbereans could not be together. Look at Fen and Sol."

"You are different, Cec," he said as his mood was now changing from angry to passionate. "You are Gaea, a goddess. You can do what you like, you are no slave! What do I have to do to prove myself to you? I got us out of the dungeon in the realm between realms."

Cecily could not help herself. "You are the reason we were there in the first place!" she said, her voice rising. "This whole sorry state of affairs is your fault! You helped Dasrus get close to us! You helped him put his plans into action! All those people dead, Jedd. That is on your conscience!"

"Oh no!" he swiftly snapped back. "Don't you put the blame on me! You have led me on for centuries!"

Again, she felt that she could not comment on this but she hoped it was not true at all.

"Jedd, let's just calm down. Why don't we talk about this tomorrow when we've both had some sleep? Things will seem better in the morning."

"Sleep? You expect me to sleep? You know, when I compared you to Purdey back in the Bramble Arms that day, I said it because I knew it would get to you. But I was right! You are just like she was, twisted."

Cecily was suddenly very aware that he was speaking about her mother in the past tense and she was not sure how she felt about that. Her mouth was gawping at the indignation of the insult, but still he continued.

"Honestly, Cec, you should have heard the screams as her soul was ripped from her body, piece by piece. They haunt me. I can still see the fear and horror on her face as she witnessed what Dasrus was doing to her. She was alive until the final piece left her body, minutes of torture that would have felt like a lifetime. Only that is nothing compared to the hell she will be experiencing in the Dark. And you are just like her, Cec! But trust me, your fate will be far worse!" And with that, he charged out of the room, slamming the door behind him.

Cecily stood for quite a while, staring at the back of the door. She once again found herself shocked by yet another revelation she did not care to know about. She had no idea that Jedd felt that way about her. He certainly had a funny way of showing it. One thing was for sure, the feeling was definitely not reciprocated. She thought she would find it hard to forgive him after all the awful things he said to her that night in the Bramble Arms, but now, knowing that his selfishness was the cause of everything that had happened, the thought of Jedd Benedict made her sick to the stomach. To top it all off, he had the nerve to blame her and he had also threatened her. She thought long and hard about the graphic description he had given her about Purdey's death. He had obviously spared her the details the first time around, but now, out of spite, he had told her the truth about her mother's demise. He could be lying to hurt her, of course, but she doubted it. She did not know how she felt about the manner in which Purdey died. She felt like she should be appalled, devastated even, but all she felt was numb. Once again, Jedd's true colours had shone through.

Eventually, Cecily made her way into the makeshift bed she had fashioned in the corner. One of the things bothering her most about what Jedd had said was the fact that she was always drawn to Dasrus. The thought repulsed her and yet something in the back of her mind, a niggling feeling, was troubling her. She tried to work it out, but to no avail. She watched the bedroom door for a long time, trying to prepare herself mentally should Jedd make a reappearance. However, for now, he had not and Cecily's exhaustion got the better of her. She drifted off to sleep, worrying about what the next day would bring.

Chapter 27

When everyone announced they would go upstairs to the bedrooms to try and get some sleep, Elisabeth noticed Jedd sneak off, so she decided to follow him. Her instincts were playing hell with her. She knew he was up to something and she certainly did not trust him yet. She saw him enter the bedroom at the end of the corridor and automatically assumed that must be the room in which Cecily was residing. She knew that she should not, but she could not help herself. She positioned herself outside the room so she could eavesdrop against the door, but also so she could hide in the shadows of the darkened corner of the landing should anyone suddenly exit the room.

She listened, heartbroken, as Jedd confessed his love for Cecily. She had always suspected it. Over time, she had watched him carefully, but to hear him say it out loud, with such zeal, shattered her heart into a million pieces and made her sick to the stomach. She felt like running away and never looking back. Then her feelings changed again as he so quickly turned spiteful and nasty when Cecily confessed that she did not return his feelings. She felt shame as he revealed the horrific details of Purdey's death to Cecily. She knew he was speaking out of hurt, but he sounded so wicked.

As he stormed out of the room, Elisabeth's agility enabled her to conceal herself swiftly and Jedd did not notice her hiding in the corner. Instead of going to the bedroom he was supposed to be sharing with Kaden and Sol, he flew down the grand staircase. Elisabeth followed him as he made his way further down the stairs and into the kitchen. She confronted him just as he was about to leave.

"Where are you going, Jedd?"

"To get some fresh air!" he snapped.

"Oh, come on," goaded Elisabeth. "What are you really up to?"

"What do you mean?" asked Jedd through gritted teeth, turning his back on the door to face Elisabeth.

"Well, are you true to the Light or are you teetering on the edge of darkness? I witnessed for myself how much Dasrus scares you. But the question is, what do you fear more, Jedd? The repercussions of betraying the Light or an eternity of hell, because that's what you'll get for betraying Dasrus. Just admit that you are out of your depth."

"I'm just going for a walk, Elisabeth. Climb down from that high horse."

But Elisabeth had no intention of stopping now she had started. "Isn't it time you made your mind up once and for all? First betraying us, then betraying Dasrus. Are you going to betray us again now you know there is no chance of getting what you want? What would the coward in you do?"

Elisabeth saw the dangerous glint in Jedd's steely eyes.

"You were listening?"

"She will never love you the way you want her to. You know that, don't you?"

Jedd's temper was quick to flare again. "What do you know? She hasn't got her memory back yet! You can't speak for her! You don't even like her!"

"That's not true, Jedd!" shouted back Elisabeth, all of her anger and resentment towards them both threatening to bubble over. "You have to be realistic. Let her go."

She knew she was in hazardous territory here, but this still did not stop her. She wanted to let everything out. She was about to carry on her tirade, but as she was speaking, she saw the glint of metal around his neck, reflecting the single candlelight attached to the wall. She could just make out the pendant in the dark, which had come untucked from his top.

"What is that pendant, Jedd? I'd never seen it before two nights ago."

Jedd looked down and stuffed the pendant back into his top. His fury finally got the better of him.

"Why don't you just mind your own business, Elisabeth? You are always interfering, sticking your nose in where it's not wanted. I've had enough! Do you not think I've noticed you watching me all the time, following me about like a lost puppy? I know how you feel about me. Well, let me put you straight. I'll never love you."

He delivered this final blow with the same malice in which he had described Purdey's death to Cecily. The shock must have been visible on Elisabeth's face as before he stormed out, slamming the door behind him for the second time that evening, he smirked noxiously at the anguish he had just inflicted.

Elisabeth turned away sharply from the door, as if he was still stood there, watching her misery. She tried not to dwell on his cruel words, but she could not help it and as a result, all she felt was hopelessness and despair. She walked over to the kitchen table and sat on one of the benches. She wearily put her head down on the table, resting it on her arms. She really must get a hold of herself and handle these emotions. She knew she felt so strongly as she was only recently reactivated, but the truth was, the more years she spent as a human on this plane, the harder the feelings were to battle during times of reactivation. She did not know how Fen and Sol did it, how they were so stoic during times of reactivation. But she also knew that their situation was very different from hers. They only had eyes for each other. Their love was reciprocated. No one else to get in the way and that was how it had always been for them. Even though they did not remember in times of deactivation, they were automatically drawn to each other, like moths to a flame. Jedd had loved her once, she was sure of that. Only now there was someone else and she resented Cecily for that, even though she knew it was not her fault. Elisabeth was glad she was downstairs in the kitchen as she did not want anyone to hear her sobs.

Chapter 28

"What a beautiful day!" sighed Cecily.

She was lying down on a soft, woollen blanket in a clearing in Bramblegate Woods. She would know these woods anywhere. She loved them so much. The scorching sun was beating down on her and she was sweltering, probably because of the full, long, linen dress she wore. But she did not care that she felt too hot, she had never been this happy before and she did not feel she could possibly ever be any happier than she was right now, in this moment. The grass was a vibrant green in colour, fresh and overgrown. Flies zipped past her ears on their way in search of tasty fare and the birdsong in the trees high above sounded like a majestic symphony. To her left, the six aged oak trees, which stood in a protective ring, flourished with lush, tender leaves. She felt such peace, like she could lie here forever.

She rolled onto her side and came face to face with him, the reason for her elation. She looked into his crystal eyes and was lost.

"I've never experienced such joy, my love," said Cecily to the young man. "Tell me it will always be this way?"

"It will always be this way, my darling. I will never leave you. We will be together for all eternity."

Her heart skipped a beat. She loved him more than anything else, more than life itself, so why could she not remember his name? It was on the tip of her tongue. Not to worry, it did not matter. He was the love of her life, her soul mate. She would do anything for him and him for her. They leaned in to kiss each other, Cecily's heart beating like a hummingbird's wings. Just as their lips were about to meet, Cecily opened her eyes to discover her love's beautiful face had gone and in its place, a black hood with glittering, unnatural eyes beyond it. Cecily tried to stop her head from moving towards the abyss beyond the hood, but she could not. She was being pulled by some strange force and before she knew it, she had entered the blackness of the hood and she was falling down, down, down, all the while, a hateful cackle resounding through her head, mocking her. After what seemed like a lifetime, the heinous crowing subsided and was replaced by an equally torturous derision. It was a voice she recognised and it was disturbingly calm.

"What's wrong, Cecily?" it said as it ridiculed her. "Do you not like what you see? After all, you made me like this. Everything I've done is for you."

"No!" screamed Cecily into the void which was this black hole, still falling all the while. "You did this to yourself! Don't you dare blame me!"

Cecily landed with a thump. When she opened her eyes, which had been tightly closed, she was back on the blanket in the blazing sun and her feelings of bliss had returned. She could not remember ever feeling this happy. But what was that niggling feeling in the back of her brain? She decided to ignore it. Nothing was going to ruin her contentment. She rolled over to face her one true love.

"I've never experienced such joy, my love," said Cecily. "Tell me it will always be this way?"

She gazed into his perfect eyes, waiting for his comforting response, when his face changed, replaced by the black hood with nothing but emptiness beyond.

"It will always be this way," the eerily calm voice mocked. "I will never leave you. We will be together for all eternity."

Once more, wicked laughter resounded in her ears.

"No!" she screamed, shutting her eyes and willing this stain on her happiness to disappear.

The laughter stopped abruptly and Cecily opened her eyes. She was relieved once more to see the loving face of her soul mate staring back.

"What's wrong?" he asked, stroking her face soothingly. "Bad dream?"

She was about to reply when her lover's face transformed into the vile demon with the black hood.

This infliction of torture continued in a vicious cycle. Each time she believed herself safe with her love, the demon would reappear, taunting her with his abuse. Every time her beloved's face changed into what it should never have been, Cecily felt like her heart had been ripped from her chest, like the beast had punched his way through her rib cage and taken it for himself. She began to feel despair and desperation. She could not withstand an eternity of this pain.

"Right now, your soul is vulnerable," he said as he taunted her. "It is time to protect yourself and remember who you are. Be what you are, as nature intended, Cecily. Or should I call you Gaea?" His wicked laughter continued to mock her. "Your soul is vulnerable, Cecily and I am coming for you!"

Out of the corner of her eye, she saw them rise up. As she turned her head, she realised that her perfect day was now besmirched by the putrid smell of the salivating shadows. She tried to move, but she was not quite quick enough. They attacked, yellow teeth poised to chomp down and devour her torso. As the razor sharp fangs snapped into place, Cecily screamed in anticipation of the agony she would feel with half of her side missing. But when she looked down, her body was still intact. She swiftly looked around her for the shadows and the black hooded demon, but she found herself alone, the woodland around her dense.

She had to run. She did not know why, but something told her to run as fast as she could. So she did and boy, could she run fast! As she whizzed past the trees, expertly dodging every obstacle in her path, little parts of lost information found their way into her head. They were snippets at first, flashbacks of a lost life. But the faster she ran, more and more images filed themselves away into her consciousness until soon, the flood of memories was too much for her. She came to an abrupt stop and fell to her knees, clutching her head and screaming. Not because it hurt, but because she did not want them. She did not want to remember. How could she block them out? She needed to stop this, but the more she concentrated and the more she tried, the more the memories came flooding back.

"No!" she cried out. "No! Please, I don't want them!"

***

Cecily awoke with a start and sat bolt upright in the makeshift bed on the floor. She hoped that she had not been screaming out loud and she listened carefully to see if she had woken anyone else. After a couple of minutes, she decided that everyone must still be asleep. She got out of the bed and made her way across the cold stone floor to the window. As she gazed out into the night, it occurred to her how the cold stone would have bothered her when she was human. Only now she was a goddess, back to her true self and she did not notice the chill of the exposed floor under foot. She felt a bit silly for her human self, trying so hard to prevent reactivation. Now her memory was back, her connection to the Light was strong and her purpose was clear, like she'd had bad eyesight corrected by a pair of glasses. It seems it had taken the argument with Jedd to eventually force her reactivation, for she knew why she had been blocking it so vehemently and for that reason, she was grateful to Cecily Stalks for her passion and strong sense of self, traits which she knew had come from her true self, from her soul.

Whilst deep in thought, she produced a small, green ball of light and toyed with it absent-mindedly. Even though her memory was back and she remembered everything, there was still one thing that she refused to think about and would not consider for as long as she possibly could. Dasrus.

Chapter 29

At first light, Cecily went to seek out Kaden. She had not slept for the rest of the night as her mind had been too active. She knew that she must learn to control this. After all, sleep was as important as food and water for her human body. Even with an immortal spirit prolonging its life, she must still look after her human casing.

She found Kaden in the Great Hall. He was replenishing the fire with bits of wood whilst eating a piece of bread.

"Morning," he said without looking at her. "Sleep well? I've been summoned by the Wise Ones, so I've got to go. It must be important, but I'll try not to be too long."

"Kaden, I'm back," said Cecily.

Kaden spun around urgently and said, "Show me!"

With ease, Cecily produced a modest ball of green glowing light.

"Will that do or do you also want to see my mark?" offered Cecily, knowing exactly what her brand would reveal; the oak leaf, which not only represented the gateway of which she was guardian, but also life, strength, wisdom and power, characteristics of her true self.

"How did it happen?" asked Kaden.

"The usual," replied Cecily, casually. "A dream about the one who haunts me."

Kaden looked at her with a worried frown.

"It's OK, I'm all right. And just for the record, I do remember everything."

"Well, I'm glad you're back, Cec…" Kaden stopped himself.

"Do you still want to be called Cecily or do you want to be called by your natural name, Gaea?"

"No, Cecily is just fine," she said. "I like it."

Kaden smiled. "I've got to go. I don't want to keep them waiting."

"We've got to get back to the present, you know," pointed out Cecily. "We've work to do and I must protect the gateway."

As Cecily was finishing her sentence, Elisabeth appeared from the doorway that housed the stairs to the kitchen. Cecily saw her distress, as did Kaden.

"Elisabeth, are you OK?" he asked.

"I'm fine," she replied.

She was trying her best to hide it with her tough exterior, but Cecily knew something had happened and before Elisabeth revealed it, she knew it was about Jedd. She was not blind to her feelings for him.

"It's Jedd. He's gone."

Cecily's stomach did a somersault. Surely this was not a coincidence? Her argument with him must have made him leave. Now she was reactivated, she remembered the last time and him confessing his feelings to her, only there was no time to tell him she did not think of him like that. He was her brother. She had certainly never led him on.

"I was the last to go up to bed. I saw him fly down the grand staircase and straight onto the kitchen stairs. He was in such a rush. I followed him and confronted him just as he was about to leave through the back door. I asked him what he was doing and if he was going to betray us again. I told him he should make his mind up once and for all, about choosing the Light or the Dark, I mean."

Elisabeth stumbled over her words and Cecily's immediate thoughts were that she was not being entirely truthful. Maybe Jedd had told her about their argument, or maybe Elisabeth had overheard.

"He was so nasty and his words were vile." Elisabeth looked to the floor before continuing. "Like he took pleasure in hurting people. I don't know what happened to him!"

Cecily could see that she was struggling to hold back her emotions and so she stepped in to rescue her.

"Jedd paid me a visit last night. I'll be honest with you all, it was a bit awkward. He told me that before our last deactivation, he gave me some very important information. This was all before I got my memory back, so I didn't know what he was talking about."

Elisabeth gasped and looked from the floor at Cecily. She must not have realised that Cecily was back to her old self.

"He confessed that he loved me and he told me that I was the reason for his betrayal. He betrayed us to force reactivation so he could get my answer. He told me that having his memory while we didn't was torture for him."

She saw Elisabeth wincing as she spoke, but if they were going to work out what Jedd was up to, she had to be honest.

"But I did have my memory and he knew that! Why didn't he say something?" said Kaden, exacerbated. "Maybe I should have realised."

"Don't beat yourself up, Kaden. It was his choice not to tell you," said Cecily.

"Anyway," she continued, "I told him I love him as a friend and he accused me of always choosing Dasrus. He then gave me some horrific details about Purdey's death and stormed out."

As she was speaking, Fen and Sol descended the grand staircase and made their way over to join them.

"I think that it took the argument with Jedd to force my reactivation."

"You're back?" asked Sol.

"Yes," replied Cecily, with a nod of her head.

Fen and Sol beamed at her.

"But Jedd has gone."

Cecily quickly filled them in on what they had missed.

"The question is, where has he gone?" asked Kaden. "I didn't even notice he was missing."

"Neither did I. Maybe he has just gone out for some fresh air," suggested Sol.

"Surely, he wouldn't betray us again," said Fen.

"He was very angry last night. He said some awful things, but it was more than just the words, it was his whole attitude. He was wicked," explained Cecily, "just like he had been with me in the months leading up to the party."

"He was the same way with me," chipped in Elisabeth. "Like the nice humble guy he turned into when he broke us out of the realm between realms was all an act, like all his caring and kindness was false. The minute he can't have what he wants, he turns nasty again."

"We all know that Jedd has always been a bit of a wild card and a law unto himself, but we know him well and we know he was fiercely loyal to both us and the Light," said Kaden, defending his old friend. "Being reborn with his memories, still activated, has obviously been too much for him to handle by himself. I still don't understand why he didn't say anything. If he had his memories, he would have known about me. And how did he not slip up? Look at Elisabeth!"

"His actions have been calculated if you ask me," said Elisabeth, now staring at the floor again. "He didn't want to forget or he would have shared his secret with Kaden. He said it himself, he planned the whole thing just so he could get the answer to his question. He is selfish beyond all measure. He has done what no warrior of Light should ever do. He has put himself first. Look at the death and destruction he has caused."

Cecily witnessed Elisabeth once again fighting her emotions.

"I should have done more," said Kaden, reproaching himself again. "Looking back, there was definitely something off with him. He was shifty and secretive, as well as unusually harsh and nasty. I should have known something was wrong."

Cecily placed a comforting arm around her friend's shoulder.

"There's something else," said Elisabeth. "A pendant. I noticed it the night he carried me into the realm between realms. I had never seen it before then. It's a black stone encased in a gold frame. He was wearing it last night too. It had obviously become untucked from his shirt by accident, as when I asked him about it, he stuffed it back in his shirt and told me to mind my own business. What could it be?"

Kaden looked worried. "That doesn't sound good."

Cecily noticed Kaden drift off and she knew he was deep in thought, trying to make sense of everything.

"Sorry to change the subject," interrupted Fen. "We've just spoken to Lady Bramble. She and the children are desperate to go home. Lady Bramble said the children are terrified. They think this place is full of ghosts."

Cecily quite understood how unnerving it must be for them. As a human, she too had felt the same way about random people walking in and out of rooms, whispered conversations and the echoes of jovial laughter. It was strange, although rather than the people of this time being the ghosts, they belonged here. It was the group of visiting companions themselves that were the spectres.

"I've really got to go," said Kaden, snapping out of his trance. "I've kept the Wise Ones waiting long enough. We'll have to work out the enigma that is Jedd later. Maybe the Wise Ones can shed some light on the situation."

His friends murmured in agreement.

"When I return, we'll form a plan and get back to the present. We've still got to ensure the safety of the Bramble family, especially Oscar. But at least now that Cec has her memory and powers back, she can shut down the gateway. That should take some pressure off. I'll be as quick as I can."

And with that, Kaden transformed into a bright ball of light.

Just before he disappeared into thin air, Cecily heard him say, "I'm so glad you are back, Cec. I've missed you."

The message was for her ears only and it resounded in her head. She smiled to herself.

After Kaden had gone, Fen and Sol announced that they would go out and have a look around to see if they could locate Jedd. Elisabeth was to stay at Bramble Hall and keep Lady Bramble and the children company, when they eventually appeared from one of the upstairs bedrooms. Cecily needed some alone time to think about their situation and to rediscover her powers before they journeyed back into real time. However, she needed to talk to Elisabeth before she went anywhere.

After Fen and Sol had left, she beckoned Elisabeth over to a couple of the comfortably upholstered chairs by the fire, which was now spitting and crackling thanks to the wood Kaden had added to it.

"Elisabeth," began Cec, "I just want you to know how truly sorry I am about Jedd."

"Don't be sorry to me," snapped Elisabeth, defensively. "He is probably in the process of betraying all of us."

"I didn't mean that," said Cecily quietly. "We don't yet know that he has betrayed us a second time and until then, we have to give him the benefit of the doubt. I meant that I'm sorry for the way he feels about me. I don't feel the same way about him. I never have and I have certainly never led him to believe otherwise."

"You don't have to explain yourself to me," sniffed Elisabeth. Cecily noticed that Elisabeth was unable to look her in the eye.

"Oh, but I do. I know how you feel about Jedd and I know those feelings are more than brotherly love. It was hard for you to hear what I said about our argument. I can see the pain on your face, Elisabeth."

"What does it matter?" she snapped again. "We can never be together anyway. We are Cerbereans."

Elisabeth started to weep silently, so Cecily got up and perched on the arm of her chair and held her friend's hand in an attempt to comfort her.

"Exactly, you can never be together as Cerbereans." Cecily did not know why, but as she spoke, she felt overwhelming sadness. "All the more reason for you to focus and regain your strength. I know you love him, but the reason your emotions are so raw is because you've only just been reactivated."

"And because of the way he has treated me, not only his hostility and the things he has said, but also the kidnapping."

She was fighting back the tears but Cecily thought it best for her to get her emotions out, and so she let her cry. At least the source of Elisabeth's hostility to Cecily was now clear. She just hoped that Elisabeth could see past it and realise that Cecily was not to blame.

They sat together for a while in silence as Elisabeth tried to compose herself. When it seemed she had, Cecily said, "Come on, get a handle on those emotions. We've a job to do and we must stick together."

Elisabeth nodded stoically, staring into the fire.

Cecily looked up and saw that Lady Bramble and the children were making their way down the grand staircase.

"Will you be all right with them?" she asked Elisabeth.

"Yes, I'm OK now," she said, her tough exterior firmly reclaimed.

Cecily said good morning to the Brambles and made her way out of the front door. She would let Elisabeth bring them up to date on the situation. Cecily needed to be outside in her world and so she headed straight for the comforting familiarity of the woods.

As she walked down the mud track that in the future would be the gravelled driveway, she thought about Jedd and she wondered if he would betray them once and for all. It was a lot for the Light to expect the Cerbereans to spend so long as humans in between activations and for them not to feel as humans feel. She did not doubt the extremes of the unrequited love that both Jedd and Elisabeth were experiencing. Just as she wished more than anything that Elisabeth could overcome her anger and resentment, she wished the same for Jedd and hoped that his feelings would not lead him down a path of revenge he might one day regret.

As she was thinking about Jedd's confession to her and how it explained how rotten he had been to her during this lifetime as humans, she suddenly realised that she and Jedd were not so dissimilar. He was bitter and angry at lifetimes he remembered that no one else did, waiting for the answer to a burning question from someone with amnesia. He was desperate. Cecily had been bitter and angry at the lot she had been given in life: her beloved father dying while she was still so young, being left with the worst mother in the world and the doldrums of the daily grind. For different reasons, they were both bitter and angry at the world, yet both Jedd and herself behaved in exactly the same way. They chose to keep their problems to themselves and pushed everyone else away.

But that was where the similarities ended. Now reactivated, Cecily could see the bigger picture. She saw the threat of the Dark looming and she knew all too well what it was capable of. She had a job to do and her job was to fight the Dark, to protect humans and the Earth, her domain. Jedd had lost sight of the bigger picture and Elisabeth was right, he had put himself before the cause. This could ultimately end in destruction. Whatever Jedd decided to do, it was now in the hands of the Universe. His deeds were already written and destiny would decide his fate. And that faith in the Universe, her true father, was why she was able to detach herself from the things happening around her. She remembered her chat with Kaden yesterday when he explained that sometimes he found it hard to get caught up in everyday human stresses and it was the same for her. She still felt some residual human anger at Jedd for the way he had treated her, in fact, the way he had treated them all, but it was out of their hands. What will be, will be. And that is what she had to focus on now. She had to ensure she was strong and ready for the battle ahead. The future was preordained, that much she knew, but she would try her upmost in the fight ahead to prevent the Dark from conquering Earth. And if they were beaten? Well, she would fight again and keep on going for as long as it took to defeat her enemy.

Cecily was now deep in the heart of Bramblegate Woods and she decided to let their beauty distract her for a while. The weather remained overcast and dull, but at least it was not raining like yesterday. In this time, they had been transported back to the beginning of spring and the trees and flowers were waking up after a long winter. The rain of yesterday had helped their blossoming on a little and today things seemed greener. She took a deep breath, revelling in the earthly smells. She thought back to her human lifetime of late, to her time as Cecily Stalks. Cecily Stalks must have been quite in tune with her spiritual side, as she had felt the comfort of the nature around her and appreciated its beauty and serenity. She felt the same affinity with nature as her goddess counterpart and was also at her happiest around it. She thought about her human mother and father.

Yesterday, her emotions about them had been so fresh and real; however, today was a different story. Today she was detached from those feelings. The life she had lived up until she got her memory back seemed so far away, like she was watching a film or reading a book about it. There was no doubt in her mind about the love and respect she felt for her human father and now she could remember everything, she realised he had been her father many times before, protecting and caring for her human self. He was a true Light Worker. However, Purdey was a tricky one. This human lifetime was her first encounter with Purdey. Cecily had a feeling that she was a new soul who had made her choice about the Dark very early on. That was the only thing that could explain her behaviour because Cecily herself was a mother, the Earth Mother, and one thing you never did was abandon your children. So Cecily felt that Purdey had got what she deserved. She had made her choice. All the hatred she had felt towards Purdey had gone as she could now think about things more objectively.

She thought back to her human experiences of the dreams, snippets of her past, true life, trying to awaken her consciousness. Everything seemed so obvious to her now. She thought about the shadow beasts that had haunted her and how terrified she had been. Getting her memory back was like waking from that nightmare and she realised she had nothing to fear. And then, even though she tried to stop herself, she thought about when she met Cian, the time they had shared together and how much human love she had felt for him. Then she thought about the pain he had caused her by his betrayal and lies. Her human self had thought that she had made herself vulnerable by baring her soul to Cian, but now she knew that was not so. There was nothing he did not know about her anyway. But she did not like where this train of thought was leading her. Somehow it was hard to be objective and see the bigger picture. These memories stirred feelings.

And there it was without warning. The niggling feeling she used to experience as a human, her brain prompting her to remember something, thoughts she should dissect and analyse. She had the feeling deep down that something was not right, that something was missing, still forgotten, but there she stopped herself. She locked away what was coming in a box, returned it to the back of her mind and threw away the key. She would not go there. She would not think about it. She decided to leave her human self, Cecily Stalks and her memories, behind. This Cecily was aware that memories make us who we are. They mould us and shape us. But not her mortal memories. She was different now and she must focus on building her strength for the battle ahead. *So, what about the memories that make you who you are now?* she thought to herself. Those she could handle by locking them away, as she just had.

Cecily found herself in the clearing by the circle of the six aged oak trees. In this time, they had already been cut down, unlike in her dream of the previous night where they had flourished, standing tall and proud. Subconsciously, Cecily knew this was where she was heading. She was drawn to this place as it was the source of so much ancient magic. It was the perfect place to practise. She decided that she should test her powers and she could not wait to get started. It was like riding a bike and she had not forgotten.

She started off with some simple spells, gradually progressing to some trickier magic. Her green light bounced playfully around the clearing. Like Kaden's blue light, hers was green for a reason. She drew her power from nature and she was the personification of the Earth itself. Her light represented growth, fertility, harmony, healing and freshness. As well as drawing on nature for her magic, she could also absorb power from the earth around her by touching it. She was like a sponge, able to suck up its energies and use their power to her advantage. Absorption gave her own powers a boost. Cecily was the Earth Mother. She was able to give life, heal and create and now as she danced around the space in the middle of the woods using her strength, speed and agility, her warrior traits, she gave life to wilting weeds and created flowers where there were none. Cecily's gift was that she could use the nature around her. She was the goddess of the Earth and all that grew in the ground were her children. They were her servants, ready to do her bidding. She alone controlled the forces of earthly nature. She caught sight of herself in a puddle left by yesterday's rain and her reflection stared back at her. Her green eyes were bright and her red hair shone in the light of the day. Her physique seemed to have filled out somewhat and the tom boy, Cecily, was no more. She was goddess again. For the first time, she recognised herself and she felt strong.

She decided to finish her drill with some sword fighting as she did not want to be rusty when facing agents of the Dark. She skilfully wielded the heavy sword with both hands, slicing and dicing the air before turning swiftly to face another imaginary adversary. She continued this playacting over to the ring of oak stumps and as she leapt onto one of them, she suddenly felt very sick to the stomach, so much so that she had to sit down. She felt energy in the air around the tree stumps, which meant that magic had recently been performed there. The residual energy left over from the spell was strong, which accounted for her nausea. She was wracking her brain, trying to remember back to the time she was in, to think what this powerful magic could have been. That was the only explanation, because as visitors to this time, only Kaden and herself could perform magic and Kaden was with the Wise Ones. No matter how hard she tried, she could not think what it was that had happened there.

When she had composed herself, she decided to use her own magic to discover the culprit. Cecily was also able to use natural energy to see into the past. She could touch organic material and see what had occurred in the vicinity, imprints of the past. As the energy from the spell was strong, she took a few deep breaths and then placed her hand on the tree stump next to the one she was sitting on and concentrated. It did not take Cecily long to find out what had happened there only hours earlier and what she witnessed not only shocked her, but filled her with dread. She needed to get back to Bramble Hall and warn the others immediately.

They were betrayed and the Dark was coming.

Chapter 30

Jedd's anger was at a pinnacle as he stomped through Bramblegate Woods. Deep down, he had already known the answer he would receive from Cecily, whether she was reactivated or not. She had never given him any reason to believe otherwise. It had all been in his head. He was deluded and he had become obsessed. He felt absolutely ridiculous and that awful feeling of rejection was just too much, because when all was said and done, he loved her deeply. She filled his head and she was all he thought about.

He had watched her carefully, looking for some indication that she felt the same way. He had waited patiently all these long years for the answer to one simple question and it took but a single moment to shoot him down in a ball of flames. It was all over now and he had his answer. The pain was too much for him to bear. For eighteen years, he had remembered his alternative life. He supposed he should be thankful it had been no longer as they had lived many lifetimes since their last reactivation. However, eighteen years was long enough to build hope that the person you loved felt the same way about you. It was long enough to feel the pain of not being with that person and being alone. It was long enough to grow angry, bitter and frustrated at your situation, especially when you had convinced yourself there may be hope.

He realised he had gone about it all the wrong way. His attitude and his betrayal had simply pushed her away, pushed them all away. He had lost their respect. He should have confided in Kaden and he would have made him forget, maybe even have sent him away, like Elisabeth. But ultimately, that had put him off and so he lied to them all and pretended he was oblivious to the solution, all because he had been scared he would forget how he felt about her. It had just not been an option at the time. The pain had been easier to live with until his emotions had got the better of him.

Deep down, he felt shame and guilt at the situation he had engineered for his own selfish reasons. Many innocents had died as a result of his betrayal. After the others had been reactivated, he felt strong again, drawn to the Light, like he had a purpose and that he needed to prove himself worthy and redeem himself. Now he realised it had been a waste of time. He could not live with the overwhelming emotions of pain, guilt and anger any longer as he did not have the will to fight them. The others would never trust him again anyway. He hated their righteousness, especially Elisabeth's. She was always sticking her nose in where it was not wanted. He knew he had hurt her and he simply did not care. He knew this highlighted his selfishness. And then there was her. She would never love him. There was only one she had ever loved and Jedd knew he could never compete. He had nothing to live for and for that reason, he was now sure of what he wanted.

Jedd had decided to stick to the undergrowth of the wood, just in case anyone resolved to follow him. As he looked down at his strong, powerful arms, cut and scratched, he realised that he had taken his frustration out on the flora and fauna around him. He pushed his way through the final knot of branches into the clearing with the six old oak tree stumps. He sat in exactly the same place as he had done in the months before his betrayal when he used to meet Dasrus there. He remembered the pure terror he had felt in those moments. However, that fear was now gone. He took a couple of deep breaths and held the pendant, whispering the magic words bestowed upon him by the demon. He thought he had hidden the jewel so well, until Elisabeth found him out. But he pushed all thoughts of his friends out of his head now. He needed to get this over with before he changed his mind.

Almost instantly, Dasrus appeared, startling Jedd and making him jump to his feet. Although Jedd was determined, he still felt his heart in his mouth as the demon glided towards him on a wave of shadow beasts, salivating and growling noisily in hope of a meal.

"So, this is where they've fled to?" said Dasrus in his eerily calm voice. "An interesting choice. So, young Cerberean, you have used the pendant. Does this mean you have made your decision?"

"Yes, Master," he said, all of the nerves and stuttering disappearing as he replied with conviction.

"And?"

"I want to serve the Dark, serve you, my Lord."

"Well I must say, this is a surprise! I thought that you would betray me after I locked you in the dungeon with your friends. I thought that once the others were reactivated, you would return to the Light. In fact, I was half expecting an ambush."

"I'll be honest, Master, I did think about it. My pull to the Light was strong, but now I am certain of what I want."

"So, I take it she refused you then?"

Jedd looked to the ground and with that gesture, he needed no words to explain what had happened. Dasrus's wicked laughter resounded around the clearing, bouncing off the trees and filling Jedd's ears.

"Poor, young, foolish boy, falling in love with a goddess. It's like a mouse falling in love with a lion!"

Jedd felt his anger rise once more and he had to try hard to push it down within him to keep it at bay. He realised he would do himself no favours by antagonising this dangerous demon.

"I've been very generous," began Dasrus, once his laughter had subsided. "I gave you a choice in that dungeon by leaving you with your powers and by helping your fellow Cerbereans escape, you did betray me."

Jedd felt himself break out into a cold sweat.

"However, I was counting on you to do that and you initiated my decoy plan perfectly. I suppose there was a lot of debate about how easy it was to escape, the urgent need to get back to Bramblegate and protect the little heir and the gateway? Maybe discussions about you being a double agent?" Dasrus began to cackle once more. "The truth of the matter is that my plan could not have gone any better! There are some things, of course, that I didn't factor in over these eighteen long years. I knew that Purdey would betray her daughter, but you betraying the Light? Well that gave me the opportunity to execute my plan while the Cerbereans were looking the other way. And the delay with Cecily not being able to retrieve her memories? Again, another unexpected extra! Although I too engineered that delay," he added proudly, accepting the blame. "But whether you betrayed me or not, your soul still belongs to me. You sold it."

The spookily calm voice turned menacing as the demon directed his unnatural stare directly at Jedd. It seemed like an eternity before Dasrus chose to speak again and Jedd began to feel nervous, wondering what price he was about to pay. When the demon began to speak once more, the twisted calm had returned to his voice.

"However, you have, although unwittingly, served me well and there is no doubt that all of that pain, anger and resentment inside you, or rather the fact that you want to forget it, could be put to good use. I see into your heart, young Cerberean. I know that more than anything you desire not to feel again and so I will reward your duplicity. Understand though, there is no going back from this."

Jedd did not need to think twice. He nodded.

Dasrus started murmuring under his breath and as the mutterings got louder, Dasrus waved his arms around in the air, with the ardour with which a conductor orchestrates his musicians. Jedd tried not to think about what was going to happen. All he knew was that he was about to get his just desserts.

The time for fear was long past. At the climax of his spell, a ball of black pulsating darkness freed itself from Dasrus's hand and fired at Jedd. A black smudge in the air, Jedd barely had time to register it before it slammed into his chest. He felt an unbearable pain as the darkness tore into his heart. He could almost feel it stop beating as it hardened and turned callous. A black veil descended before his eyes and his spirit departed his body, taking a harrowing journey into the dark. He was falling deeper and deeper into obscurity and as he fell, his soul burnt up and ripped apart, like a rocket re-entering the Earth's atmosphere. The fragmented soul fell faster and faster and as it did, the remnants of who he had been were torn away: the Cerberean, the Warrior of Light, all the good he had done and the love he had felt. But also, all of the anger, pain and resentment lifted until there was nothing. In the oblivion of nothingness, the pieces of his broken spirit reconvened, coming together with an almighty crash, as once again they formed one body. And then his ascent began, only this time, the darkness around him did not fill his very being with despair. It felt comfortable, like home. He still remembered who he had been and the slippery slope that had led him down this path, only it did not matter now. He did not feel anymore. He had only one goal, one desire and he was focussed solely on that; to serve his master and destroy the Light.

His dark spirit found itself back in Bramblegate Woods. It was not yet returned to his body. His recently blackened soul watched on as the human body he had once inhabited now mutated before his eyes. It contorted this way and that as the already large frame began to get bigger, bones popping out and disjointing themselves before returning to their new positions. The muscles in his legs, arms and chest transformed, becoming immense and more defined until the body was much stronger and more powerful than it had been before, pure brawn. The hair on both his head and body fell out, leaving him bald and the eyes which had once been a steely grey, were now black. The face he had known so well was now disfigured and distorted. His bodily transformation into demon was now complete and he had witnessed his own rebirth. With a flick of his hand, Dasrus sent the spirit sweeping back into its newly formed exterior.

"Welcome, my child! My warrior of darkness!" cried Dasrus, as he greeted his new creation. "Come, we have much work to do."

Jedd grunted in agreement.

Chapter 31

As Kaden arrived in the familiar frosty blue environment, he sensed the others were already waiting for him. Sure enough, he was soon surrounded by six bright balls of light, just like himself.

"Hello, Masters. I am sorry to keep you waiting."

"No matter, brother. The importance of our meeting is such that we do not mind waiting."

"The Earth Mother has regained her memory?" chimed another of the Wise Ones.

"Yes, that is why I am a little late," replied Kaden.

"That is good news. We fear that she is the only one who can help now."

Kaden felt his heart sink. He said nothing and let his Masters continue. He listened intently as their voices sang, one after the other.

"We have now been given instruction to intervene, young one."

"Last time you were here, we told you to think about the bigger picture."

"Time is running out."

"We must guide you, tell you what we have learned."

Kaden waited with bated breath.

"You have been focussing on protecting your gateway while behind the scenes, Dasrus has been administering a much larger design."

"He is in the process of successfully convening the three gateways protected by the other elements: Fire, Water and Air."

"If he is successful, he will not need the Earth gateway. He will be able to release Dark on the Earth plane without it."

"And what of the Cerbereans protecting those gateways?" asked Kaden. "Have they been corrupted, like Jedd?"

"Dasrus's methods are unorthodox," replied one of the Masters.

"He has help this time."

"The demons of the Dark are coming together."

"Instead of fighting their own selfish battles in an attempt at individual power and glory, they are presenting a united front."

"Dasrus is at the helm of this army."

"What would once have been impossible is now conceivable."

"You must shut down the Earth gateway as quickly as possible."

"Although if the Dark is successful in opening the other three gateways, it will not matter."

"The elements must join forces to defeat the Dark."

"They are currently fragmented."

"The balance must be kept."

"Mother Earth is the only one with enough power over Dasrus to stop him."

"He knows this which is why he has not attempted to open the Earth gateway this time."

"Lessons have been learned."

"He has simply been toying with her, with all of you."

"His actions up until now have been nothing but a decoy, while his real plan has been bubbling under the surface."

"The Earth Cerbereans must stop him."

"You are the only ones who can."

Kaden was about to speak, but the Wise Ones had not yet finished.

"There's one more thing, young one."

"Some sensitive information."

"A closely guarded secret."

"There is a fifth element."

"In the Realm of Light."

"If Dasrus and the Dark gain access to the fifth element, they will be able to destroy the Realm of Light and then all will be lost."

"The Earth plane will plunge into eternal darkness and there will be no coming back from that."

"A fifth element?" questioned Kaden. "I thought that was just a myth?"

"Keep it to yourself for now, Light Doer. You will know when the time is right to reveal our secret to the others."

"How? How do we stop this from happening?" enquired Kaden, as he was digesting the enormity of the task ahead.

"In every age, there are those who battle evil."

"Be as you are, as nature intended."

"Celestial forces are at work."

"The Light will guide you."

"Go forth, Light Doer."

"What will be, will be."

Kaden knew there was no point in asking any more questions, as the essences of the Wise Ones were fading with their words.

Kaden knew he did not have much time. He needed to get back to the others as soon as possible and they had to return to the present in order to shut down the Earth gateway. However, he needed a moment. He was still reeling from what the Wise Ones had revealed. How could they have been so wrong? The guardians had been lulled into a false sense of security, so used were they to Dasrus's endless attempts to open the Earth gateway in his incessant pursuit of the torture of Cecily.

He had been so angry with the Wise Ones after his last visit, thinking that they had abandoned the Cerbereans, letting all those people die at the party by giving no warning. He now grasped that the party was just the warm-up act and there was, in fact, a much bigger picture. He realised that the warnings were in place, he had simply failed to act on his gut feeling. He must trust his own judgement more, trust in the Wise Ones and in the Light. He must not let his human emotions get in the way. It was destiny that he and his fellow Cerbereans were placed on the Earth plane. They must find a way. And with a renewed sense of purpose, he began the journey back to the Middle Ages.

Chapter 32

As Kaden was returning to Bramble Hall, things seemed a lot livelier than the last time he had returned after visiting the Wise Ones. Through the icy blue haze of his ball of light, he could see Sol pacing up and down at the end of the Great Hall they had set up as their living and eating area yesterday. Lady Bramble was sat on one of the comfortable chairs, the children stood by her side, clinging to her and crying. Elisabeth was sat on a bench at the long, wooden table, her head in her hands. Cecily and Fen were having a discussion and both had worried looks on their faces.

As Kaden materialised back into his humanoid form, Cecily said, "Thank goodness!"

"What's going on?" he questioned. He did not like the atmosphere in the room. Something had happened. Cecily leapt straight into her tale about what she had seen.

"I went to the clearing earlier to practise with my powers, just to make sure I wasn't rusty," she began. "As I entered the circle of oaks, I felt a residual energy left by magic. This magic was powerful stuff. It made me feel sick. So I had a look into the not so distant past and I saw Dasrus. With Jedd."

Cecily paused and Kaden could see she was choosing her words carefully.

"We've been betrayed," she continued. "Jedd is no more."

"What? Dasrus killed him?" Kaden immediately thought this is why everyone must be so upset and he too felt the same emotion coming over him.

"In a way, yes," said Cecily. "He's a demon. Dasrus turned

him into a demon. I saw it happen with my own eyes."

Kaden sat down on the bench next to Elisabeth.

"Are you sure? Maybe the vision was a trick, planted by Dasrus."

"Impossible!" cried Cecily. "Firstly, how would Dasrus know where we are in order to leave the vision? Secondly, he doesn't know I am reactivated and I'm the only one with the power to look into the past. Finally, the imprint of the residual energy matched the spell and magic he used, very dark and powerful magic, which is what he would need to transform someone into a demon. Jedd has betrayed us."

"I can't believe he would do this!" wailed Elisabeth through her fingers. Kaden noticed that her face was red and he could see she was devastated by this news.

"Did you see anything else, Cec? Could you hear what they were saying?"

"No nothing. Just enough to give me the gory details. Dasrus must have masked the rest of their conversation. He probably wanted to leave just enough to taunt us, in case I should happen over it. Just enough to show us the path our friend has chosen. I mean, being a demon has got to be better than hanging around with us, hasn't it?" Sarcasm laced her words. "We've got to get back to Bramblegate now!" she continued, urgently. "I've got to shut down the gateway. Plus, Dasrus knows we are here now thanks to Jedd. It's no longer safe."

Kaden could tell she was back. She was very different from her human counterpart. The goddess was a leader, strong and in charge.

"But that is what Dasrus is going to expect, for us to leave here and go directly to the gateway," suggested Sol.

"Not necessarily," replied Cecily. "He doesn't know I'm reactivated. Jedd left before it happened."

"Sorry to interrupt," said Lady Bramble. "But why can't you shut the gateway down permanently to stop anything like this from happening again. It would also remove the need for a human protector."

She looked down sadly at her son who was visibly petrified, while Delilah cried, "Mummy! I want to go home!"

"We can't, Lady Bramble," explained Kaden. He truly felt for them. "Trust me, we've tried. All we can do is a spell to temporarily prevent the use of magic in the area and Cecily is the only one powerful enough to do that. Neither can we destroy the Dark. We can lock them away, again with magic, but they find a way out eventually."

"And death always becomes the Bramble family as a result," said Lady Bramble, angrily. Oscar gasped.

"Not always," replied Kaden, trying to make her feel better. "Anyway, I don't think Dasrus will be waiting for us at the gateway. By all accounts, he has much bigger fish to fry. This whole situation has been an elaborate decoy, a red herring. That is why the Wise Ones summoned me, to put us back on the right track again. We've been focussing on the wrong problem."

"What?" said Cecily, who seemed very shocked. "What is his true plan then?"

Kaden was about to relay what the Wise Ones had told him when he saw something move out of the corner of his eye. He turned and jumped at the sight of the shadow beasts in the darkened corners of the Great Hall.

"It's OK," said Fen. "They've been hanging around all morning. They are of this time. Sol and I checked them out."

"Do you not think it is a bit strange that Jedd gave us up only last night and now the place is crawling with shadows?"

"They have been benign," said Elisabeth. "They have just been patrolling."

"Trust me," added Sol. "We've been keeping our eye on them!"

But Kaden was not convinced. He walked over to one of the darkened corners, reached over his head to the space between his shoulder blades, retrieved his sword with a blast of light and came down hard on one of the beasts lurking in the shadows with one swift swipe. As he suspected, the shadow dissipated and the other seemingly benign beasts turned their attention on Kaden.

"Spies!" he shouted, although he could see that the others had already drawn their swords and were running to his aid, all except Elisabeth, who was guarding the Brambles.

The friends fought furiously, slicing this way and that, until all of the beasts had dissipated. They checked every inch of the Great Hall, in all the dark places, to ensure that no shadows were creeping there and when they were sure, Kaden added a protective shield to the boundaries of the Great Hall, ensuring that no more could enter.

"Kaden, we are so sorry!" began Sol. "We checked them this morning. They weren't real!"

"Don't worry," said Kaden. "Dasrus was bound to send spies sooner or later. When those bottom feeders report back to him, he'll know that Cecily is back and that we know about Jedd, but also that the Wise Ones have disclosed what Dasrus is really up to."

"And what is that, exactly?" asked Cecily, sounding rather agitated.

Within the privacy of the shield, Kaden informed the group of what the Wise Ones had told him, omitting the part about the fifth element.

"He tricked us?" said Cecily, incredulously. "How could we have been so blind?"

"Look, we have to have faith," explained Kaden. "Events were supposed to play out like this. Whatever we feel about the party and what happened in Bramblegate, we've got to put it behind us. In the grand scheme of things, those events were just a drop in the ocean." Kaden saw Lady Bramble wince, but he carried on regardless. "It is nothing compared to the devastation that will happen if we don't stop the Dark."

"Devastation?" questioned Lady Bramble curtly, obviously upset that her husband's death was described as a mere drop in the ocean.

"As long as Dasrus can convene the remaining three elements, then he can release Dark on Earth. The Earth plane will be overrun with demons bringing with them pain and suffering. Human souls will be corrupted. They will have no choice. They will stop choosing the Light and as a result, no more souls will pass to the Light. Trust me, whatever vision you have of what hell might be like, it will be nothing compared to this. The Dark will be much harder to defeat if they gain control. It could take centuries, even millennia. The balance between good and evil must be kept. The Earth plane must be neutral."

Lady Bramble said nothing, she simply stood there gawping, which told Kaden he had answered her question. He wondered if he had overdone it, although everything he said was true.

"What signs are we looking out for, Cec?" asked Sol.

"Well," began Cecily, "the four elements are the very substance of the Earth plane, its entire composition. If they are in conflict with one another, the Earth plane will be plunged into chaos. Without the cooperation of Water or Air, Earth cannot flourish. Fire will make Earth arid and dry. When our natural surroundings begin to wilt and die, that will be the signifier it has started."

"I think we'd better get out of here," said Kaden, sensibly.

"I agree," said Cecily. "We need to move fast. Let's go straight to the clearing and shut down our gateway, like the Wise Ones suggested."

"What if he's waiting for us?" asked Elisabeth.

"When Dasrus finds out we have discovered his true plan, he knows that we will try to stop him. Therefore, he will be waiting for us at every twist and turn to prevent us from doing that. We have already lost the element of surprise. The fight has begun and this one is not going to be easy. He's never tried anything on this scale before, which tells me that he is more determined than ever to release Dark on Earth."

The others nodded in agreement with Kaden. However, the Brambles looked terrified. Kaden could see their fear and so he set about comforting them.

"Lady Bramble, you and the children will have to remain in the safe room for now, just until we can stop Dasrus. I will ask the Fanes to bring you daily supplies and leave them in the organ loft. As you know, they will not be able to enter the room. Do not give that spell to anyone, Lady Bramble, not even the Fanes. Make sure you are not seen and communicate with no one. That room is the safest place to be, providing as few people as possible know about it."

"But how long do you think we will be in there for? It is rather small and claustrophobic!"

"Better that than dead!" snapped Elisabeth, which started the children crying again. Elisabeth folded her arms and rolled her eyes.

"I know what Elisabeth said was harsh," said Kaden, glaring at Elisabeth, "but it is true. As soon as we get rid of the threat, things can return to normal." And then he added, "Well, as normal as possible," as he realised that for the Brambles, things would never be normal again with the absence of their father.

"Won't people be looking for us?" asked Lady Bramble. "Family, friends, staff?"

"The Purification Unit will take care of all that, in fact, they probably already have. They will have planted a story, like you've gone on holiday or something. Please, don't worry about the details. Just concentrate on getting through this difficult time."

Lady Bramble said, "OK," and hugged her children tightly to her side.

"Right!" said Kaden, springing into action. "In a minute, I'm going to start the spell and then drop the shield. Cerbereans, you know what to do! Swords at the ready, just in case they are waiting for us on the other side."

Kaden began murmuring under his breath, arms and legs outstretched. As his spell came near to its end, he dropped the shield and became a ball of pale blue glowing light.

"Quick!" he heard Cecily say.

First, Fen and Sol went into the light with the children, followed by Elisabeth. Cecily was in the process of ushering Lady Bramble through when he heard the lady scream. With an almighty shove, Cecily pushed her into the light while with the other hand, Kaden could see her fighting the shadows single-handedly as they attacked. Through the blue haze, Kaden could see that she was backing her way towards him as she was dealing with the onslaught of beasts and Kaden was willing her to hurry. When he saw that she had an opportunity, he communicated it to her in such a way so that his voice could be heard loud and clear in her head.

"Come on, Cec! Now! Hurry!"

She dived into the ball of light and when she was safe, Kaden disappeared into thin air, leaving the salivating shadows at the medieval Bramble Hall.

Chapter 33

Kaden had taken the group directly to the clearing. Cecily exited the ball of light, alert with sword at the ready for whatever may be awaiting them. But she could see no signs of the shadow beasts and the others were crowding around something on the ground. This time, rather than clinging to their mother, the children were grasping each other. Delilah was sobbing and Oscar seemed to be hyperventilating. Cecily knew what they were crowding around as she had been there when it had happened. There was no way she could have prevented it; there were too many and they were bound to attack as soon as the shield fell. Cecily bent down and took Oscar by the shoulders.

"Come on, nice deep breaths. Your mum will be fine."

And then Oscar spoke for the first time in a couple of days.

"I don't want her to die too!"

"Your mum is going to be OK," said Cecily, comforting the boy and his sister. "I'm going to fix her."

Kaden, now back in his humanoid form, took over from Cecily and stood with the children. Cecily gestured for Fen and Sol, who had been stemming the blood flow with Lady Bramble's scarf, to move to one side. Elisabeth was at Lady Bramble's head, dabbing it with her sleeve and trying to keep her still. Cecily removed the scarf and had a look at the wound. It was quite a nasty bite and it was losing a lot of blood, but she knew that blood loss was not their biggest problem. The fangs of those putrid smelling monsters contained poison and she knew that was why Lady Bramble was writhing. Cecily knew that she must get to work quickly. There was not much time.

She would need a lot of magic for this healing spell, so she placed one hand firmly on the ground in order to absorb the Earth's power and one hand over Lady Bramble's leg. Cecily closed her eyes and began muttering the spell under her breath. Cecily's green light ran up the arm that was placed on the ground, the light ran across her body and into the other arm that was hovering over Lady Bramble's leg. The green glow emitting from her hand shone down on the bite mark and it had a cauterizing effect. After a minute or two, the wound was sealed and not even a scar remained.

"Good as new!" said Cecily, cheerily.

The children rushed to their mother's side and were weeping again, this time with relief.

"Oh, thank you!" cried Lady Bramble. "How can I ever repay you?"

"Don't worry about it," said Cecily, rather embarrassed at the prospect.

Elisabeth, who had now relinquished her hold on Lady Bramble's shoulders, said, "This is all Jedd's fault! I still can't believe he betrayed us a second time. I thought he was intelligent?" She was very angry.

"Dasrus can see into people's hearts," explained Kaden. "He offers them their greatest wishes and deepest desires. Who knows what Jedd wanted so badly?"

"I'm going to start the magic to shut down the gateway," said Cecily. "We need to get Lady Bramble and the children to safety, before there are more surprise attacks."

Kaden nodded. "Yes, you are right."

Cecily walked over to the far corner of the clearing and closed her eyes in concentration. She had not uttered these words in a long time, but she had not forgotten them. As she murmured the spell, her utterance was directed at the trees and shrubbery. She was talking to them, commanding them to do her will. Her green light glowed all around her as she pulled her hands in an upward motion, controlling the nature in front of her. The trees, bushes, plants and flowers began to weave themselves together, intertwining to form a barrier of thicket. The natural shield grew further and further into the sky and eventually began to curve over, cocooning the clearing safely under a natural awning. Cecily ran over to the next corner and began the spell again. As the trees and shrubbery came together in a defensive screen, they blocked out the dappled sunlight that had been shining through their branches, shading the clearing from the warm June sun. When the flora and fauna from the two corners met each other in unison, she ran to the third corner and repeated the magic. The clearing was now safeguarded on three sides. The group of companions were enclosed by an impenetrable fortification of nature that stood guard against the gateway to the Dark. Cecily ran over to the fourth and final corner in order to complete the spell. The underbrush and timber were so tightly woven that the clearing was becoming deeper under shadow as the spell progressed. As the woods fused together in the last corner of the clearing, they rose up to meet the dome-like natural roof that would defend the clearing and gateway until it was no longer needed.

Cecily was inwardly breathing a sigh of relief when she heard a noise on the other side of the thicket that was still weaving and growing. It sounded like something was punching its way through.

"I can hear something!" she shouted to her friends.

She thought to herself that this could not be good. The spell was not yet complete. The others came over to the corner of the clearing where Cecily was stood.

"It's getting louder," said Fen, drawing her sword.

The others followed suit.

"It's OK. We might make it," said Cecily. "Look!" she said, pointing upwards. "The spell is almost complete. A few more seconds and the clearing will be protected…"

But as she was uttering these words, the demon that was Jedd pushed his way into the clearing. Cecily recognised him instantly as she had seen his transformation in the vision, but it took the others a few seconds to realise.

Kaden was the first to speak. "Jedd? Is that you?"

The beast did not reply, so Cecily decided to answer for him. "Yep, that's Jedd alright! Handsome fellow!"

Elisabeth ran forward and grabbed the demon by the arm. "Why?" she asked, frantically. "Why have you done this to yourself?"

The monster simply shook her off as if she were a rag doll. She hit the floor so hard, she bounced and the look of shock and devastation on her face was evident.

Fen, Sol and Kaden took turns in trying to reason with the demon formerly known as Jedd, but it was clear that he was gunning for one person and one person only. His eyes, now black like puddles of tar, were set firmly on Cecily and it seemed that the efforts by her friends to reason with him went unnoticed. Cecily knew that his mission was to finish her and she was sure he would not stop until he had achieved it. She suddenly felt very responsible for what had happened to her fellow Cerberean, her brother. She must have hurt him deeply to make him think this was his only option.

His sword had been replaced by a new weapon which he dragged along the floor behind him. It seemed that with his new-found strength and bulk, he was able to wield a huge ball made of iron, with lethal looking spikes protruding from it, on a long cumbersome chain. He started towards Cecily, walking at first, but then moving with surprising speed, despite his newly formed mammoth frame. As he took his first swing with the enormous spiky ball and chain, Cecily was able to shift out of its way easily, because she too was fast. He struck again for a second time, but again, she dodged the attack. Out of the corner of her eye, she could see her friends coming to assist, swords out in front ready to strike, but at that moment, she heard the unmistakable growling of the shadows, succeeded by their rancid smell.

A quick look left and right confirmed that the beasts were gathering as a dark mass and descending swiftly on the clearing. The Cerbereans turned their attention to the hell beasts while Cecily continued to avoid Jedd's swings. She did not want to hurt him. In the back of her mind, she was hoping there was some way they could bring him back from this. But neither could she avert his onslaught forever. She needed to help her friends get rid of the shadows before someone else ended up with a deadly bite, or worse.

As she was considering the best way to hold off Jedd, something else caught her eye. Entering the clearing was Acantha, quite obviously still possessed. Only this time, Acantha was not alone. Cecily groaned out loud as Dawn and Cherry, two of the weekend staff from the Dairy and members of the Kaden Quinn fan club, stumbled into the clearing behind their manager. All three of them had their arms outstretched, ready to grab and bite, snarling and drooling as they went.

"Don't hurt them!" Cecily shouted over to the others as they clocked the zombie-like creatures. "We might still be able to help them!"

Cecily was becoming annoyed. She decided that this charade had gone on for long enough. As she continued to dance around Jedd like a boxer in a major title fight, she began a spell. Her hands glowed with their green light as she talked to her newly formed shield that was still holding around three sides of the clearing. The tightly bound thicket bowed to Cecily's command, doing her bidding as she coaxed it out of the sky. Before Jedd the demon knew what was happening, he had been snatched by the flora and fauna forming part of the natural roof. It wrapped him up tightly so he was unable to move and lifted him high into the air as it retracted. Jedd was now part of the organic canopy that protected the clearing and although he struggled, he could not free himself from his woody captor.

Now that she had temporarily dealt with Jedd, she made her way over to Acantha, Dawn and Cherry, which did not take long as they were unable to move quickly with their slow and unnatural footsteps, one leg dragging behind the other. When the three possessed creatures saw Cecily in front of them, it was as if they had noticed her for the first time. They smiled their evil and distorted grins and immediately made a beeline for her. She began another spell, only this time, tree roots exploded from the ground and took down the crazed humans by the ankles. The shadow beasts noticed what was happening and they turned their attention on Cecily. She drew her sword and skilfully fought the shadows with one hand, while ensuring that with the other hand, she completed her spell. The tree roots wound up the zombies' bodies from the ankles to their necks, binding them fixedly, rendering them incapacitated. Although they really did not seem to mind as they continued to grin, evilly, like it was a big joke, snarling and drooling all the while.

The Cerbereans were fighting well, even though they were severely outnumbered and one Cerberean down. But Cecily knew that was why they were guardians and protectors; because they were skilled warriors and because they could handle it. But she also knew they were stronger because of her, their leader. And true to form, she was about to demonstrate how quickly Mother Nature could change.

"Kaden! We've got to get rid of the demons so I can finish the spell!"

She turned to see where Fen, Sol and Elisabeth were and nodded in their direction.

"Tell them to get down and cover their heads on my signal!"

Kaden put his thumbs up to show that he had understood and Cecily watched him fight his way over to the far side of the clearing where the others were battling back the shadows. When they had all shown her the thumbs up, she began her spell. She knew she had to be careful as she only wanted to expel the shadows, not Jedd or her three zombie prisoners, as she was hoping to return them to their former selves. She closed her eyes in concentration and thought about how she wanted to phrase her magic.

But before any words could leave her mouth, she felt an excruciating pain in her head, which travelled all the way down her body like a river flowing over a waterfall. It rendered her powerless and all she could do was curl up in a ball on the floor. She was half expecting the shadow demons to attack her while she was down, but she knew they would not dare as their master was coming. She could feel him. She willed her fellow Cerbereans to be all right, but there was nothing she could do. He had caught her off guard, although this was nothing he was doing to her; she was doing it to herself.

She could feel him coming because he was a part of her and her a part of him. That niggle at the back of her brain was now free and everything she had been trying to block out, both as Gaea, the goddess and as Cecily Stalks, the human, was at the forefront of her mind, playing itself out like a silent movie. She was now forced to face the very things she had been avoiding thinking about since her memory had returned. She felt the gut wrenching pain of the past as her stomach tied itself into knots. She felt the eternity of agony that lay before her in her immortal life. She cursed having to spend time as a human, because it gave her the ability to think and feel this way. She rather wished she could stay awake and activated forever, learn to deal with the torment and develop the heart of stone she so wished for. She wanted to feel no love in her heart for him, nothing. But then there was the relief of deactivation and the knowledge that she would not know him until she was needed once again in the battle between good and evil. She craved the simplicity of a human life and subsequently found herself wishing she could live and die that way, rather than the immortality she had wished for only moments earlier.

Cecily was two things: immortal goddess, yet also human until the time came for reactivation. These two parts of herself were in conflict with one another and she felt incomplete; half of something, neither one thing nor the other. And this was what had caused the trouble in the first place, because the past never leaves us. It is who we are. He will never leave her alone. He will torment her forevermore. And yet knowing this, she still mourns his love. She knows it is her duty to the Light to destroy the Dark, but she is torn. She is always torn where he is concerned. It was all her fault. Deep down, the last thing she wanted to do was hurt him more, so does that, in fact, make her as bad as him? Another war that rages, but within her.

Dasrus was her soul mate, her one true love and by the time she was able to look up again, once the pain had subsided, he was standing there, right in front of her.

Chapter 34

"Hello, Gaea dear! Miss me?" he said in his eerily calm voice. "I must admit, it has taken me quite a while to put this plan into action. Who would have thought that it would be your own mother and one of your friends who ultimately helped things to run as smoothly as they have? What do you think of the new improved Cerberean?"

With his last question, he pointed up to the canopy at Jedd, who was wriggling frantically in an attempt to liberate himself. Cecily was glad her spell was still holding. She said nothing to Dasrus. She could not bring herself to speak and instead simply stared into the hood, thinking about what was there before the darkness. It broke her heart.

"Anyway, I just thought I would pop by and say 'Hello' now that you actually remember who I am. Although we had fun as Cian and Cecily, didn't we?"

Cecily stared at the demon, remaining stoic and silent. She refused to rise to his taunts.

"Nothing to say? OK, I'll collect my demons and be on my way then. I'll let you finish your spell to shut down the gateway." Up until now, although his voice had retained its eerie calm, it had had a lilt of joviality about it. But with his next words, the malevolence returned. "It won't make a difference, protecting the gateway. By the time I've finished I won't need it. Dark will already be upon the Earth and it will be me locking you away, until I find a way to destroy you for good, that is. You are already too late." He turned his attention to the Bramble family and spat, "Don't think I've finished with you either!"

Cecily had never seen such fear as the family simultaneously jumped and gasped at his address. Kaden, who was standing nearest to them, put a comforting arm around Oscar's shoulder. He was visibly shaking. Cecily knew Dasrus had achieved the required effect.

"See you soon, Gaea, or I believe you now prefer, Cecily?"

His mocking, evil cackle filled the clearing and in an instant, he was gone, as too were the shadows. However, not without leaving Cecily a little reminder of the torture he could inflict on her. She could no longer see him, but his voice resounded around her.

"Remember, it will always be this way. I will never leave you. We will be together for all eternity."

Cecily, who had not managed to make if off her knees throughout the entirety of Dasrus's visit, now slumped down onto her bottom, exhausted. The others remained silent for a few moments after Dasrus's message had finished and although her friends knew what the demon's final words represented, she could see the puzzled look on Lady Bramble's face. Every time Cecily saw Dasrus, he stirred such a flurry of conflicting emotions in her. She knew she must pull herself together. She did not want to appear weak. Kaden came over to where she was sat, grabbed both of her hands and helped her to her feet.

"Are you ok?" he asked quietly, so the others would not hear.

"I'm fine," she lied. "Just a bit shocked. It's the first time I've truly seen him in a while."

The growling and slobbering noises made by the zombie ladies refocused Cecily to the task at hand and she knew she must regain charge over this situation. She looked up.

"Well he's taken Jedd, but at least he's left these three. Hopefully, the Purification Unit will be able to help them."

"We still have to find out if there's a way of helping Jedd!" cried Elisabeth. "We can't just abandon him!"

Cecily could see that Elisabeth was not taking Jedd's

transformation well.

"We will, Elisabeth," said Cecily. "It is also up to Jedd though. He has to want our help."

"Of course he wants our help! Who would choose to become like that!"

Cecily knew that Elisabeth was upset and so she said nothing. She felt partly responsible for Jedd's defection, even though she knew it was not really her fault.

"I'm going to finish the spell. At least the gateway will be protected and that will be one less worry for us."

"But you heard the demon," interjected Lady Bramble, shaking. "He said there is no point, that he doesn't need this gateway!"

"We can't trust everything Dasrus says. He's a demon," pointed out Fen.

"We are the guardians of this gateway. It is our job to protect it in times of trouble," explained Kaden.

Cecily could see the panic on the faces of the Bramble family, so she decided she must reassure them. "You will be perfectly fine in the safe room, as long as you do as we say. You must not worry."

"Not worry?" replied Lady Bramble, her voice becoming high-pitched and more neurotic with every word. "I've an army of demons threatening my family. They've already killed my husband and had a good go at me. How can I not worry? I feel… powerless." She paused while she found the right word.

"We understand," said Fen, soothingly. "We will get you some help so you can cope with those worries."

"We will find a way to stop them, Lady Bramble," said Sol, confidently. "The balance of good and evil on Earth must be preserved in equal measure."

Cecily loved Sol's confidence. It was infectious.

She walked over to the edge of the clearing where the green wall made of thicket was half-grown into the sky. She completed the spell and watched as the natural canopy sprouted and met with the other corners to form a dome-like roof. The clearing fell dark and Cecily was satisfied that the gateway was guarded. Nothing magical could take place there now and Cecily was the only one with the power to enter or exit the clearing and lift the spell. With a green light emanating from her finger, Cecily carved a doorway in the newly grown protective wall. The companions left the clearing, with the three zombies, and Cecily then sealed the doorway they had just exited. As the zombies were bound from the ankles up, Cecily thought the best way for them to travel was by tree, so she whispered softly to the trees of Bramblegate Wood and once again, branches bowed down to lift the possessed creatures up and the trees carried them through their bows, one branch at a time, following the path of the Cerbereans. However, the friends were careful not to walk beneath the drooling zombies, as for the second time in as many days, Sol found himself covered in gunk falling from their slobbering mouths above.

The group headed towards the dell and before long they found themselves at the Fanes. True to form, the Watchers were waiting and the Cerbereans had to go to the trouble of identifying themselves again. Only this time around, Cecily knew exactly what to do. When it was her turn, she stepped forward and said, "My name is Gaea."

In his characteristic sharp tone, Mr Fane said, "Show me!"

She reached behind her head with one hand to the place in between her shoulders and grabbed the hilt of her sword. She felt the brand sizzle on her palm, only it did not hurt. Before it disappeared into obscurity, she brandished the tall proud oak at him. And then just for good measure, she allowed a small, green glowing light to dance playfully between her fingers.

"Welcome back, lass," said Mr Fane, winking at her.

Once they were inside the house, Kaden erected his icy blue shield so they could talk freely. The Cerbereans, the Brambles and Mr Fane made their way through to the sitting room, while the zombies remained at the back of the kitchen by the door. Mrs Fane was preparing tea for the visitors and every now and then, her voice could be heard loud and clear.

"Now do be quiet, dears!" as she addressed the zombies' growling and snarling.

While they were waiting for Mrs Fane, the group filled Mr Fane in on everything that had happened since they left: about Jedd, the ambush, Cecily getting her memory back, the decoy plan and Dasrus's real plan. They also told him about the surprise visit from Dasrus.

"Heavens above! Things have certainly moved on in the last day or so! It looks like you young guardians are going to have to work out a solid plan of action, especially if you are going to track Dasrus down to the other gateways."

"We've certainly a lot to consider and not much time to consider it," said Kaden.

"Well, you are welcome to stay here till you sort things out and we'll help if we can."

He gestured towards Mrs Fane who had just entered the room with a tray of tea, cake and biscuits.

"Thanks, Abram. We appreciate that," said Kaden, gratefully.

"And I'm sorry about young Jedd. I was hoping matters would turn out differently, but I'm afraid that once a traitor, always a traitor."

The group said nothing. They all averted their eyes, except for Elisabeth, whom Cecily had noticed was wearing a look of defiance on her face. Mr Fane appeared not to have observed this.

"But first things first, we need to get the Purification Unit here to sort out our cases of possession in the kitchen," pointed out Cecily.

"Don't worry, dear," said Verena. "I'll call them."

And off she went into the next room. Cecily smiled to herself as she remembered the last time she was here and how she had wondered how such a call to the Realm of Light would be made. She had imagined Verena using a telephone. Now of course, she knew that you just needed a quiet space to concentrate and all you did was simply ask the Light out loud for what you needed. You had to be specific though!

A few minutes later, Mrs Fane re-entered the room with a tall, thin man with white blond hair and pale skin, dressed in a long white coat, white trousers and white shoes. Some other members of the Unit dressed in the same way waited outside the sitting room door. When they had greeted each other, Cecily explained about the possessions in the kitchen.

"Please do your best to save them," said Cecily.

"Well of course, we always try our best," replied the pale man, "but you know what those shadow demons are like. They slowly devour their prey from the inside out. It's all a big game to them. We'll have to take them outside into the garden, beyond the shield. We can arrive and depart while the shield is up, but we can't purify."

Cecily nodded in agreement and watched as the members of the Purification Unit picked up the slobbering zombies like rolls of carpet and took them outside.

It was a while before Cecily heard the Purification Unit come through the back door, by which time, the tea and sweet treats had all been wolfed down by the hungry guests. Cecily walked into the kitchen to meet them.

"It was tough," began the tall man with the white blond hair, "but we managed to get rid of the demons. The beasts had taken a firm hold of their victims. They had been incubating for a few days. Usually, we like to get them straight away."

"Is there any damage?" enquired Cecily.

"Not that I can tell. Maybe there will be some problems with short-term memory, but nothing too serious."

"That is good news," said Cecily, somewhat relieved. She really did not want any more casualties from that dreadful party.

"We've helped them to come to terms with what happened and sent them on their way. They should be fine, but as always, we'll monitor their progress."

"And the demons?"

"Dissipated."

"Great!" said Cecily, meaning it. "While you're here, I've one more favour to ask."

Cecily explained the Brambles' predicament to the Purification Unit. She did not want them to yet accept what had happened to Lord Bramble or to become complacent; she needed them to stay alert and be afraid of Dasrus and the Dark so they would be sure to stay in the safe room. But she did want to remove some of their pain and the shock they'd had from being hurtled into this world that they did not understand. She knew what that felt like as she had been in the same position only yesterday."

"Do you think you can help?" she asked the pale man. "Just until they can complete the whole purification process."

"Of course," smiled the man, revealing beautifully straight white teeth.

Cecily beckoned the Bramble family to the kitchen. The Purification Unit once more proceeded to leave out of the back door of the cottage and into the garden.

"Wait!" cried Cecily. "I'll ask Kaden to take down the shield, just in case there are any unwelcome guests lurking outside who might fancy their chances. We will all be safer inside, even without the shield."

Cecily then left, closing the kitchen door behind her.

When they returned, Lady Bramble said, "What charming men! When do we return to the safe room?"

Kaden muttered under his breath and reinstated the shield. "Tonight, under the cover of darkness," he said. "We don't want anyone to see you going into the house."

Lady Bramble looked in high spirits and even the children

were smiling.

"We'll be going now," said the pale man from the sitting room door.

Cecily beamed at him. "Thanks!" she said.

"No problem. Just call if you need anything else."

"Oh we will dear, we will!" said Verena, as she ushered them into the next room ready for departure.

While the Brambles had been with Purification Unit, the Cerbereans decided between themselves that they would not discuss their plans in front of the family. The fewer people who knew how they were going to approach the situation, the better. So, for the next few hours, while waiting for the summer sun to set, idle chitchat and tales of old dominated the conversation, mainly provided by Mr Fane. Mrs Fane was busy in the kitchen preparing a home-cooked feast. Cecily was so glad of Abram and the fact that he was such a good talker as it meant she did not have to say much. She wanted to consider her position.

Cecily noticed that she was not the only one who was quiet. Elisabeth was painfully silent. She had not said much since they were at the clearing earlier and Jedd had been revealed to her for the first time. Elisabeth had to get a handle on her emotions before her bitterness and rage lead her down the same unsavoury path as Jedd. But how could Cecily talk about handling feelings after her episode in the woods earlier that day? She felt hypocritical. The truth was they were all susceptible.

As night fell, the Cerbereans got ready to deliver the Brambles back to the safety of the organ loft. Mrs Fane sent the family on their way with enough things to make their stay there a bit more comfortable and she promised that Mr Fane and she would leave a package with fresh food in the organ loft every other night for their retrieval.

"Aye, I'll sneak up to the bedrooms too and get you some fresh clothes. There's not much call for medieval clothing round here. Folk'll think you're going to a fancy-dress party. Same goes

280

for you lot," he said, nodding at the guardians.

They all laughed.

"Don't worry, Abram! We'll get changed tomorrow so we don't show you up!" said Kaden, jokingly.

Thanks to Mr Fane's jovial attitude, the group left feeling positive with Mrs Fane's warnings to be careful ringing in their ears. However, such cautioning was not needed as their mission was highly successful and they delivered the Brambles to their safe room without incident. In fact, they did not see a soul. When the family were settled and Kaden had repeated what they should and should not do several times, Cecily felt happy about leaving them. They did not seem as fragile after the Purification Unit's intervention. They said their farewells and promised to get them out as soon as possible.

The five Cerbereans headed back to the dell and to the Fanes' cottage, where they would be staying for the next day or so. They had to regroup and decide on a course of action. This would also give them the opportunity to consult with the Wise Ones if necessary, although they did not have much time to spare. Once back at the cottage, Mr Fane completed his customary checks while Kaden reinstated the shield that would keep out things that go bump in the night, or in the very least, warn them against any impending attacks. The five friends were dotted around the Fane's sitting room in makeshift beds on the floor.

Soon, everyone was asleep, exhausted after the events of the past few days. Cecily, however, could not sleep. Her mind was reflecting on such events and the rollercoaster ride they had embarked on. So much had happened: the doomed party, reactivation, the betrayals by Purdey and Jedd, being kidnapped and imprisoned, escaping from the realm between realms, a trip back to medieval Bramblegate in search of her memory and to top it all off, ambushes and attacks. But the thing that concerned Cecily the most was that they had been infiltrated from within by people close to them. And it was her fault. She had refused to acknowledge the warning signs and her subconscious had tried its best to block reactivation in an attempt to stay human. As a result, Dasrus had managed to get close to her as Cian and not only that, a lot of people had died because they, the protectors, were slow to react.

She looked down at the gold cuff she had been unconsciously fiddling with, turning it around on her wrist and tracing the smooth shape of the bejewelled petals. When Kaden had said it was one of her favourites that had been an understatement on his part. She recalled the moment he had given it to her.

"Gaea, a token of my eternal love and worship. The gold symbolises wealth, but not a wealth in monetary terms; the wealth is that of a spiritual value and of your importance to me. I am indeed a wealthy man as I possess your heart and that is all I will ever need. The flowers represent you, Gaea; Mother Earth, queen of all that is natural and beautiful in the world. And the jewels? Well, they are precious stones, to remind you that you will always be treasured."

As everyone was now asleep, she allowed the tears to fall silently over her cheeks. She had to make up her mind once and for all. She could no longer allow emotions or feelings of confusion to get in the way of what she really wanted more than anything. She knew what she must do.